TALES OF THE HIDDEN WORLD

TALES OF THE HIDDEN WORLD

SIMON R. GREEN

OPEN ROAD
INTEGRATED MEDIA
NEW YORK

Cover design by Neil Alexander Heacox

ISBN 978-1-4804-9116-8

Published in 2014 by Open Road Integrated Media, Inc.
345 Hudson Street
New York, NY 10014
www.openroadmedia.com

CONTENTS

TALES OF THE HIDDEN WORLD

QUESTION OF SOLACE

There really are monsters out there. But you don't need to worry about them, because the Droods are out there, too. This very, very old family exists to protect Humanity, to stand between you and all the secret things that threaten you. From their hidden home at Drood Hall, tucked away somewhere in the wilds of England, they watch over the world, monitor the secret frequencies, and stand ready to do . . . whatever's necessary. They have field agents in every major city, in every country, ready to throw down with all the supernatural or super-science menaces . . . that you're better off not knowing about.

The Droods, your last chance for protection, and peace of mind. They answer to no one but themselves. The shamans of the human tribe, the shepherds of human civilization. And no, you don't get a say in the matter.

Jack Drood, Armourer to the Drood family for many years now, sat slumped in his special chair before his personal workstation, looking at his latest invention and wondering whether it was worth all the time and effort he'd put into it. As Armourer to the Droods, it was his job to come up with all the powerful weapons, sneaky gadgets and nasty surprises that the family's field agents needed, to help them bring down the bad guys. The Armourer had been doing that very successfully for decades now, and he was getting really tired of it.

He looked middle-aged but was actually a lot older. He kept up appearances by following a carefully balanced diet of protein and pasta, doing as little regular exercise as he could get away with, and abusing a whole bunch of exotic medications of dubious provenance. He liked to joke that when he died there'd be so many pills in him they'd have to bury him in a coffin with a childproof lid. He was tall and thin, growly and grumpy, and not nearly as full of nervous energy as he used to be. Two shocks of tufty white hair jutted out over his ears, below a bulging, bald pate. He had bushy white eyebrows, a prominent nose, and steely gray eyes. His face looked lived-in and hard-used, and he scowled a lot. Particularly when he had to talk to people.

He did have people skills. He just mostly couldn't be bothered.

When he occasionally forced himself up out of his chair, to go prowling around the massive stone cavern that held the Armory, and all its dangerous wonders, it quickly became obvious he was bent over in a pronounced stoop, legacy of so many years spent leaning over workbenches, creating things designed to make people place nicely with one another, whether they wanted to or not. He wore a long white lab coat, decorated with stains and chemical burns, and the occasional explosives residue, over a grubby T-shirt bearing the legend *Guns Don't Kill People, Unless You Aim Them Properly.* Armourer humor.

He still liked to think of himself as an engineer, rather than a weapons designer.

He sat there in his favorite chair, right at the back of the Armory, where people wouldn't bother him. The Armory was buried deep in the bedrock under Drood Hall, so that when things inevitably went wrong, usually suddenly and loudly and violently, the damage wouldn't reach the hall. The Armourer was thinking, and scowling, and doing his best to ignore the general racket going on around him. Dozens of lab assistants filled the Armory, working on dozens of projects, their terribly inventive minds limited only by the laws of science and probability. The laws of the land, or even basic morality, didn't get a look in. To become one of the Armourer's lab assistants, a young Drood had to prove they were way above average intelligence, incredibly and indeed foolishly brave, and basically lacking in all the usual self-preservation instincts. Their job was to produce all kinds of weird weapons, and outside-the-box inventions. And then test them extensively, often on one another, before they could be passed on to the field agents. Output was high, and so was the turnover of assistants.

The Armourer couldn't help noticing that not quite far enough away, two lab assistants equipped with personal teleport devices were dueling inside a circle. They flickered in and out, appearing just long enough to throw a blow, or dodge one. Obscenities, blasphemies, and sounds of pain hung on the air long after they were gone. Beyond them, a statue in a corner moved, ever so slightly. From when a lab assistant had slowed down his metabolism so much that for him, decades passed between each tick and tock of the clock. He'd gone under in 1955, and showed no signs of coming out. The Armourer kept him around as a cautionary example. Beyond the statue, two invisible fighters were trying to find each other inside a circle. And someone . . . had just blown up the firing range again.

Lab assistants. Always in such high spirits.

The Armourer mostly just left them to it. Safer that way. He considered his workbench. His personal computer, wrapped in long strings of mistletoe. (It had seemed like a good idea, at the time.) Set out in no particular pattern were a bonsai wicker man, a working miniature Death Star that he'd built for a bet (with himself), a stuffed poltergeist with a very startled look on its face, and an iPod full of music he never seemed to have the time to listen to. Along with all kinds of bits and pieces from half a dozen projects he was still tinkering with. On and off. Some of the electronic workings and alien-derived tech had been there so long he'd forgotten what they were for. Though of course he'd never admit that.

He glared again at his latest project, sitting insolently on the edge of his desk. A long metal rod, with all kinds of spiky projections, ending in a precarious array of lenses and crystals, powered by a miniature reactor with rather less safety features than was probably wise. It looked like a hand torch that had just limped home from an evening out at the local BDSM club. The Armourer called it a Boojum Projector, because when you pointed it at someone, or something, they softly and silently vanished away. So far, so good. The problem was: the Armourer didn't know where the projector sent them. Or, if they might come back again, someday. The math remained stubbornly ambiguous. So until he could work out some answer to this very basic problem, the Armourer couldn't in all good conscience sign off the damned thing.

And besides, when you got right down to it, the Boojum Projector was really just another gun. He'd made so many guns, down the years. And they couldn't have been that good, because the family kept coming back to him, demanding he come up with new ones. Bigger, better, badder guns . . . The Armourer sniffed, sourly. Ideas for things used to come to him so easily. They still did, but more slowly now, like squeezing blood out of a stone. He could still do it. He still had it. But when did it all become such a strain . . . ?

Somebody close by cleared their throat; quietly and politely and just a bit relentlessly. A real *I'm not going away till you notice me* noise. The Armourer sighed, inwardly, and looked up. If anything his scowl deepened, just a little. Standing before him were two of his most intelligent, and irritating, lab assistants. Maxwell and Valerie Drood. Bright and cheerful and endlessly enthusiastic, and full of enough nervous energy to run a small country between them, they both wore gleaming, pristine white lab coats. Entirely unmarked and unaffected by all the messy mayhem going on around them. The lab coats were one of Maxwell and Victoria's most useful, if boring, creations. The coats never caught on. The other lab assistants refused to wear them, because they saw their accumulated electrical burns and chemical stains and the odd bullet hole, as badges of honor and experience. *Look what I survived!* Maxwell was tall, dark, and handsome, Victoria was tall, blonde, and sweetly pretty. They held hands all the time and didn't care who noticed.

"Sorry to bother you, Armourer," said Maxwell, once it became clear the Armourer had nothing to say to them. "But we really do need to get our hands on the Boojum Projector thingy. To try it out, see what it can do. All that sort of thing . . ."

"Love the name," said Victoria. "We love classical allusions, don't we, sweetie?"

"Well, of course!" said Maxwell. "But . . . You have been hanging on to it for rather a long time. Armourer. Sir."

"So we've been sent to . . . take it off your hands," said Victoria. Who could get away with not calling people sir because she was so pretty.

"Not our idea!" Maxwell said quickly. "We wouldn't bother you for all the world, but the pressure is coming down. From above."

"From on high, actually," Victoria said diffidently. "You know how it is."

"I held them off for as long as I could," said Maxwell. "Made all kinds of excuses, on your behalf . . ."

"He did! He really did!" said Victoria. "You wouldn't believe how brave and steadfast he was, on your behalf!"

"Well," said Maxwell, "I wouldn't say that, exactly . . ."

"Well, you should, Maxwell!" Victoria said immediately. "You mustn't put yourself down, because I won't have it. You need to stand up for yourself, Maxwell sweetie."

"You're so supportive, Victoria. I don't know what I'd do without you."

They smiled into each other's eyes, lost in each other, completely forgetting the Armourer and why they'd come to see him.

"Young lab assistants in love," growled the Armourer. "The horror, the horror . . . Who's been putting the pressure on you? As if I didn't know?"

"The Matriarch has been very insistent that we move the Boojum Projector on to the next stage of testing," said Maxwell.

"Mother is always impatient, when it comes to new weapons she's taken a fancy to," said the Armourer. "You tell her she'll just have to wait, until it's ready. Still more work to be done yet."

Maxwell and Victoria looked at each other. Maxwell cleared his throat, searching for the right tactful tone.

"I'm very sorry, sir, but . . . Your mother, Martha, hasn't been Matriarch for some time. She died, a few years back."

"We have a new Matriarch now, Armourer," said Victoria. "Margaret. Remember?"

"Ah," said the Armourer. "Yes. Of course." He squeezed his eyes tight shut, just for a moment. "Of course I remember. Just, force of habit . . ." He sniffed loudly and glared at them both. "You're getting a little old to be lab assistants, aren't you? You must be well into your twenties. More? Damn, how Time flies. And takes advantage, when you aren't looking. . . . Why haven't you left the Armory, like all the others? You need to specialize in . . . something, and move on! Fly the nest!"

"We like it here," said Maxwell. "Don't we, Victoria?"

"Oh yes, Maxwell! Ever so much! It's all so exciting. . . . I don't think we'll ever want to leave the Armory!"

"Well, you should," the Armourer said crushingly. "Get out while you can. I used to think like you, and look what happened to me. I got old when I wasn't looking."

Maxwell and Victoria looked at each other again. They thought he didn't notice.

"We'll come back again later, Armourer," said Maxwell. "When you're feeling a bit more . . . focused."

The Armourer kept his gaze fixed on the Boojum Projector on his workbench until he was sure they were both gone. And then he sighed, just a little, to himself. Of course his mother was dead. He'd been to her funeral. And now, news of his little slip would be all over the Armory in minutes. Gossip moved so quickly among the lab assistants that sometimes it arrived before the event that triggered it. The Armourer leaned back in his special chair and looked around the great stone cavern that just about contained the Drood family Armory. Huge machines crowded up against one another, like animals competing for territory, surrounded and interrupted by long rows of workstations, combat areas, and proving grounds. Plus a whole bunch of snack machines and soft drink dispensers.

The Armourer was pretty sure there was a working still, somewhere. There certainly had been, when he'd been a lab assistant. He built it himself.

And lab assistants, lab assistants everywhere, running around doing unwise things, raising hell and havoc and generally having a good time. They did so love to test out a new theory, often suddenly and violently and all over the place.

The Armourer was pretty sure they all respected him, in their own way. If only for his seniority and his proven track record in creating weapons of mass unpleasantness. But it did worry him, just a little, that he had no idea how they felt about him, otherwise. He'd never cared about being liked, or popular. That wasn't the job. He wasn't even there to oversee discipline. That wasn't what the assistants needed. He was there to inspire them, drive them on, and provide the right reckless atmosphere for them to function in. But how long had it been, since he just sat down and had a talk with any of them?

His gaze drifted back to the Boojum Projector. Bloody thing. Maybe the family could use it for garbage disposal. . . .

Did it matter where garbage went, once you made it disappear? Well, yes, he supposed it might. If you didn't know where you were sending it, and whether someone there might object. And there was always the chance it might reappear . . . unexpectedly. No, no . . . Forget the projector. Too many unanswered, and perhaps unanswerable, questions. Not every idea is a winner. Like the time he'd crossed chocolate and cheese to provide the perfect snack. He could still make people vomit, just by reminding them of how it has tasted. . . . The Armourer sniffed moodily. He hated it when Good Ideas turned out not to be practical.

He tugged thoughtfully at the tuft of hair protruding over his right ear and then stopped abruptly when some of the hairs come away in his hand. He studied the loose white hairs for a while, before opening his hand and letting them fall away. He'd have to be more careful. He didn't have much hair left to lose. It didn't seem that long ago, that he used to have a fine head of hair. Like his brother, James. But he lost it all years ago, to stress. The Armourer pouted, sulkily. He missed having hair. But then, he missed a lot of things.

One hell of a loud explosion shook the entire Armory. Things fell over, cables dropped down from the ceiling, and a dusty cloud of smoke rose up everywhere. Lab assistants ran frantically back and forth, yelling at one another to do something, instead of doing it themselves. A few fires flared up, briefly, before the targeted sprinklers cut in and put them out. A voice rose above the general chaos.

"Sorry . . ."

Order was quickly restored, someone was smacked hard around the back of the head, and everything returned to normal as everyone went back to work. Sudden loud noises and material damage came as standard when you worked in the Drood family Armory. That's why there were always stretchers and body bags piled up unobtrusively in one corner. If only because they helped concentrate the mind wonderfully. The Armourer hardly enough noticed the explosion. He had other things on his mind.

There was a time, when he had been a field agent. People tended to forget that Jack Drood had been one of the best secret agents the family ever had, back when he and the world were a lot younger and things seemed so much simpler. And those who did remember what he did out in the world preferred to forget the kind of things field agents had to do, back in the day. In that Coldest of Wars. All the hard and necessary things Jack Drood did to keep the world safe.

All those years, running around broken Europe, chasing and being chased back and forth across the Iron Curtain. Stamping out supernatural brushfires, before they could get out of hand. Blowing up super-science villains in their hidden bunkers, before they could let loose something unspeakable, if they couldn't get their own way . . . Killing people who needed killing. But had any of it really made any actual difference? Had he even killed the right people?

They'd made such a great team, Jack and his brother, James, fighting the good fight, in all the right places. But the family broke up the team. Separated them, sent them off on different missions, in different places, because there was just so much going on in the hidden world, in those days. And not nearly enough field agents to go around. The world made a legend out of James, and his amazing exploits. They called him the Gray Fox. The greatest secret agent of his time. Guns, girls, and gratuitous violence, and he always got the job done. It seemed like wherever Jack went, everyone had heard of the Gray Fox. In all the secret retreats and the back alley bars, the corridors of power and the loneliest places in the world. And the family . . . went along. Because the Gray Fox's success reflected well on the family, and it was always useful to have a legend on their side.

Jack Drood did just as much good work, but he always believed a secret agent's job was not to be noticed. Get in, do what needed doing, and get out; and if you'd done your job properly, no one should ever know you were even there. So Jack . . . got overlooked. No legend for him. Hardly anyone knew about him, outside the family. And he was fine with that, mostly. He never saw himself, or James, as any kind of legend or hero. Just secret agents, doing a hard, necessary, and sometimes distasteful job. So everyone else could sleep safely in their beds.

The Drood family has only one code, and one motto: *Anything, for the family*. Droods serve the family, because the family serves a greater purpose. Droods get the best of everything, because they have to give up everything else that matters. No one gets to walk away, or have their own life. No one gets to know peace, not while the world still needs saving. But there are many ways to serve in the Droods.

The Armourer didn't mind giving up being a field agent. Not really. There was excitement and glamour, out in the field. A sense of being right at the heart of things, doing something that mattered . . . but there was also blood and horror and death. Far too much death. Jack never enjoyed the work, the way James did. The Gray Fox was born to do fieldwork. Born to break into hidden bases, steal the secret plans, seduce the villain's mistress, and walk away with a smile on his face. Jack did that, too, sometimes, but he couldn't seem to separate the heady moments of triumph from all the dark and nasty stuff that went with it. The innocents betrayed and the people left behind, the bodies left slumped in alleyways and the lives of families ruined. James never looked back, but Jack couldn't seem to look away from all the collateral damage that went with his successes.

He didn't like most of the people he had to deal with, out in the field, and he really didn't like some of the things he had to do to keep the world safe. The villains who cried before he shot them in the face; the women who cried when they discovered they'd been used by both sides, just for what they knew; the allies you betrayed to get the information you needed and the politicians the family wouldn't let him touch, even though it was clearly the only sane and reasonable thing to do. *Our atrocities were acceptable, because theirs were so much worse.* Was it Churchill who said that? The Armourer had believed that for a long time. He had no problem with killing people who needed killing. But the old certainties of World War II were quickly eroded by the increasing ambiguities of Cold War politics. When today's enemy could be tomorrow's friend, or at least ally. And, far too often, vice versa.

The Armourer closed his eyes to rest them, just for a moment. He felt awfully tired. It seemed like he always felt tired, these days. The work never ended, no matter how much you put into it. Even if you worked every hour God sent, and then some, trying to keep up with the family's demands. Knowing a good man could die, out in the field, if you didn't get just the right weapon or gadget to him, in time. The Armourer had considered retiring now and again. But it wasn't like there was anybody ready to step up and replace him. No one he'd trust to be up to the job, and its responsibilities. No one who could protect all the good men and women out in the field, the way he did. And besides, if he did retire, what would he do with himself?

He forced his eyes open and sat up straight in his chair, grunting loudly at the effort involved. He rummaged through his desk drawers, until he found a fresh packet of Chocolate Hobnobs. Best cookies in the world. He cut open the package with a handy switchblade, scattered half a dozen Hobnobs across his desktop, and then picked one up and dunked it carefully in his tea mug. He stirred the cookie around a few times. A mug that provided you with tea at always just the right temperature was definitely one of his better inventions. Now, if he could only create a packet of Hobnobs that was constantly refilling itself . . . Put it on the To Do list. The Armourer bit carefully into the tea-soaked cookie. Marvelous. One of the life's more important little pleasures.

His computer made a loud self-important noise to let him know he had an important message coming in. The Armourer glared at the machine till it shut up.

"Well?" he said.

The computer monitor turned itself on and presented him with an urgent e-mail from the Matriarch. Who had clearly decided it would be more diplomatic, and probably safer, to address him from a distance. The e-mail wanted to know why he was so behind on so many important projects. Including the much awaited and anticipated Boojum Projector. The e-mail then reminded the Armourer that he had promised the family the following important items (there followed a depressingly long list) that should have been ready for field testing by now. That Matriarch wanted him to know she was very disappointed in him. The Matriarch didn't want to have to take responsibilities away from him, and she really didn't want to have to. . . . The Armourer got bored with the message, even while he was reading it, and deleted the e-mail, before he got to the barely veiled threats he knew would be coming at the end. The monitor screen shut itself down. The Armourer smiled briefly. It wasn't like he hadn't heard it all before. It would all be ready when it was ready, and not before. The Matriarch should know that. He'd told her often enough. But that was mothers for you; they always believed their sons could do anything.

He went back to looking around the Armory. Packed full of lab assistants, eagerly risking their lives and sanity in the pursuit of knowledge and things that went bang. So many young men and women . . . half of whom he didn't recognize, or remember. Hell, he didn't even know what half of them were working on. It was a big place, there was a lot going on . . . But there was a time he would have known. When he would have known all their names and faces, and what they were up to. It was just . . . there had been so many lab assistants, down the years. So many come and gone, risen to greatness or sent to an early grave. He was getting used to middle-aged men coming up to him in the hall, greeting him with loud voices and hearty handshakes, expecting him to remember them from when they'd briefly worked for him, during their time in the Armory. Before leaving, to do something more important for the family. The Armourer always smiled and nodded, and assured them that of course he remembered, but mostly he didn't. The trouble was . . . lab assistants tended to blend into one another. They arrived, they did good work, and they moved on. Which was how it should be. Only he stayed and grew older while the lab assistants seemed to grow younger every year. They moved on because they had ambition, and the Armourer thought he could remember a time when he did, too.

He used to know, and care about, every assistant and every project in his Armory. He took a pride in it. He was always striding up and down, peering over shoulders, offering a helping hand, handing out useful criticism and the occasional commendation. But these days he just didn't seem to have the energy. And, if he was honest with himself, he just didn't care as much as he used to. It was hard to get excited about a new gun, or gadget, when he'd seen so many before. When an Armourer stops caring about the work . . . then maybe it was time for him to step down. But he wasn't ready just yet . . . to give it all up and spend the rest of his life in the dayroom, watching television with all the other old fossils. He still had ideas. Still came up with things new enough and important enough to get his blood racing. He still had it.

He finished his cookie, took a long drink of hot tea, and sank back in his special chair. And the sights before him drifted away, replaced by older visions from another Time. He looked back over his long life; trying to decide, needing to know . . . Whether he did more good for the family, and the world, during his time as a secret agent out in the field, or afterward, as the family Armourer, creating things to keep field agents alive, and kill people who needed killing . . . It suddenly seemed very important to him, to be able to understand his life, if only on that level. Such a long life . . . so many things achieved . . . But did any of them really matter?

Why did he give so much of his life to his work? Because that's what he had.

His work mattered. He was convinced of that, at least. People were alive today because of what he'd done. He'd been involved in saving Humanity, and the entire world, on many occasions. Even quite recently, with the Hunger Gods War, and the invasion of the Hall grounds by the army of Accelerated Men. He could still put on the family armor and fight the good fight. All through his life, he'd always been ready to put his life on the line, for others. That had to mean something. . . . But what did it mean? If he hadn't done the work, if he hadn't gone out to fight, somebody else would have. What might his life have been like if he had never given up being a field agent? Had made himself a legend, like his brother, James? What if he'd never taken on the burden of the Armory and buried himself underground? What if . . . he'd found the strength to turn his back on the family, and his work, and his damned duty, and just walked away? No . . . No, he could never have done that. He believed in the family, and what it stood for. Sometimes in spite of himself and the family.

Eddie had been the only one to successfully tell the family to go to Hell, and make it stick. His nephew, Edwin, son of his sister, Emily and her husband, Charles. Good people, all of them. And even Eddie kept coming back, to be the family's conscience and take on the missions no one else could. Eddie even ran the family for a while, when the old system grew corrupt, and then he gave it all up to go back into the field, where he belonged. He left, but he kept coming back, because he knew he was needed.

The same mistake Jack made.

The Armourer wondered just how many deaths he was responsible for, throughout his long career as the Armourer. Far more than he ever killed personally, as an agent out in the world. As a field agent, he'd dispatched his fair share, but as Armourer, his deadly touch had spread across the whole world. Every time a Drood agent killed an enemy, it was because the Armourer had made it possible. If all the ghosts of his slaughtered dead came looking for him, would they fill the Armory? Or the hall? Would even the massive grounds outside Drood Hall be big enough to contain them all? And if he walked up and down the rows of ghosts on parade, looking into their dead reproachful faces, would he still believe they'd all needed killing?

It had all seemed so much simpler when he was younger, running wild in a world full of people who wanted him dead. Like his first job, not long after World War II, when he was sent chasing after missing Nazi gold, in Bavaria, at Lake Walchensee. A huge lake set right in the middle of the Bavarian mountains. Martin Bormann had been sent there with tons of gold bullion, to fund a Fourth Reich. The idea had apparently been that Bormann would seize and occupy the mountains, as a base for the Nazis to relaunch themselves. Instead, he ran away and disappeared. Supposedly, he dumped the tons and tons of gold bullion into Lake Walchensee first, because it would just have slowed him down. He probably meant to come back for it later, with a new face and a new identity, when he no longer had the world snapping at his heels. But that never happened.

The family sent Jack Drood to Bavaria, and to the lake, to see if the gold was there. Not because they needed it, they just didn't want anyone else to have it. Because a lot of gold can buy a lot of trouble.

Surrounded on all sides by jagged gray mountains without a hint of personality, Lake Walchensee's waters shimmered like living silver, under the light of a full moon. Jack Drood stood at the edge of the shore, looking out over the waters. A young man, full of vim and vigor, determined to do well and make his family proud of him. His hand went to the golden collar around his throat, the family torque. He muttered the right activating Words, and just like that, golden armor spilled out of the torque and covered him completely from head to toe. The greatest, most secret weapon of the Droods—the marvelous living armor that made them stronger, faster, and completely untouchable. Jack Drood stood for a while, thinking, like a golden statue, his face a featureless mask, a living symbol of implacable duty. And then he strode slowly forward into the shimmering waters, making quiet splashing sounds that didn't carry any distance at all. Jack knew the waters were icy cold, deadly cold on that still wintry night, but he didn't feel the cold at all. The armor saw to that. He strode on until the waters closed over his head, and he disappeared beneath the surface of the lake.

He descended steadily, following the curved bank beneath his armored feet, until finally he was walking along the bottom of Lake Walchensee. He'd left the light from above behind long ago, and now he moved through dark, still waters. He made his armor glow brightly, to give him some light to move in, but even so he was lucky to see more than ten feet in any direction. The bottom of the lake was scattered with objects, none of them particularly unusual or important, and he couldn't see a scrap of gold anywhere. His heavy armored feet sank deep into the muddy bottom, every step disturbing dirt and sediment, sending it rising up into the dark water, before falling slowly back again.

Jack carried a special device of his own invention, set into the armor of his left hand. He'd promised the family it would detect gold bullion at up to a hundred yards radius, but so far the damned thing wasn't reacting at all. Jack shook his hand a few times, just on general principles, but it made no difference. He moved slowly, steadily forward, covering a grid of the lake bottom he'd memorized previously. Looking carefully about him and doing his best not to trip over things.

He'd been underwater for more than an hour, supported and protected by his armor, not feeling the cold or any need for air, when he suddenly became aware that he wasn't alone down there. He'd been getting glimpses of things moving, just on the edge of the light his armor radiated, but he only knew for sure he had company when a steel harpoon came flying at him out of nowhere at incredible speed. It ricocheted harmlessly off his armored chest and fell slowly away through the water. Jack concentrated, and his armor blazed up, spreading new golden light through the dark waters. And there they all were, suddenly revealed in the new light, standing huddled together in their little groups, surrounding him. Caught completely unaware.

For a while they all just stood there, looking blankly at one another. Three different groups of half a dozen men each, wearing various kinds of underwater gear. Bubbles rose up in sudden bursts, as the divers talked to one another. And off on the very edge of the golden light; , a small yellow submersible. Probably the Americans; , they always had the budget to do things in style. Most of the divers were holding pressurized harpoon guns, and a few had over-sized guns adapted for underwater warfare. The various groups tried out every weapon they had on Jack, because they all knew they had to take out the Drood agent first, before they could turn on one another. Most agents would have had the sense to turn and run, rather than annoy a Drood, but the possible proximity of so much gold had turned their minds.

Jack just stood where he was, at the bottom of Lake Walchensee, and let the harpoons and bullets bounce uselessly off him. He hoped they'd get the hint and just go away, once it became clear they couldn't hurt him. He still believed in playing the game and doing the right thing. But even after the yellow submersible had fired an explosive rocket at him, and he'd had to catch the thing and hold it against his armored chest, to smother the explosion . . . When the waters calmed down again, and it was clear he hadn't been forced back so much as a step . . . Even then, they wouldn't give up. Duty, or greed, had got a hold of them.

They came at him from all sides, with vicious knives in their hands. Big, heavy blades with serrated edges. They stabbed and cut at him and got nowhere, and Jack realized he had no choice but to deal with them. Because they weren't going to go away and leave him alone, and abandon the gold. So he killed them all. He smashed in heads and ribs with his heavy golden fists. He punched holes in their scuba tanks, and ripped away their breathing tubes, and held them in place till they drowned. He grabbed the knives out of their hands and stabbed them through their black rubber diving suits. He had to chase after the last few when they finally turned to run. He caught them easily, his golden armor driving him through the dark waters at superhuman speed.

Bodies floated everywhere, falling slowly to the lake bottom in awkward, spread-eagled poses. Blood rose up here and there in drifting streams.

The yellow submersible tried to flee while he was occupied. He soon caught up with it, pulled himself up onto its roof, and punched great holes in its sides with his golden fists. Air bubbled out thickly. The motors strained to lift the small craft, even with Jack's extra weight, until he ripped them away. The submersible sank slowly back through the dark waters to settle on the muddy bottom. Jack found the escape hatch and held it closed, until he was sure everyone inside was dead. He didn't feel good about it. The family had warned him what being a field agent could mean, but he hadn't realized it would feel like this. So . . . easy.

He didn't examine any of the bodies, or the submersible, to discover who they'd been working for. It didn't matter. His orders had been clear. No one else could be trusted with that much gold. The other agents could have been CIA, KGB, or any of the many alphabet soup groups operating all over divided Europe, in those days. So many organizations, operating on either side of the Iron Curtain. Searching for treasure, or power, or just something they could turn to their advantage. Except . . . Jack spent hours, walking back and forth on the bottom of the lake, and he never found so much as a single gold coin. The only gold in those dark waters was the armor he was wearing.

He left the dead behind and walked up out of the dark waters, and that was Jack Drood's first mission as a field agent.

East Berlin was the dark side of that separated city, and Jack Drood sent his car racing through the back streets, hitting the brakes at the very last minute so he could screech around corners. This was some years later, after he'd made a reputation, if not a legend, for himself. Nothing to match his brother, James, the Gray Fox, but enough that he could still rely on being given the more interesting missions.

Jack glanced quickly at the rearview mirror. He was still being pursued by half a dozen official cars at speed. They swayed back and forth behind him as the gray anonymous men took it in turns to lean out the side windows and open fire on him. Jack grinned. They were having to go all out just to keep up over treacherously uneven roads, and even when they did manage to hit him, the bullets just bounced off his specially reinforced chassis. He felt so safe; he didn't even bother to armor up. Just kept his head down, kept his foot down hard, and sent his car hammering through the narrow back streets and alleyways of East Berlin, heading for Checkpoint Charlie and safe passage back to civilization.

Jack was driving one of his favorite cars, his very own lovingly restored 1933 open-topped, four-and-a-half-liter Bentley, in racing green with red leather interiors. Not exactly an inconspicuous car, for a secret agent out in the field. Just smuggling it into East Berlin had been a real pain in the ass. But when it came to holding its own in a car chase, the Bentley had no equal. Jack liked a car he could depend on. The Bentley had a bulletproof chassis and windows, hidden machine guns, front and back, and a whole bunch of other nasty little secrets tucked away about its person, which Jack had designed and installed himself.

There was a long waiting list at Drood Hall, just to look at the specs.

Jack sent the Bentley racing up and down the back streets

and alleyways, some of them so narrow the sides of the car brushed against the cheap concrete and brickwork. Dark streets under a dark sky, no moon up above, and hardly any working streetlights. Only the Bentley's headlights, blazing fiercely before him, showed Jack the way through East Berlin. He hung onto the steering wheel with both hands, laughing aloud as the car bounced and jumped. Nothing like a good old-fashioned hot pursuit to get the adrenaline going. He concentrated on the city map he'd memorized and sent the Bentley slamming around sudden corners, hitting the supercharger now and again, when he needed to open up a little more space between him and his pursuers. The sound of so many roaring engines in the confined spaces was almost unnaturally loud in the night, but no one looked out a window to see what was going on. Jack peered ahead into the glare of the headlights. Either the map he'd been given was wrong, or someone had been doing a lot of unauthorized building around here. A whole bunch of turnings he'd been relying on just weren't there.

He kept his foot down, gunning the motor. He was heading in the right direction, and that was all that mattered.

It didn't help that most of East Berlin looked the same. Dull, faceless, characterless buildings on every side, thrown up in a hurry to hold a subservient population in place. Hardly any lights in the windows, and no one about on the streets. Not at that hour. The only people out and about at this time of the night in East Berlin were agents like him, and the East German secret police following him. The cars behind were catching up, despite everything Jack could do to throw them off, and more and more bullets were slamming into the rear of the Bentley. Jack kept his head well down and grinned across at his companion, curled up in a ball in the passenger seat.

Greta was a pretty young secretary who worked for the secret police because she liked eating regularly. She'd managed to get word to a Drood representative that she would tell them everything she knew (and it promised to be quite a lot, and worth the knowing) if the Droods would get her safely out of the country. And save her soul from Hell.

"So," he said, raising his voice just a bit to be heard over the roar of the car's engine and the sound of bullets hammering into the rear. "How long have you and your friends been allowing yourselves to become possessed by demons?"

"It all started out as a game," she said. "Just a few of us, doing it for fun. For the thrill of it all. We called out to spirits, through the Ouija board, and they came. And then we called out to other things, and they came, too. We let them in, just for a while, and it felt good, so good. With a thing from Hell inside us, we weren't afraid to do anything. You don't understand how powerful a feeling that can be, not to have to be afraid . . . And then the demons spoke to us and encouraged us to do things, and we did. I liked being possessed. I liked it so much I let seven demons come inside me, and then I couldn't get them out. I can feel them, squirming inside me, like barbed wire slicing through my thoughts . . . I'm holding them down for the moment, but every day it feels like there's less and less of me, and more and more of them. I was told you can help me."

"Don't worry," said Jack, in his best calm and reassuring voice. "We have people standing ready, who know how to deal with things like this. What about your friends?"

"What about them?"

"Well, what happened to the other people who were possessed by demons?"

"I killed them," said the little secretary, still curled up in a ball in the passenger seat. "I had to clean up after myself, before I could leave."

And then the Bentley was suddenly slammed to one side, right across the road and into the far wall, as a hidden gun emplacement opened up. The heavy bullets hammered all along the length of the car, and Jack had to fight the steering wheel for control. The Bentley bounced back off the wall, hardly damaged by the impact, and swerved back and forth across the road. Jack laughed out loud and kept going, hitting the supercharger for all it was worth. He'd designed the Bentley to be a tank, unstoppable. But when he looked around at his passenger, to say something cheerful and reassuring, he found the gun emplacement must have been specially designed, too. Its unusually heavy bullets had punched right through the Bentley's reinforced side, leaving a long series of jagged holes. In the car and in the passenger. The little secretary sat slumped in her seat, almost torn in half. Blood soaked her whole side of the car. She was dead. With that much damage, she had to be. But she still turned her head around to look at Jack and smile at him with bloody teeth.

Jack checked the road ahead was clear and looked back at her. Demons from Hell looked back at him through her unblinking eyes.

"Get us out of here," said the secretary, with her dead mouth. "Get us back to Drood Hall, and we will teach you all the secrets of Hell."

"I don't think so," said Jack. "We know all we need to know about the Pit."

He hit a large red button set into the dashboard and filled the car with a blast of exorcist radiations. A bit basic, a bit down and dirty, but it did the job. The secretary's body shook and shuddered, horrible screams emerging from her slack mouth, and then she was still. The car stank of blood and brimstone, the stench of Hell. Jack reached across, opened the opposite door, and pushed the body out. It hit the ground hard, in a flail of limbs, and was quickly left behind. The door shut itself, and Jack drove on.

He tried to feel sorry for the poor little secretary, but he hadn't known her long enough. Nobody told her to play with fire.

Jack drove on through the empty East Berlin night, roaring through the deserted streets. No one was chasing him anymore. They'd all stopped to check the body. Jack hoped they'd be properly appreciative that he'd cleaned up for them, but he rather doubted it. He drove on, heading for Checkpoint Charlie and home, and he never looked back once.

Jack went walking in solitary silence, on the gray dusty surface of the Moon, surrounded by mountains and craters, snug and secure inside his golden armor. The dimensional Door had dropped him off exactly where he was supposed to be. He was there to retrieve Professor Cavor's last mooncraft, crash-landed back in Victorian times, so its presence wouldn't embarrass the Americans when they landed their ship in a few years' time. Jack took his time, looking around him, grinning broadly behind his featureless mask. Enjoying the magnificent scenery by Earthlight.

He found the crashed vehicle easily enough, right where it was supposed to be. He peered through the porthole at the mummified body inside, and then dragged the craft back to the Door, great clouds of dust billowing up around him, and then falling slowly back again. He forced the craft through the expanded Door, and then turned away, and walked back across the gray land to one particular crater, mentioned in Cavor's last communication. He found the stone stairway, cut into the interior side of the crater, and proceeded carefully down the rough steps, following them around and around and down and down, until finally he came to the abandoned ruins of the Selenite city. They were all long gone, of course. All that remained of Selenite civilization was rot and ruin. He walked cautiously on through the great stone galleries, past massive crystal installations, feeling very small against the sheer scale of the surrounding structures. He had hoped to find some last remnants of their unearthly science, but everything he touched crumbled to dust under his golden fingers.

He'd got there too late. Millennia too late.

The Armourer stirred restlessly in his chair. He had a strong feeling he should be somewhere else, doing something else, but he couldn't think what. He seemed to have spent most of his life feeling that way. When he was out in the field, he couldn't wait to get home. When he was stuck in the hall, he quickly got bored. And when he finally left the field and settled down in the Armory . . . he pined for the adventures he'd left behind.

Which might well be why he so often went truant, on a little walkabout, to places he knew he shouldn't be. Places like the Nightside, where he knew the family wouldn't come looking for him. It was only small disobediences like that, he often thought, that kept him sane.

It had been different, at first. When he had a family of his own. A wife and a child. Both of them gone now. He brought Natasha back to the Hall so they could be together, but it didn't last. All too soon she was taken from him and he was left alone, with nothing left but his job, and his duty. There had been . . . affairs, dalliances, down the years. Mostly with pretty young lab assistants, with daddy issues. The Armourer smiled, briefly. James might be the one with the reputation as a lady-killer, but Jack had done all right for himself. In his own quiet way. And he hadn't always been alone. He'd had a dog once. Until it exploded. Poor little Scraps.

Jack remembered his wife, Natasha. He met her in Moscow while he was working a mission there, alongside the resident Drood agent. So long ago now . . .

He punched a masked man in the face, kneed him briskly in the nuts, and then threw him off the edge of the building. The masked man screamed all the way down, but Jack was already moving on to his next target. There had to be twenty or more of the enemy, clattering over the steeply sloping tiled roof, with only Jack and Natasha to stand against them. The Moscow field agent, Erin Drood, was down below, defusing the bomb. Jack ducked a flailing fist and punched the masked man savagely in the side. He felt ribs break under his fist. He knocked the man down, and then braced himself as he turned and found another masked man pointing a gun at his head. Natasha stepped in and kicked the man's legs out from under him, with one broad sweep of her leg. She waited till he hit the roof, hard, and then stamped on his hand till he let go of the gun. And then she stamped on his head. Jack and Natasha exchanged a grin and moved on to new targets.

Slipping and sliding across the steep uneven roof, far above the Moscow streets.

The masked men called themselves the Children of Vodyanoi. A small but very determined group that wanted to make mankind over into something better. The Russian authorities thought they were just another suppressed religious sect, but Drood intelligence knew better. Which was why Jack had been sent to help the resident field agent, Erin Drood, stop the Children of Vodyanoi, before they did something that couldn't be undone. Natasha was their local contact, but she insisted on getting involved. And seeing her fight overwhelming odds with just spiked brass knuckles and a cheerful smile, Jack was glad she was there. He couldn't armor up for fear of setting off the bomb, so he was having to rely on old Drood fighting techniques. He thought he was doing okay. The Children of Vodyanoi all had the strength of fanatics, but they hadn't a clue how to fight on a professional level.

Jack and Natasha fought their way from one side of the roof to the other, and when they finally stopped and looked back, there was no one else left standing. Jack and Natasha leaned on each other, companionably, breathing hard.

"Explain to me again, please," Natasha said finally. "Just what the hell these idiots thought they were doing?"

"They wanted to transform Humanity," said Jack. "Make us all superhuman. Using alien DNA stripped from the dead crew of a crashed starship. Unfortunately, they didn't know the DNA acted like a virus. It infected them and changed their thinking, so they would want to infect others. With alien DNA programmed to override any other DNA, so we would end up like them. Invasion and colonization, by proxy."

Natasha looked around the roof, counting quietly. "This is it. This is all of them. A very small group."

"Then all that's left is to burn the bodies," said Jack. "With these very special incendiaries provided by the family Armourer. Burns right down to the genetic level, or so I'm told."

"What about the bomb?" said Natasha.

"I defused that ages ago," said a cheerful voice behind them. "I just enjoyed watching you fight."

"Piss off, Erin," said Jack. "Just for that, you can carry the bomb out of here."

Erin laughed and disappeared. Jack and Natasha looked at each other.

"Is there any chance that you or I could be infected with alien DNA?" said Natasha. "After all, we did come into close contact with those idiots. Briefly."

"The injections we took earlier will protect us," said Jack. "My family has antidotes for everything."

"I'd still feel safer if you were to look me over," said Natasha. "Personally."

Jack grinned. "I can do that."

They weren't supposed to fall in love, but they did anyway. Jack brought Natasha back to Drood Hall and married her. Natasha became pregnant within a year and gave birth to a fine baby boy. And they were so happy together . . . for a while.

Natasha died some two years after Timothy was born. Nothing special, or out of the ordinary, her kidneys just stopped working, and she died while the Drood doctors were still trying to figure out why. Things like that happen, even to Droods. By the time Jack got back from his latest mission, it was all over. He stood looking down at her grave, holding his confused young son by the hand, and swore he would never leave the Hall again. Because he hadn't been there for his wife and son when they needed him. He would stay, because his son needed him.

Though of course by then, it was already too late.

Jack took up a position in the Armory. He'd always been fascinated by the weapons and devices he'd been supplied with as a field agent, and had come up with a few useful things himself. He was a bit old to be a lab assistant, but the Armory was happy to have someone with firsthand experience of how their various creations actually operated under field conditions. Jack just wanted something to occupy his mind. To keep him from thinking about the happy life he used to have.

He trained under the previous Armourer, his aunt Eloise, sister to the Matriarch. Eloise had been Armourer for decades. She was a real terror, working everyone hard, always shouting and swearing and carrying on, not prepared to let anyone get away with anything. Or take the credit for anything she could take the credit for. And God help you if you didn't keep all your paperwork strictly up-to-date. Jack wasn't sure anyone actually liked her, but everyone did good work under her unwavering glare. They didn't dare do anything else.

Eloise was a great believer in weaponizing unnatural forces, an idea that had been all the rage back in the 1920s and 1930s. But definitely starting to feel a bit old hat by the time Jack joined the Armory. He tried to steer the work in a more scientific direction, but Eloise would have none of it. She was getting old and slow and past it, but wouldn't admit it. The quality of the work coming out of the Armory started to suffer, though Eloise made sure the blame fell everywhere except with her. Until she blew herself up. Jack was then promoted to Armourer. So he could put in place all the changes he'd been advocating for so long. Things improved immediately.

Did she fall or was she pushed? The Armourer smiled. He'd never tell. Anything, for the family.

He looked at the chair opposite him, and smiled at Natasha. She smiled sweetly back at him. She was sitting very straight and upright, as she always did, with her hands folded neatly in her lap. Still wearing her usual long black leather coat and her knee-length boots. Long, dark hair fell out from under her fur cap. She sighed and shook her head.

"What are you still doing here, Jack? This was only ever supposed to be a temporary position."

"I came back to the Hall to look after Timothy," said Jack. "So he wouldn't be alone. I did mean to leave here, move on, as soon as he was old enough to look after himself. But everyone knows how that worked out. After he went rogue, I didn't want to leave the hall and the family. They were very supportive. And they were all I had left."

"You should have gone back out into the world again," said Natasha. "Back where you belonged."

"I was busy," said the Armourer. "There was always so much work to do. And besides, if you weren't in the world, I wasn't interested in it anymore."

"So you stayed here and got old," said Natasha.

"Yes," said the Armourer. "I miss you so much, Natasha."

"I know. Why didn't you marry again?"

"Because I never felt about anyone else, the way I felt about you."

The Armourer looked away, thinking, remembering, and when he looked back, she wasn't there anymore. And neither was the chair she'd been sitting on.

Timothy Drood . . . His son, his only child. Not like his brother, James, who had so many children by so many women, out in the field. You can't go tomcatting around like James did and not expect there to be consequences. James produced so many illegitimate half-Droods they formed their own organization, the Gray Bastards. The Armourer tried to keep in touch with as many of them as he could, because they were his nephews and nieces, after all. But there were just so many of them. All determined to go their own way and make a name for themselves, like their illustrious father. So many of them died, trying to prove themselves worthy of the family name. Like Harry, and Roger, and . . .

If the Armourer had a son now, he supposed it would have to be his nephew, Eddie. A good man, a better field agent, and a credit to his family. Eddie Drood, the man responsible for the death of the Armourer's beloved brother, James, and his estranged son, Timothy. There was no one in the family the Armourer felt closer to than Eddie, but there was no denying that closeness came with a cost.

Timothy Drood . . . or Tiger Tim, the name he took for himself when he went rogue, and disappeared into the African jungles. What they used to call a bad seed. Bad to the bone. Or could it all have been the Armourer's fault, did Timothy Drood become Tiger Tim because of parental neglect? The Armourer thought he'd done his best, but he'd never known what to make of his odd, unruly son. A strange child, even from an early age. The Armourer never knew how to be a father to him. Timothy had always been resistant to every form of authority, or affection. And so more and more the Armourer just left him to his own devices and buried himself in his work. Because he understood his work. Was it because of that turning away, that his son had gone to the bad?

"Still blaming yourself, after all these years?" said Timothy. He sounded pleased at the idea. "Hello, Daddy. Here I am, back again, like the traditional bad penny. You're looking old."

He sat in the chair opposite the Armourer, where his mother had been, lounging bonelessly, almost arrogantly relaxed. A man heading into middle age and fighting it all the way. He had that kind of aesthetic musculature that only comes from regular workouts with professional equipment in expensive private gyms, and the skin on his face, especially just around the eyes, looked suggestively taut. He was wearing a rich cream safari suit, topped off with a white snap-brimmed hat, complete with tiger-skin band. He looked very inch the Great White Hunter and gloried in it. He smiled a lot, but it never reached his cold blue eyes.

"Why did you always prefer the jungles, boy?" said the Armourer. "Dangerous places, jungles."

"Not for me," said Tiger Tim, smiling easily. "When I walk

through a jungle, you can always be sure that I am the most dangerous thing in it."

"Well?" said the Armourer. "Tell me, was it my fault that you turned out bad? Did I let you down?"

"Typical you," said Tiger Tim. "Everything has to be your responsibility. It's a form of arrogance, really."

"Answer me!"

"I never thought of myself as bad. . . . I just wanted to have fun."

"Did you ever love me, son?" said the Armourer. "I tried to love you. I really did."

"Love . . ." said Tiger Tim. "Sorry. Never really got the hang of love."

"You nearly killed me," said the Armourer. "Trying to force me to open the family's Armageddon Codex for you."

"So I did," said Tiger Tim, nodding cheerfully. "Now that one was your fault. You didn't have to fight me."

The Drood family keeps its most secret depository of its most dangerous weapons, the Armageddon Codex, locked away in a pocket dimension only loosely linked to the Armory. For security reasons. Only the Armourer can even approach it, let alone enter it, without setting off all kinds of alarms. But Timothy Drood, not yet Tiger Tim, wanted in. So he lured his father off to a private place, with an urgent message, and beat the crap out of him. Timothy had laid his plans well, found all the right loopholes in the security measures that would let him access the pocket dimension, but he still couldn't open the Codex without the knowledge locked away in his father's head.

Timothy kicked his father in the ribs, again and again, and then knelt down beside him. "Come on, Daddy dearest! I'm on a deadline here! Give me the secret! Tell me how to unlock the Lion's Jaws!"

The Armourer lay curled up in a ball on the cold stone floor.

He ached all over from the beating he'd taken. He spat out a thick mouthful of blood and glared up at his son. Above and behind the two of them stood the Lion's Jaws, a great stone carving of a lion's head, complete with mane, perfect in every detail. Twenty feet tall and almost as wide, it towered over them, carved out of a dark blue-veined stone that made the head seem eerily alive. Timothy drew back his foot to kick his father again, and the Armourer flinched despite himself. Timothy laughed breathily.

"I know I need a brass key, Daddy," said Timothy. "The key opens the Jaws, but everyone knows that. I need to know how to open the Jaws so I can pass though them safely! Just give me the key and tell me how to use it, and I'll stop hurting you. Won't that be nice? Why do you always have to fight me, Daddy? You don't think I'm enjoying this, do you?"

"Yes," said the Armourer.

Timothy considered the point. "Well, all right, yes; you've got me there. I always enjoy punishing things that get in my way. But I promise you, I'd enjoy kicking the crap out of whoever had the key to the Lion's Jaws. Don't take this personally, Daddy."

"You sure you want to pass through the Jaws?" said the Armourer. Slowly, painfully. "You must know the legend, that only the pure in heart and pure in purpose can pass safely through to the Codex. Anything else, and the Jaws will slam down. And eat you."

"Oh, please," said Timothy. "That's just family fairy tales, to keep the weak of spirit from trying to do something like this. I am not so easily put off. I want the weapons from the Armageddon Codex, Daddy. I want the Time Hammer and the Juggernaut Jumpsuit. I want Oathbreaker, and Sunwrack, and Winter's Sorrow. I want to walk up and down in the world and make it dance to my tune."

"Why?" said the Armourer.

"I just want to have some fun," said Timothy.

"But these weapons are powerful enough to destroy the whole world!"

"What could be more fun?" said Timothy. "Oh, the things I will do . . ."

Except he didn't, in the end, because the Gray Fox appeared out of nowhere to save the day. As he so often did. He saved the Armourer's life, that day, although he let Timothy get away. Because the Armourer asked him to. That small piece of kindness had come back to haunt him many times, down the years. As he heard of some new slaughter, with his son's name attached to it. As Timothy Drood turned himself into Tiger Tim, slowly and deliberately, one cruel decision at a time. Spreading his evil like a plague, laughing delightedly as he walked through rivers of blood. Until finally, he went up against Eddie Drood, and Eddie killed him. Far and far away from home, in the icy wastes of the Antarctic. Eddie said afterward that Tiger Tim had died well, and the Armourer had pretended to believe him.

Timothy wasn't there anymore, and neither was the chair he'd been sitting on. The Armourer was surprised to find he was crying. For places and people lost. For things that might have been. He hauled out a handkerchief and dabbed at his face. His hand shook.

"I always tried to do my best for the family," he said. "I tried. . . . Doesn't that count, for something?"

"Of course it does," said James.

The Armourer looked up, and there was the Gray Fox, standing before him, smiling broadly. James Drood, in his prime. Tall and darkly handsome, effortlessly elegant in his expertly tailored tuxedo, wearing his usual sardonic expression. He looked every inch his legend.

"Come along, Jack," said James. "No time to be lounging around when there's important work that needs doing."

"Oh James," said Jack. "I've missed you so much."

"Of course you have," said the Gray Fox. "But now, we're back together. The old team! And we'll never be parted again."

The Armourer looked at him and nodded slowly. "It's over here, isn't it?"

James smiled. “You’ve done all you can, here. Time to go. You didn’t think I’d leave you to make the last great journey on your own, did you?”

“Do I get to rest at last?” said the Armourer.

“Where would be the fun in that?” said James. “We have better and far more important work waiting for us now! And far more fun than you’ve ever known. . . . Come along, James. It’s time to do things that really matter.”

He put out a hand to the Armourer, who clasped it with his own. And just like that Jack and James stood together, both of them young and in their prime again. They laughed out loud and hugged each other fiercely.

“Good work?” said Jack. “Work that really matters? Lead me to it!”

And then he paused, and looked at his brother.

“What is it?” said James.

“Can you answer the question?” said James. “Did I do more important work as a field agent, or working here in the Armory?”

“You already know the answer,” said James, kindly. “Anything, for the family. You always did good work, Jack, and everything you did was designed to save people’s lives, in the long run. And that is all that matters.”

The two young men walked forward through the Armory, and lab assistants came forward from all sides to form two great crowds for them to walk through. Ranks and ranks of faces, smiling and waving to the Armourer as he passed. And he knew all their faces, and all their names, even the ones who’d left the Armory long ago. They were all there to say good-bye to him. The Armourer hadn’t realized how many lives he’d touched.

A dog ran forward to greet them and danced eagerly in front of Jack.

“Is that you, Scraps?” said Jack.

“Of course,” said James. “Everyone you ever lost is waiting to meet you again.”

Jack and James Drood, reunited at last, walked on together and never looked back once.

Maxwell and Victoria found the Armourer sitting slumped in his chair at his desk. Quite dead. Maxwell checked for life signs, didn't find any, and sent the nearest lab assistant hurrying off to inform the Matriarch. Maxwell and Victoria looked at the dead man.

"At least he died still working," said Maxwell.

"He gave his life to the Armory," said Victoria.

It must have seemed like a nice thing to say.

What better way to start off a collection of stories than with an upbeat piece about death? The Armourer, Jack Drood, is a long-standing character from my Secret Histories novels first introduced some ten years ago, in The Man with the Golden Torque. He was an old man even then and has grown increasingly frail ever since, and it just seemed the right time to let him go. Jack Drood never really got the same respect as his more famous brother, James Drood, the Gray Fox, but he was a major player in the Cold War and a great secret agent in his own right. I wanted to show him at the end of his life, looking back and trying to decide whether he did more good for his family, and Humanity, as a field agent fighting the bad guys, or as an Armourer producing weapons and devices to keep other agents alive. I wanted to give him one last big adventure.

STREET WIZARD

I believe in magic. It's my job.

I'm a street wizard, and I work for the London City Council. I don't wear a pointy hat, I don't live in a castle, and no one in my line of work has used a wand since tights went out of fashion. I'm paid the same money as a traffic warden, and I don't even get a free uniform. I just get to clean up other people's messes and prevent trouble when I can. It's a magical job, but someone's got to do it.

My alarm goes off at nine o'clock sharp every evening, and that's when my day begins. When the sun's already sliding down the sky toward evening, with night pressing close on its heels. I do all the usual things everyone else does at the start of their day, and then I check I have all my bits and pieces, before I go out. The tools of my trade: salt, holy water, crucifix, silver dagger, and wooden stake. No guns. Guns get you noticed.

I live in a comfortable enough flat, over an off license, right on the edge of Soho. Good people, mostly. But when the sun goes down and the night takes over, a whole new kind of people move in: the tourists and the punters and every other eager little soul with more money than sense. Looking for a good time, the fools. They fill up the streets, with stars in their eyes and avarice in their hearts, all looking for a little something to take the edge off, to satisfy their various longings.

Someone has to watch their backs to protect them from the dangers they don't even know are out there.

By the time I'm ready to leave, two drunken drag queens are arguing shrilly under my window, caught up in a slanging match. It'll all end in tears and wig pulling. I leave them to it and head out into the tangle of narrow streets that make up Soho. Bars and restaurants, nightclubs and clip joints, hot neon and cold hard cash. The streets are packed with furtive-eyed people, hot on the trail of everything that's bad for them. It's my job to see they get home safely, or at least, that they only fall prey to the everyday perils of Soho.

I never set out to be a street wizard. Don't suppose anyone does. But, like music and mathematics, with magic it all comes down to talent. All the hard work in the world will only get you so far, to be a Major Player, you have to be born to the Craft. The rest of us play the cards we're dealt. And do the jobs that need doing.

I start my working day at a greasy spoon café called Dingley Dell. There must have been a time when I found that funny, but I can't remember when. The café is the agreed meeting place for all the local street wizards, a stopping-off place for information, gossip, and a hot cup of tea, before we have to face the cold of the night. It's not much of a place; all steamed-up windows, Formica-covered tables, plastic chairs, and a full greasy breakfast if you can stomach it. There's only ever thirteen of us, to cover all the hot spots in Soho. There used to be more, but the budget's not what it was.

We sit around patiently, sipping blistering tea from chipped china, while the Supervisor drones on, telling us things he thinks we need to know. We hunch our shoulders and pretend to listen. He's not one of us. He's just a necessary intermediary, between us and the Council. We only put up with him because he's responsible for overtime payments. A long, miserable streak of piss, and mean with it, Bernie Drake likes to think he runs a tight ship. Which basically means he moans a lot, and we call him Gladys behind his back.

"All right! Listen up! Pay attention and you might just get through tonight with all your fingers, and your soul still attached!" That's Drake. If a fart stood upright and wore an ill-fitting suit, it could replace our supervisor and we wouldn't even notice. "We've had complaints! Serious complaints! Seems a whole bunch of booze demons have been possessing the more vulnerable tourists, having their fun and then abandoning their victims at the end of the night, with really bad hangovers and no idea how they got them. So watch out for the signs, and make sure you've got an exorcist on speed dial for the stubborn ones. We've also had complaints about magic shops—that are there one day and gone the next, before the suckers can come running back to complain the goods don't work. So if you see a shop front you don't recognize, call it in! And Jones, stay away from the wishing wells! I won't tell you again. And Padgett, *leave the witches alone!* They've got a living to make, same as the rest of us.

"And, if anybody cares, apparently something's been eating traffic cops. All right, all right! That's enough hanging around! Get out there and do good. Remember: you've a quota to meet."

We're already up and on our feet and heading out, muttering comments just quietly enough that the supervisor can pretend he doesn't hear them. It's the little victories that keep you going. We all take our time about leaving, just to show we won't be hurried. I take a moment to nod politely to the contingent of local working girls, soaking up what warmth they can from the café, before a long night out on the cold, cold streets. We know them, and they know us, because we all walk the same streets and share the same hours. All decked out in bright colors and industrial-strength makeup, they chatter together like gaudy birds of paradise, putting off the moment when they have to go out to work.

Rachel looks across at me and winks. I'm probably the only one there who knows her real name. Everyone else just calls her Red, after her hair. Not much room for subtlety in the meat market. Not yet thirty, and already too old for the better locations, Red wears a heavy coat with hardly anything underneath it, and stilettos with heels long enough to qualify as deadly weapons. She crushes a cigarette in an ashtray, blows smoke into the steamy air, and gets up to join me. Just casually, in passing.

"Hello, Charlie boy. How's tricks?"

"Shouldn't I be asking you that?"

We both smile. She thinks she knows what I do, but she doesn't. Not really.

"Watch yourself out there, Charlie boy. Lot of bad people around these days."

I pay attention. Prossies hear a lot. "Anyone special in mind, Red?"

But she's already moving away. Working girls never let themselves got close to anyone. "Let me just check I've got all my things: straight razor, brass knuckles, pepper spray, condoms, and lube. There, ready for anything."

"Be good, Red."

"I'm always good, Charlie boy."

I hold the door open for her, and we go out into the night.

I walk my beat alone, up and down and back and forth, covering the streets of Soho in a regular pattern. Dark now, only artificial light standing between us and everything the night holds. The streets are packed with tourists and johns, in search of just the right place to be properly fleeced, and then sent on their way with empty pockets and maybe a few nice memories to keep them going till next time. Neon blazes and temptation calls, but that's just the Soho everyone sees. I see a hell of a sight more, because I'm a street wizard. And I have the Sight.

When I raise my Sight, I can See the world as it really is, and not as most people think it is. I get to See all the wonders and marvels, the terrors and the nightmares, the glamour and magic and general weird shit most people never even know exists. I raise my Sight and look on the world with fresh eyes, and the night comes alive, bursting with hidden glories and miracles, gods and monsters. And I get to See it all.

Gog and Magog, the giants, go fist fighting through the back streets of Soho; bigger than buildings, their huge misty forms smash through shops and businesses without even touching them. Less than ghosts, more than memories, Gog and Magog fight a fight that will never end till history itself comes stumbling to a halt. They were here before London, and there are those who say they'll still be here long after London is gone.

Wee-winged fairies come slamming down the street like living shooting stars, darting in and out of the lampposts in a gleeful game of tag, leaving long, shimmering trails behind them. Angels go line dancing on the roof of Saint Giles's Church. And a handful of Men in Black check the details of parked vehicles, because not everything that looks like a car is a car. Remember the missing traffic cops?

If everyone could See the world as it really is, and not as we would have it, if they could See everything and everyone they share the world with, they'd shit themselves. They'd go stark staring mad. They couldn't cope. It's a much bigger world than people imagine, bigger and stranger than most of them can imagine. It's my job to see the hidden world stays hidden, and that none of it spills over into the safe and sane everyday world.

I walk up and down the streets, pacing myself, covering my patch. I have a lot of ground to cover every night, and it has to be done the traditional way, on foot. They did try cars, for a while. Didn't work out. You miss far too much, from a car. You need good heavy shoes for this job, strong legs, and a straight back. And you can't let your concentration slip, even for a moment. There's always so much you have to keep an eye out for.

Those roaming gangs of Goths, for example, all dark clothes and pale faces. Half of them are teenage vampires, on the nod and on the prowl, looking for kicks and easy blood. What better disguise? You can always spot the real leeches, though. They wear ankhs instead of crucifixes. Long as they don't get too greedy, I let them be. All part of the atmosphere of Soho.

And you have to keep a watchful eye on the prossies, the hard-faced working girls on their street corners. Opening their heavy coats to flash the passing trade, showing red, red smiles that mean nothing at all. You have to watch out for new faces, strange faces, because not everything that looks like a woman is a woman. Some are sirens, some are succubae, and some are the alien equivalents of the praying mantises. All of it hidden behind a pleasing glamour until they've got their dazzled prey somewhere nice and private, and then they take a lot more than money from their victims.

I pick them out and send them packing. When I can. Bloody diplomatic immunity.

Seems to me there's a lot more homeless out and about on the streets than there used to be. The lost souls and broken men, gentlemen of the road, and care in the community. But some have fallen further than most. They used to be Somebody, or Something, living proof that the wheel turns for all of us, and if you're wise, you'll drop the odd coin in a cap, here and there. Because karma has teeth, all it takes is one really bad day, and we can all fall off the edge.

But the really dangerous ones lurk inside their cardboard boxes like tunnel spiders, ready to leap out and batten onto some unsuspecting passerby in a moment, and drag them back inside their box, before anyone even notices what's happened. Nothing like hiding in plain sight. Whenever I find a lurker, I set fire to its box and jam a stake through whatever comes running out. Vermin control, all part of the job.

From time to time, I stop to take a breath and look wistfully at the more famous bars and nightclubs, that would never admit the likes of me through their upmarket, uptight doors. A friend of mine, who's rather higher up the magical food chain, told me she once saw a well-known sit-com star stuck halfway up the stairs, because he was so drunk he couldn't remember whether he was going up or coming down. For all I know, he's still there. But that's Soho for you, a gangster in every club bar and a celebrity on every street corner doing something unwise.

I stoop down over a sewer grating, to have chat with the undine who lives in the underground water system. She controls pollution levels by letting it all flow through her watery form, consuming the really bad stuff and filtering out the grosser impurities. She's been down there since Victorian times and seems happy enough. Though like everyone else, she's got something to complain about; apparently, she's not happy that people have stopped flushing baby alligators down their toilets. She misses them.

"Company?" I ask.

"Crunchy," she says.

I laugh, and move on.

Some time later, I stop off at a tea stall, doing steady business in the chilly night. The local hard-luck cases come shuffling out of the dark, drawn like shabby moths to the stall's cheerful light. They line up politely for a cup of tea or a bowl of soup, courtesy of the Salvation Army. The God-botherers don't approve of me any more than I approve of them, but we both know we both serve a purpose. I always make a point to listen in to what the street people have to say. You'd be amazed what even the biggest villains will say in front of the homeless, as though they're not really there.

I check the grubby crowd for curses, bad luck spells, and the like, and defuse them. I do what I can.

Red turns up at the stall, just as I'm leaving. Striding out of the night like a ship under full sail, she crashes to a halt before the tea stall and demands a black coffee, no sugar. Her face is flushed, and she's already got a bruised cheek and a shiner, and dried blood clogging one nostril.

"This john got a bit frisky," she says dismissively. "I told him that's extra, darling. And when he wouldn't take the hint, I hit him in the nads with my brass knuckles. One of life's little pleasures. Then when he was down I kicked him in the head, just for wasting my time. Me and a few of the girls rolled him for all he had, and then left him to it. Never touch the credit cards, though. The filth investigate credit cards. God, this is bad coffee. How's your night going, Charlie boy?"

"Quiet," I say, and work a simple spell to heal her face. "You ever think of giving this up, Red?"

"What?" she says. "And leave show business?"

More and more drunks on the street now, stumbling and staggering this way and that, thrown out of the clubs and bars once they run out of money. I work simple spells from a safe distance. To sober them up, or help them find a safe taxi, or the nearest Underground station. I work other protections, too, that they never know of. Quietly removing weapons from the pockets of would-be muggers; driving off minicab drivers with bad intent, by giving them the runs; or breaking up the bigger street gangs with basic paranoia spells, so they turn on one another instead. Always better to defuse a situation, than risk it all going bad, with blood and teeth on the pavement. A push here and a prod there, a subtle influence and a crafty bit of misdirection, and most of the night's trouble is over, before it's even started.

I make a stop at the biggest Chinese Christian Church in London and chat with the invisible Chinese demon that guards the place from troublemakers and unbelievers. It enjoys the irony of protecting a Church that officially doesn't believe in it. And since it gets to eat anyone who tries to break in, it's quite happy. The Chinese have always been a very practical people.

Just down the street is an Indian restaurant once suspected of being a front for Kali worshippers. On the grounds that not everyone who went in came back out again. Turned out to be an underground railroad, where people oppressed because of their religious beliefs could pass quietly from this dimension to another. There's an Earth out there for everyone, if you only know where to look. I helped the restaurant put up an avoidance spell, so only the right kind of people would go in.

I check out the Dumpsters around the back, while I'm there. We've been having increasing problems with feral pixies, just likely. Like foxes, they come in from the countryside to the town, except foxes can't blast the aura right off you with a hard look. Pixies like Dumpsters; they can play happily in them for hours. And they'll eat pretty much anything, so mostly I just leave them to get on with it. Though if the numbers start getting too high, I'll have to organize another cull.

I knock the side of the Dumpster, but nothing knocks back. Nobody home.

After that, it's in and out of all the pokey little bars in the back streets, checking for the kind of leeches that specialize in grubby little gin joints. They look human enough, especially in a dimly lit room. You know the kind of strangers, the ones who belly up to the bar next to you with an ingratiating smile, talking about nothing in particular, but you just can't seem to get rid of them. It's not your company or even your money, they're after. Leeches want other things. Some can suck the booze right out of you, leaving you nothing but the hangover. Others can drain off your life energy, your luck, even your hope.

They usually run when they see me coming. They know I'll

make them give it all back, with interest. I love to squeeze those suckers dry.

Personal demons are the worst. I hate demons. They come in with the night, swooping and roiling down the narrow streets like leaves tossed on the breeze, snapping their teeth and flexing their barbed fingers. Looking to fasten on to any tourist whose psychic defenses aren't everything they should be. They wriggle in, under the mental barricades, snuggle onto your back and ride you like a mule. They encourage all their host's worst weaknesses, greed or lust or violence, all the worst sins and temptations they ever dreamed of. The tourists go wild, drowning themselves in sensation, and the demons soak it all up. When they've had enough, they let go and slip away into the night, fat and engorged, leaving the tourists to figure out where all their money and self-respect went. Why they've done so many things they swore they'd never do. Why there's a dead body at their feet and blood on their hands.

I can See the demons, but they never see me coming. I can sneak up behind them and rip them right off a tourist's back. I use special gloves; I call them my emotional baggage handlers. A bunch of local nuns make them for us, blessed with special prayers, every thread soaked in holy water and backed up with nasty silver spurs in the fingertips. Personal demons aren't really alive, as such, but I still love the way they scream as their flimsy bodies burst in my hands.

Of course some tourists bring their own personal demons in with them, and then I just make a note of their names, to pass on to the Big Boys. Symbiosis is more than I can handle.

I bump into my first group of Gray aliens, and make a point of stopping to check their permits are in order. They look like ordinary people to everyone else, until they get up close, and then they hypnotize you with those big black eyes, like a snake with a mouse, and you might as well bend over and smile for the probe. Up close, they smell of sour milk, and their movements are just *wrong*. . . . Their dull gray flesh slides this way and that, even when they're standing still, as though it isn't properly attached to the bones beneath.

I've never let them abduct anyone on my watch. I'm always very firm: no proper paperwork, no abduction. They never argue. Never even react. It's hard to tell what a Gray is thinking, what with that long, flat face and those unblinking eyes. I wish they'd wear some kind of clothes, though. You wouldn't believe what they've got instead of genitals.

Even when their paperwork is in order, I always find or pretend to find something wrong, and send them on their way, out of my area. Just doing my bit, to protect humanity from alien intervention. The Government can stuff their quotas.

Not long after, I run across a Street Preacher, having a quiet smoke of a hand-rolled in a back alley. She's new: Tamsin MacReady. Looks about fifteen, but she must be hard as nails or they'd never have given her this patch. Street Preachers deal with the more spiritual problems, which is why few of them last long. Soon enough they realize reason and compassion aren't enough, and that's when the smiting starts, and the rest of us run for cover. Tamsin's a decent enough sort, disturbed that she can't do more to help.

"People come here to satisfy the needs of the flesh, not the spirit," I say, handing her back the hand-rolled. "And we're here to help, not meddle."

"Oh, blow it out your ear," she says, and we both laugh.

It's not long after that I run into some real trouble: someone from the Jewish Defense League has unleashed a Golem on a march by British Nazi skinheads. The Golem is picking them up and throwing them about, and the ones who aren't busy bleeding or crying or wetting themselves are legging it for the horizon. I feel like standing back and applauding, but I can't let this go on. Someone might notice. So I wade in, ducking under the Golem's flailing arms, until I can wipe the activating word off its forehead. It goes still then, nothing more than lifeless clay, and I put in a call for it to be towed away. Someone higher up will have words with someone else, and hopefully I won't have to do this again. For a while.

I take some hard knocks and a bloody nose, before I can shut the Golem down, so I take time out to lean against a stone wall and feel sorry for myself. My healing spells only work on other people. The few skinheads picking themselves up off the pavement aren't sympathetic. They know where my sympathies lie. Some of them make aggressive noises, until I give them a hard look, and then they remember they're needed somewhere else.

I could always turn the Golem back on, and they know it.

I head off on my beat again, picking them up and slapping them down, aching quietly here and there. Demons and pixies and golems, oh my. Just another night, in Soho.

Keep walking, keep walking. Protect the ones you can, and try not to dwell on the ones you can't. Sweep up the mess, drive off the predators, and keep the world from ever finding out. That's the job. Lots of responsibility, hardly any authority, and the pay sucks. I say as much to Red when we bump into each other at the end of our shifts. She clucks over my bruises and offers me a nip from her hip flask. It's surprisingly good stuff.

"Why do you do it, Charlie boy? Hard work and harder luck, with nothing to show but bruises and bad language from the very people you're here to help? It can't be the money; I probably make more than you do."

"No," I say. "It's not the money."

I think of all the things I See every night, that most of the world never knows exists. The marvelous and the fantastic, the strange creatures and stranger people: gods and monsters and all the wonders of the hidden world. I walk in magic and work miracles, and the night is full of glory. How could I ever turn my back on all that?

"Why don't you just walk away?" says Red.
"What?" I say. "And leave show business?"

I've never made any secret of the fact that the Nightside is based on London's Soho, or at least Soho as I knew it back in the day, when history was already turning into legend—when the bad old days were mostly over, but there was still plenty of sin to go around if you knew where to look. With this story, I wanted to show an ordinary working stiff, cleaning up the supernatural messes other people leave behind. The people and the setting are probably the closest I've ever come to describing the Soho I knew.

DEATH IS A LADY

I once had a near-death experience. This was back in 1972, before they became fashionable and everyone was having them. Which is probably why mine bears little or no resemblance to latter descriptions. Or perhaps I just need to be different in everything.

I was on a walking holiday in the Lake District. Seventeen years old, bright and bushy-tailed, hair halfway down my back. Well, it was 1972. I walked fifteen miles a day and spent every evening in the pub. I couldn't do that now; it would kill me.

Halfway through the week, I took a nasty fall, split my head open, and woke up in hospital. But while I was out, I had a dream that was not a dream. It did not feel anything like a dream, but it was some years, before I was able to put a name to it.

There was darkness, and then I was sitting in a stuffed leather chair before a crackling open fire in an old Victorian study. Books on the walls, gas lamps, blocky old Victorian furniture. Slow ticking clock. A bit dark, but not gloomy. Peaceful. It was a place I had never seen before or since, but I felt immediately at home there.

Sitting in the chair on the other side of the fire was a tall, dark-haired, pale-faced woman, dressed in black. The height of Victorian fashion. She was beautiful and, although I had never seen her before, I trusted her immediately. I can see her face as clearly now as then, but it is no one I have ever known. I fell in love with her at first sight. She knew and smiled, understanding.

She was Death. I knew that as clearly as I know my own name.

She told me in a warm, reassuring voice that I had arrived there too soon. It was not my time yet, and I had to go back. I did not want to go, but she was sympathetically insistent. I could not stay. It was not my time. She would see me again, eventually.

And I woke up in hospital with stitches in my head.

The experience was as real to me then as anything else I had ever known. It is real to me now. Every moment of the experience remains clear and distinct to me. And I know that when my time does finally come, she will be waiting to greet me again. As she promised.

Death is a lady.

This is a true story. It all happened, just the way I've written it. I was on a school walking-and-climbing holiday, when I was seventeen. I took a bad fall and smashed in the side of my head. I'm told I was technically dead for several seconds, before I snapped back. I actually woke up some time later, at the hospital, while they were putting stitches in my head. But this is what I remember happening in between. My very own Near Death Experience. It all happened long ago, before such things became fashionable and everyone was having one. Which is probably why mine is a bit different. Is this a real experience? I don't know. I think so. All I'll say is this: when Neil Gaiman introduced his Lady Death in the Sandman comic, it was like a validation. . . .

DOROTHY DREAMS

Dorothy had a bad dream. She dreamed she grew up and grew old, and her children put her in a home. And then she woke up and found it was all real. There's no place like a rest home.

Dorothy sat in her wheelchair, old and frail and very tired, and looked out through the great glass doors at the world beyond. A world that no longer had any place, or any use, for her. There was a lawn, and some trees, all of them carefully cut and pruned and looked after to within an inch of their lives. Dorothy thought she knew how they felt. The doors were always kept closed and locked. Because the home's residents—never referred to as patients—weren't allowed outside. Far too risky. They might fall, or hurt themselves. And there was the insurance to think of, after all. So Dorothy sat in her wheelchair, where she'd been put, and looked out at a world she could no longer reach. As far away . . . as Oz.

Sometimes, when she lay in her narrow bed at night, she would wish for a cyclone to come to carry her away again. But she wasn't in Kansas anymore. Her children told her they chose this particular home because it was the best. It just happened to be so far away that they couldn't come to visit her very often. Dorothy never missed the weather forecasts on the television, but it seemed there weren't any cyclones here, in this part of the world.

Dorothy looked down at her hands. Old, wrinkled, covered with liver spots. Knuckles that ached miserably when it rained. She held her hands up before her and turned them back and forth, almost wonderingly. *Whose hands are these?* she thought. *My hands don't look like this.*

A young nurse came and brushed Dorothy's long gray hair with rough, efficient strokes. Suzie, or Shirley, something like that. They all looked the same to Dorothy. Bright young faces, often covered with so much makeup it was a wonder it didn't crack when they smiled. Dorothy remembered her own first experiences with makeup, so many years ago. *Been at the flour barrel again,* Uncle Henry would say, trying to sound stern, but smiling in spite of himself. So long ago . . .

Suzie or Shirley pulled the brush through Dorothy's fine gray hair, jerking her head this way and that, chattering happily all the time about people Dorothy didn't know and things she didn't care about. When the nurse was finished, she showed Dorothy the results of her work in a hand mirror. And Dorothy looked at the sunken, lined face, with its flat gray hair pulled back in a tight bun, and thought, *Who's that old person? That's not me. I don't look like that.*

Eventually, the nurse went away and left Dorothy in peace. To sit in a chair she couldn't get out of without help. Though that didn't really matter, because it wasn't as though there was anything she wanted to do. . . . To sit, and think, and remember, because her memories were all she had left. The only things that still mattered.

Don't get old, dear, her auntie Em had said, back on the farm. *It's hard work, being old.*

Dorothy hadn't listened. There was so much she could have

learned, from wise, old Aunt Em and hardworking Uncle Henry. But she was always too busy. Always running around, looking for mischief to get into, dreaming of a better place far away from the grim gray plains of Kansas. She dreamed a wonderful dream, once, of a magical land called Oz. Sometimes she remembered Oz the way it really was, and sometimes she remembered it the way they showed it in that movie. . . . She'd seen the movie so many times, after all, and only saw the real Oz once. So it wasn't surprising that sometimes she got them muddled up in her mind. The movie people made all kinds of mistakes, got so many of the details wrong. They wouldn't listen to her. *Silver shoes,* she'd insisted, not that garish red. All the colors in the movie Oz had seemed wrong: candy colors, artificial colors. Nothing like the warm and wonderful world of Oz.

Dorothy dozed in her wheelchair, and fell asleep; and dreamed a better dream.

She woke up, and she was back where she belonged: in Oz. A country of almost overwhelming beauty, bright and glorious as the best summer day you ever yearned for. Great stretches of greensward ranged all around her, dotted here and there with groves of tall, stately trees bearing every fruit you could think of. Banks of flowers in a hundred delicate, delightful hues. All kinds of birds singing all kinds of songs, in the trees and in the bushes. Wonderfully patterned butterflies fluttered on the air, like animated scraps of whimsy. A small brook rushed along between the green banks, sparkling in the sunshine, and the open sky was an almost heartbreakingly perfect shade of blue.

Dorothy was just a little disappointed. When she'd imagined returning to Oz in the past, she'd always thought there would be a great crowd of Munchkins waiting for her, with flags and banners and songs, happy to welcome her back. Those marvelous child-sized people, in their tall hats with little bells around the brim. But there was no one there to greet her. No one at all.

Dorothy was surprised to find herself a young woman, in a smart blue-and-white dress and silver shoes, rather than the small child she'd been the last time she visited Oz. Though this was how she'd thought of herself for many years, long after she stopped seeing that image in the mirror. She patted herself down, vaguely, and was surprised at how solid and real she felt. And not a pain or an ache anywhere . . .

She jumped up and down and spun around in circles, waving her arms around and laughing out loud, glorying in the simple joy of easy movement. And then she stopped abruptly, as a dog came running up to her, wagging its tail furiously. A little black dog, with long, silky hair and small black eyes that twinkled so very merrily. It danced around her, jumping up at her, almost exploding with joy, and Dorothy knelt down to smile at it.

"You look just like the dog I used to have when I was just a little girl," she said. "Its name was Toto."

The dog sat back on its haunches and grinned at her. "That's because I am Toto," said the dog, in a rough breathy voice. "Hello, Dorothy! I've been waiting here for such a long time for you to come and join me."

Dorothy stared at him blankly. "You can talk?"

"Of course!" said Toto, scratching himself briskly. "This is Oz, after all. . . ."

"But you're dead, Toto," Dorothy said slowly. "You died . . . a long time ago."

"What does that matter, where Oz is concerned?" said the little dog. "Aren't you glad to see me again?"

Dorothy gathered the little dog up in her arms and hugged him to her tightly, as though to make sure no one could ever take him away from her again. Tears rolled down her cheeks, and Toto lapped them up gently with his little pink tongue.

Finally, she had to let him go, if only so she could look at him again, and Toto backed away, to regard her seriously with his head cocked on one side.

"You have to come with me now, Dorothy."

"Where?" said Dorothy.

"Along the yellow brick road, of course," said Toto. "To where all your old friends are waiting, to meet you again."

Dorothy straightened up and looked, and sure enough there it was: a long straight road stretching off into the distance, paved with yellow bricks. A soft, butter yellow, easy and inviting on the eye. Nothing like the gaudy shade in the movie. Dorothy smiled and set off briskly down the road, with Toto scampering happily along beside her. She had no doubt the road would lead her to answers, just as it always had.

The sun shone brightly, with not a cloud anywhere in that most perfect of skies. Birds sang sweetly, a cool breeze caressed her face, and Dorothy's heart was so full of simple happiness it felt like it might break apart at any moment. It felt good to be just striding along, stretching her legs, after so long in that damned wheelchair. Neat fences stretched along either side of the yellow brick road, painted a delicate duck's-egg blue, just as she remembered. Beyond them lay huge open fields full of every kind of crop, so that the whole land was one great checkerboard of primary colors.

Soon enough, she came to a small summerhouse of gleaming white wood, standing stiff and upright all on its own at the side of the road. Bright green jade and rich blue lapis lazuli made delicate patterns over the gleaming white. And there, inside the summer house, sitting at a table, were two women she recognized immediately. Glinda the Good Witch, and the Wicked Witch. They were taking tea together and chatting quite companionably. They stopped their conversation and put down their teacups to smile brightly at Dorothy.

She stopped a cautious distance away and studied them both carefully. Toto sat down at her feet, apparently entirely undisturbed. The witches looked pleasant enough: two cheerful young women who didn't seem any older than Dorothy was. Now. Glinda wore white, and the Wicked Witch wore green, but otherwise there wasn't much to choose between them. They might have been sisters. Dorothy remembered them as being much older the first time she encountered them, but then, she had been just a small child at the time. All adults seemed old, then. Dorothy crossed her arms tightly and gave both witches her best hard look.

"It seems to me," she said firmly, "that an explanation is in order."

Glinda and the Wicked Witch shared an understanding smile and then both of them beamed sweetly at Dorothy.

"You were just a child when you came here, my dear," said Glinda. "And you wanted an adventure. So we provided one. In a form you could understand. You can have anything you want here."

"Glinda played the Good Witch, so I played the Bad," said the witch in green. "Though you were never in any danger, of course."

"So nothing that happened here was real?" said Dorothy.

"Well," said Toto, carelessly, "there's real; and then there's real. I always found reality very limiting. I couldn't talk when I was real."

"When you were alive . . ." said Dorothy, slowly.

"Yes," said Toto. He waited a minute, as though for her to grasp something obvious, and then he sighed and got to his feet again. "Look! Here come some more of your old friends!"

Dorothy looked around, and her heart jumped in her breast as she saw the Scarecrow, the Tin Woodman, and the Lion, hurrying down the yellow brick road to join her, waving and laughing. They all looked just as she remembered them. The Scarecrow was out in front, lurching along, all bulgy and misshapen in his blue suit and pointed blue hat, his head just a sack stuffed with straw with the features painted on. She jumped up and down on the spot, clapping her hands together, until she couldn't wait any longer, and ran forward to grab the Scarecrow and hug him fiercely, burying her face in his yielding shoulder. He scrunched comfortably in her arms.

The Tin Man was waiting for her when she finally let go of the

Scarecrow. All shining metal, with his head and arms and legs jointed on, and not an ounce of give in him anywhere, but she still hugged him as best she could. He patted her back carefully with his heavy hands. And finally, there was the Lion. He towered over her, standing tall on his two legs, a great shaggy beast; and when Dorothy went to hug him, she couldn't get her arms halfway around him. His breath smelled sweetly of grass.

But when she finally stepped back from her friends, Dorothy was shocked again when they strolled over to the summerhouse and greeted both witches warmly, as old friends. Dorothy's heart ran suddenly cold. She folded her arms again and hit them all with her hard stare.

"So," she said harshly. "If you two just pretended to be Good and Bad Witches, does that mean you three just pretended to be my friends?"

"Of course we were your friends," said the Scarecrow, in his soft, husky voice. "That's what we were there for. To keep you company, so you wouldn't be alone and scared. So you could enjoy your adventure."

"Right," said the Tin Man. "A doll to hug, a metal man to protect you, and a cowardly lion to feel superior to."

"Wait just a minute," said the Lion. "There was a lot more to my role than that. . . ."

"I don't understand," said Dorothy, suddenly close to tears.

"Then let me explain," said a familiar voice.

And when Dorothy looked around, there he was, of course. Oz, the Great and Terrible. The Wonderful Wizard of Oz. A little old man with a bald head and a wrinkled face, in the kind of clothes no one had worn . . . since Dorothy was a child. He smiled kindly on Dorothy, and there was such obvious warmth and compassion in the smile that she couldn't help but smile back. She felt better, in spite of herself.

"I thought you went back to Omaha," said Dorothy. "In your balloon."

"Just another part of your adventure," said the Wizard. "I never really left. I'm always here, in one form or another."

"Then . . . you were just playing a role, like all the others?"

"I am Oz, the Great and Terrible, the Kind and Beneficent, and everything else you need me to be. I am the man with all the answers. Come walk with me, Dorothy, and all will be made clear."

Reluctantly, Dorothy allowed the little old man to lead her out along the yellow brick road, and they walked along together, the little old man moving easily beside her. It bothered her, on some level, that all her old friends stayed behind. That even Toto didn't come with her. As though the little old man had things to tell her that could only be said in private. Or perhaps, because they already knew. As though . . . they shared some great and terrible secret that only the Wizard himself could tell her.

"I always was the one with all the answers," said the Wizard. "Even if I wasn't necessarily what I seemed."

"When I first met you, I saw a huge disembodied Head," said Dorothy. "The Scarecrow said he saw a lovely Lady. The Tin Woodman, he saw an awful Beast, with the head of a rhinoceros, and five arms and five legs growing out of a hairy hide. And the Lion saw a Ball of Fire. But in the end, you turned out to be just an old humbug, a man hiding behind a curtain. Why do you insist we had to kill the Wicked Witch, before we could all have what we needed?"

"Because gifts must be earned, and good must triumph over evil, if an adventure is to have an end," said the Wizard. "Did you never wonder why the Wicked Witch, so afraid of water, would keep a bucket of water nearby?"

"It was a dream," said Dorothy. "You don't question what happens in a dream."

"Do you remember being old, Dorothy?" the Wizard said gently.

"Yes," she said slowly. "Though that seems like the dream, now."

"You have finally woken up from that nightmare and come

home. Where you belong. This is the good place, Dorothy. Where good things happen every day, and the day never ends. Unless you want it to, of course. Look . . . See . . ."

Dorothy looked where he was pointing, out across the great green plain before them. Off in the distance, two young girls were dancing with a huge and noble Lion. A young girl in sensible Victorian clothes was conversing solemnly with a great White Rabbit. And a boy and his Bear played happily together at the edge of a great Forest.

"I know them . . ." said Dorothy. "Don't I . . . ?"

"Of course," said the little old man. "Everyone knows them, and their stories. Just as everyone knows you, and your story. All these children dreamed a great dream, of a wonderful place where magical things happened. And some author wrote the stories down, to share their dreams with others. All of you, in your own ways, caught just a glimpse of this place, this good place yet to come. For a moment, you left your world and came to mine. And because all of you are my children, you all get to come home again, in the end."

Dorothy looked steadily at the Wizard. "Who are you . . . really?"

He smiled on her, his eyes and his smile full of all the love there is. "Don't you know? Really?"

"And this is . . . ?"

"Yes. This is Heaven, and you'll never have to leave it again."

"I'm dead, aren't I? Like Toto."

"Of course. Or to put it another way, you have woken up from the dream of living, into a better dream. Everyone you ever loved, everyone you ever lost, is here waiting for you. Look: there is your auntie Em, and your uncle Henry."

Dorothy looked down the road, to where four young people were waiting. She recognized Em and Henry immediately, though they didn't seem much older than she.

"Who's that with them?" she said.

"Your mother and your father," said the old man. "They've

been waiting for you for so long, Dorothy. Go and be with them. And then we'll all go on to the Emerald City. Because your adventures are only just beginning."

Dorothy was already off and running, down the yellow brick road, in that perfect land, in that most perfect of dreams.

I was asked to write a story about Dorothy and Oz, and it started me thinking about all the famous stories of children who went off to have amazing adventures in fantasy lands. Where were they going, really? What if they were all going to the same place . . . ? Another happy story about an old person dying.

DOWN AND OUT IN DEAD TOWN

Why don't the dead lie still?

I suppose everyone remembers where they were, and what they were doing, the day the dead came back. Mostly, I still remember it as the day I got laid off. It came out of nowhere, just like the newly risen dead. The boss called me into his office and told me I didn't have a job anymore. The company was sending all our jobs abroad, where they wouldn't cost as much. And that was that. One minute I had a job and a regular wage, a future and prospects, and the next my whole life was over. I went home early, because nobody cared anymore, and watched the dead walk on television. Just like everyone else.

It was pretty scary at first. We all gathered together in front of the set, the whole family, to watch blurred pictures of dead people stumbling around with blank faces and outstretched arms, trying to eat people. Luckily, that didn't last long. Just a few last hungers and instincts firing in damaged brains, the experts said. The dead calmed down soon enough, as they forgot the last vestiges of who and what they had been. They stopped being scary and just stood around looking sad and pitiful, hanging around on street corners with nowhere to go.

At first, their families were only too happy to reclaim them, to have their lost parents and children, husbands and wives back again, and take them home. But that didn't last long. They soon found out you couldn't talk to the dead. Or you could, but they would never answer. They were just bodies, nobody home. They didn't know anyone, or remember anything. Didn't want to say anything, or do anything. And they smelled bad, so bad . . .

Soon enough, the dead started turning up on the streets again, put out by their horrified and terribly disappointed families, and the Government had to do something. They couldn't just leave the dead standing around, stinking up the place, getting in everyone's way. And so they built the dead towns, thrown up quickly, as far away from the rest of us as they could get, and put the dead there. And the world . . . just went on with business as normal.

I didn't. I had experience and qualifications and a good attitude; it never even occurred to me I wouldn't walk right into another job. But it turned out we were in a recession, or a depression, or whatever it is when there just aren't enough jobs to go around. There was a glut on the market for people with my experience and qualifications, and apparently I was too old and overqualified for what entrance-level jobs there were. And every time I turned up for an interview, my clothes were just that little bit shabbier and my manner was just that little bit too desperate, and after a while no one would see me anymore.

My savings ran out, I lost my house, my wife went back to live with her parents and took the kids with her, and almost before I knew it, I was living on the streets. With all the other people who'd lost everything. It's a lesson you should never forget. It doesn't matter how hard you work, or how much you have; there's nothing you've got that the world can't take away. The only thing standing between people like you and people like me is one really bad day.

It's not so bad, really, living on the streets. It comes as something of a relief, finally, when you realize you can stop struggling, stop fighting. That it's all over. You don't have to worry about your job or paying the bills, look after your family or make decisions. No more responsibilities, no more lying awake in the early hours of the morning, worrying about the future. On the streets, everything comes down to what's right in front of you: finding something to eat and drink, something to keep the warmth in and the rain out, and locating somewhere reasonably safe to sleep. You don't have to worry about yesterday or tomorrow, because you know they're going to be exactly like today.

It's interesting that you don't call us homeless anymore. Just street people. Like the street is where we chose to be, that the street is where we belong. You don't call us homeless, because that might imply that someone should give us a home. If you came across a stray dog in the street, wet and shivering and hungry, you'd take it home with you, wouldn't you? Give it food and drink, and a blanket in front of the fire. Been many a cold night I'd settle for that. But no, you just walk straight past, ignoring our outstretched hands and handwritten signs, careful not to make eye contact because then you'd have to admit that we are real and that our suffering is real.

We're dead to you.

I don't know why I left the city. No particular reason. Just started walking one morning and didn't stop. Walked till I ran out of streets and just kept going. Are you still a street person, if there aren't any streets? The countryside was pretty, and entirely unforgiving. The elements are just that bit closer, and more pressing, and you miss the company of people. Eventually, I came to a dead town. I stopped to look it over. There aren't any fences around a dead town: no gates or barbed wire. Nothing to keep the dead in, because they don't want to go anywhere. They have no purpose, no ambition, no curiosity. They're dead. They don't want or care about anything, anymore. Just bodies, called up out of their graves and given a bit of a push to set them going. We put them in dead towns because they had to be somewhere, and that's where they stay.

I'd never been inside a dead town, so I went in. Just to see what there was to see.

The dead took no notice of me, looked right through me as though I wasn't even there. But I was used to that. Wasn't much of a town, just blocky houses in straight rows on either side of a dirt street. No lights, no amenities, no comforts. Because the dead don't need them. They didn't even walk, just stood around, looking at nothing. A few still stumbled or staggered from one place to another, driven by some vague impulse, some last dying memory of something left undone. Their clothes were rotten and ragged, but most of the bodies persevered. They didn't acknowledge one another or the world around them. Their brains were dead in their heads, bereft of reason or meaning.

Their town was a mess and so were they. The dead don't care about appearances. They didn't smell that bad, so far from their graves, just a dry, dusty presence, like autumn leaves in the wind. I was used to the stench of people who live on the streets. Life smells worse than death ever will. I walked down the dirt street, picking my way carefully between the dead. Not because I was afraid of them, but because I didn't want to be noticed. I still half expected someone to come up and tell me to leave, that I didn't belong there, that I had no place in a dead town. But no one looked at me as I passed or reacted to the sound of my footsteps in the quiet street. The dead had this much in common with the living: they didn't give a damn that I was there.

I never saw the dead make much use of the houses they'd been given. Sometimes they might lie down on a bed for a while, though of course they didn't sleep; as though that was something they remembered doing, even if they no longer knew why. And sometimes they would walk in and out of a door, over and over. Presumably for the same reason. I never really saw them do much of anything. Mostly they just stood around, as though waiting for something. As though they felt there was somewhere they should be, something they should be doing, but no longer knew what, or why.

I found a bed in a room in a house that was still reasonably intact. I barricaded the door so I wouldn't be disturbed and got some sleep. Even a damp and dusty bed can be the height of comfort when you're used to shop doorways and cardboard boxes. The dark didn't bother me, or the dead outside. In the morning, I went looking for food and drink, but of course there wasn't any. I walked up and down and back and forth, but there were only the dead and the houses they didn't need.

I watched one dead man just fall over, for no obvious reason. None of the other dead noticed. I went over to him and crouched down, a cautious distance away. His face was empty and his eyes saw nothing. He was dead and gone, now. Nobody home. I could tell. His boots looked to be much the same size as mine, and in much better condition, so I took them. Good footwear is important when you do a lot of walking.

I knew why he'd fallen over, why he'd stopped moving. It meant the last living person who knew or cared about him was gone. Nobody remembered him, so there was no one to hold him here anymore. That is why the dead came back, after all. Because we just couldn't let them go. Because we all had this selfish need to hang on to our loved ones, even after their time was up. We thought of our friends and family and loved ones as ours, our possessions, and we wanted them back so much we called them back up out of their graves. Unfortunately, the part we cared about, the personalities, or souls, had passed on to wherever personalities or souls go. Beyond our reach. All we could bring back was their bodies.

I'd seen people try to talk to the dead, speaking earnestly and emotionally to blank faces, trying to reach someone who wasn't there anymore. Heard people raise their voices, in anger and anguish, trying to force or cajole a reaction of some kind from their returned loved ones. Sometimes the living even hit the dead and screamed abuse at them. For not being what the living wanted them to be. The dead didn't react. The dead didn't care.

I didn't stay long in dead town. I had some thought of bringing other street people here, to make use of the empty homes. It was a lot safer in the dead town than it was in the city. The dead had no reason to attack us, or insult us, or steal from us. But I left, because even as far down as I had fallen, I was still better than the dead. I still had hope, and dreams, and somewhere to go. My life wasn't over till I said it was.

I went back to the city, and to the people I knew. Because even if people like you won't admit we exist, street people still have one another.

I've been watching zombie films, and reading zombie books and zombie comics, for many many years, and I'm pretty much zombied out. So if I was going to write a zombie story, it had to be something different, something new. Less apocalyptic, and more about living through the end of the world. Because every day is the end of the world for someone, when they lose their job, or their wife, or their children. And the connection between how we treat zombies and homeless people was just too clear. . . .

FROM OUT OF THE SUN, ENDLESSLY SINGING

This is the story. It is an old, old story, and most of the true details are lost to us. But this is how the story has always been told, down the many years. Of our greatest loss and our greatest triumph, of three who were sent down into Hell forever, that the rest of Humanity might know safety and revenge. This is the story of the Weeping Woman, the Man with the Golden Voice, and the Rogue Mind. If the story upsets you, pretend it never happened. It was a very long time ago, after all.

This goes back to the days of the Great Up and Out, when we left out mother world to go out into the stars, to explore the Galaxy and take her fertile planets for our own. All those silver ships, dancing through the dark, blazing bright in the jungle of the night. We met no opposition we couldn't handle, colonized every suitable world we came to and terraformed the rest, remaking them in our image. It was a glorious time, by all accounts, building our glittering cities and proud civilizations, in defiance of all that endless empty Space. We should have known better. We should have sent ahead, to say we were coming. Because it turned out, we were trespassing and not at all welcome.

They came to us from out of the Deep, from out of the darkest part of Deep Space, from far beyond the realms we knew, or could ever hope to comprehend. Without warning, they came, aliens as big as starships, bigger than anything we had ever built, and far more powerful. Endless numbers of them, a hoard, a swarm, deadly things of horrid shape and terrible intent, blocking out the stars where they passed. They were each of them huge and awful, unknown and unknowable, utterly alien things moving inexorably through open Space on great shimmering wings. They came from where nothing comes from, and they thrived in conditions where nothing should live. Their shapes made no sense to human eyes, to human aesthetics. They were nightmares given shape and form, our darkest fears made flesh. We called them the Medusae, because wherever they looked, things died.

They destroyed the first colonized planets they came to, without hesitation, without warning. They paused in orbit just long enough to look down on the civilizations we had built there, and just their terrible gaze was enough to kill every thing that lived. We still have recorded images from that time, of the dead worlds. Cities full of corpses, towns where nothing moved. Wildlife lying unmoving, rotting in the open, and fish of all kinds bobbing unseeing on the surfaces of the oceans. The Medusae moved on, from planet to planet, system to system, leaving only dead worlds in their wake.

We sent the Fleet out to meet them, hundreds and hundreds of our marvelous and mighty Dreadnaughts, armed to the teeth with disrupters and force shields, planet-buster bombs and reality invertors. The Fleet closed with the Medusae, singing our songs of glory, ravening energies flashing across open Space, and all of it was for nothing. We could not touch the Medusae. They passed over the Fleet like a storm in the night and left behind them mile-long starships cracked open from stem to stern, with streams of dead bodies issuing out of cracked hulls, scattering slowly across the dark. Occasionally, some would tumble down through the atmosphere of a dead world, like so many shooting stars with no one to see them.

The Medusae moved on through the colonized systems, wiping clean every world we'd colonized or changed, as though just our presence on their planets had contaminated them beyond saving. One by one, the planetary comm systems fell silent, voices crying out for help that never came, fading into static ghosts. Some colonists got away, fleeing ahead of the Medusae on desperate, overcrowded ships; most didn't. There is no number big enough that the human mind can accept, to sum up our losses. All the men, women, and children lost in those long months of silent slaughter. All the proudly named cities, all the wonders and marvels we built out of nothing—gone, all gone. And finally, when they'd run out of planets to cleanse and people to kill, the Medusae came looking for us. All that great swarm, hideous beyond bearing, complex beyond our comprehension, beyond reason or reasoning with . . . they followed the fleeing ships back to us, back to the home of Mankind.

Back to Old Earth.

We sent up every ship we had, everything that would fly, loaded with every weapon we had, and we met the Medusae at the very edge of our solar system. And there, we stopped them. The aliens looked upon our worlds but came no closer. And for a while we rejoiced, because we thought we had won a great victory. We should have known better. The Medusae had stopped because they didn't need to come any closer. Hanging there in open

Space, silent and huge and monstrous, out beyond the great gas giant planets, they looked on Old Earth and reached out with their incomprehensible energies to touch our world. They poisoned our planet. Changed her essential nature, so that our world would no longer support human life. They turned our home against Humanity. A fitting punishment, from the Medusae, they terraformed us.

And that . . . was when we got really angry and contemplated revenge.

The Lords and Ladies of Old Earth came together in Convocation, for the first time in centuries. They met at Siege Perilous, that wonderful ancient monument to past glories, shaped like a massive hourglass, towering high and high over the bustling starport of New Damascus. Immortal and powerful, relentless and implacable, the Lords and Ladies represented Concepts, not Countries. They spoke for all the various aspects of Humanity, and their word was Law. Made immortal, so that they could take the long view. Denied peace or rest, because they were needed. Cursed with conscience and damned with duty, because that's how we always reward the best of us.

Only the Lords and Ladies knew the secret truth of our poisoned estate: that we would have to leave Old Earth and find a new home somewhere else. The continuance of Humanity itself was at threat, but only the Lords and Ladies knew. Because only they could be trusted to know everything. The Lords and Ladies of Old Earth were given dominion to do anything and everything necessary, to serve and preserve Humanity. In an acknowledged Emergency, the Lords and Ladies were authorized and enjoined to call upon any human being, anyone anywhere, for any necessary purpose. Humanity gave them this power and trusted them to use it well and wisely. Because only they could take the truly long view, and because everyone else was just too busy.

There were checks and balances in place, of course. And truly terrible punishments.

They came to Convocation in the last hours of evening, their personal ships drifting down like so many falling leaves, settling easily onto the crystal landing pads set out on top of Siege Perilous. And then they made their way down to the single reserved meeting hall: a bare and sparse chamber, isolated from the world. They had no use for seats of state, for the trappings of power or the comforts of privilege. Exactly one hundred Lords and Ladies stood in a great circle, looking openly upon one another, in their traditional peacock robes of vivid colors. Their faces were naked and unmasked, so that everyone could see and be seen. Outside, combat androids programmed with the deposited memories of rabid wolves patrolled the perimeter, ready and eager to kill any living thing they encountered.

There were other, less noticeable protections in place, of course.

Lord Ravensguard spoke for War, so he spoke first. Tall and grave he was, with cool, thoughtful eyes. He spoke of the horrors the Medusae had committed, of what they had done and might do yet. And then he spoke of possible responses and tactics.

"There are always the Forbidden Weapons," he said calmly. "Those ancient and detestable devices locked away for centuries, because they were deemed too terrible for Man to use upon Man. I speak of the Time Hammer and the Despicable Childe. The Nightmare Engines and the Hour from Beyond."

"Could we use such things, and still call ourselves human?" said Lord Zodiac, representing Culture. "You cannot defeat evil with evil methods. You cannot stop monsters by becoming monsters."

"The enemy we face has no understanding of such concepts," Lord Ravensguard said firmly. "They do not seek to destroy us because they are Good or Evil. They do not think like us. They see us only as . . . an infestation."

"Have we exhausted all means of communicating with them?" said Lady Benefice, who spoke for Communications.

"We have tried everything, from all the many forms of technology, to the most extreme reaches of psi," said Lord Ravensguard. "They do not hear us. Or, more likely, they choose not to."

"Weapons are not the answer," said Lady Subtle, who represented Security. Small she was, compact, determined. "We have tried weapons, and they have failed us. We must sink lower than that. We will fight the Medusae with guile and betrayal, and they will not see it coming. Because they would never stoop so low."

"You have a plan?" said Lord Ravensguard.

And everyone smiled, politely. Because Lady Subtle always had a plan. She spoke to them at length of a trap, and a punishment, and Humanity's final revenge. The Convocation then deliberated. They did not have the luxury of being shocked, or offended. Their duty demanded only: Was this awful plan practical? There was much discussion, which ended when Lord DeMeter, who spoke for the soul of Humanity, raised the only question that mattered.

"Do we have the right?" he asked. "To make such a sacrifice, and place such a stain upon the collective conscience of Humanity?"

"We can do this, we must do this," said Lady Shard, who represented Duty. Vivacious, she was, full of life and deadly in her focused malice. "We will do this because we have no other choice. Humanity will be saved, and avenged, and that is all that matters."

And so the decision was made, and the order given. Lord Ravensguard and Ladies Subtle and Shard went out from Convocation to cross the world and acquire the three necessary elements for Humanity's last blow at the Medusae.

Lord Ravensguard went to the Grand Old Opera House, set among the gleaming spires and shimmering towers of the city Sydney, in Australia. Samuel DeClare was singing there, that night. There was no greater singer among all Humanity, at that time. They called him the Man with the Golden Voice. When he sang, everyone listened. He could break your heart and mend it, all in a single song. Make you cry and make you cheer, weigh you down and lift you up, and make you love every moment of it. His audiences adored him and beat their hands bloody in applause at the end of every concert. And this night was his greatest appearance, before his biggest audience. Afterward, everyone there said it was his finest moment. They were wrong, but they couldn't know that. Lord Ravensguard stood at the very back of the massive concert hall, and listened, and was moved like everyone else. Perhaps more so, because he alone knew what Samuel DeClare's final performance would entail.

He went backstage to meet with DeClare after the concert was over. The greatest singer of all time sat slumped, unseeing, before his dressing room mirror, surrounded by flowers and gifts and messages of congratulation from everyone who mattered. He was big and broad-shouldered and classically handsome, like some god of ancient times come down to walk among his worshippers. He sat slumped in his chair, tired, depressed, lost. He could barely find the energy to bow his head respectfully to Lord Ravensguard.

"What is wrong?" said the Lord. "Your audience loved you. Listen: they're still cheering, still applauding. You sang magnificently."

"Yes," said DeClare. "But how can I ever follow that? There will be other songs, other performances, but nothing to match tonight. It hits hard, to reach the peak of your career and know there's nowhere left to go but down."

"Ah," said Lord Ravensguard. "But what if I were to offer you the chance for an even greater performance? One last song, of magnificent scope and consequence, before an audience greater than any singer has ever known?"

DeClare raised his heavy head and looked at Lord Ravensguard. "How long would this performance last?"

"Just the one song," said Lord Ravensguard. Because he was allowed, and even encouraged, to lie when necessary.

Lady Subtle went to meet the infamous Weeping Woman in that most ancient of prisons, the Blue Vaults. That wasn't her real name, of course. She was Christina Valdez, just another face in the crowd, until she did what she did, and the media called her *La Llorona,* the Weeping Woman. The authorities put her in the Blue Vaults for the murder of many children. She wept endlessly because she had lost her own children in an awful accident, which might or might not have been of her own making. And then she went out into the night, every night, drifting through the back streets of dimly lit cities, to abduct the children of others, to compensate her for her loss. None of these children ever went home again.

Lady Subtle went down into the Blue Vaults, those great stone caverns set deep and deep under the Sahara Desert, and there she gave orders that one particular door be opened. Inside, Christina Valdez crouched naked in the small stone cell, covered in her own filth, blinking dazedly into the sudden and unexpected light. Because normally, when criminals came to the Blue Vaults, they were locked away forever. No clothes, no windows, no light, food and water through a slot and a grille in the floor. The door only opened again when they came to take out the body. Lady Subtle dismissed the guard and spoke, and the Weeping Woman listened.

"You have a chance to redeem yourself, Christina," said Lady Subtle. "You have the opportunity to save all Humanity."

Valdez laughed in the Lady's face. "Let them all die! Where were they, when my children died? Did any of them weep, for my lost babies?"

"The Medusae have murdered millions of children," said Lady Subtle. "You could weep for them and avenge them, too."

The argument went around and around for some time,

because Lady Subtle was patient and wise, and Christina Valdez was distracted and quite mad. But eventually, an agreement was reached, and Lady Subtle led La Llorona out of her cell and into the light. And if Lady Subtle felt any guilt at what was going to happen to Christina Valdez, she kept it to herself.

Lady Shard tracked down that most dangerous of fugitives, Damnation Rue, to a sleazy bar in that maze of crisscrossing corridors called the Maul, deep in the slums of Under Rio. The media called him the Rogue Mind, because he was the most powerful telepath Humanity had ever produced, and because he would not be bound by Humanity's rules, or the psionic community's rules, or even the rules of polite conduct. He went where he would, did what he wanted, and no one could stop him. He built things up and tore them down, he owed money everywhere, and left broken hearts and minds in his wake, always escaping one step ahead of the consequences, or retribution.

Lady Shard watched him cautiously from the shadows at the back of the packed bar, a foul and loathsome watering hole for the kind of people who needed somewhere to hide from a world that had had enough of them. The Rogue Mind was there to enjoy the barbaric customs and the madder music, the illegal drugs and the extremely dangerous drinks . . . and to enjoy the emotions of others, secondhand. For Damnation Rue, there was nothing more intoxicating than just a taste of other people's Heavens and Hells. He could always stir things up a little if things looked like getting too peaceful.

The air was full of drifting smoke, and the general gloom was broken only by the sudden flares of discharging energy guns or flashing blades. There was blood and slaughter and much rough laughter. The Rogue Mind loved it. Lady Shard watched it all, hidden behind a psionic shield.

She brought Damnation Rue to book through the use of a preprogrammed pleasure droid, with a patina of artificially overlaid memories. She was beautiful to look at, this droid, in a suitably foul and sluttish way, and when Damnation Rue persuaded her to sit at his table and watched what he thought were her thoughts, she drugged his drink.

When he finally woke up, he had a mind trap strapped to his brow, holding his thoughts securely inside his own head. He was strapped down, very securely, in a very secure air ship, taking him directly to the Blue Vaults. Lady Shard sat opposite him, told him where he was going, and observed the panic in his eyes.

"You do have another option," she said. "Save all of Humanity, by performing a telepathic task no other could, and have all your many sins forgiven. Or, you could spend the rest of your life in a small stone cell, with your mind trap bolted to your skull, alone with your own thoughts until you die. It's up to you."

"Money," said Damnation Rue. "I want money. Stick your forgiveness. I want lots and lots of money and a full pardon and a head start. How much is it worth to you, to save all Humanity?"

"You will have as much money as you can spend," said Lady Shard. "Once the mission is over."

The Rogue Mind laughed. He didn't trust the deal and was already planning his escape. But no one escaped the clutches of the Lords and Ladies of Old Earth. Lady Shard hid her smile. She hadn't actually lied to him, as such.

And so the three parts of Humanity's revenge on the Medusae came together at Siege Perilous, brought there by Lord Ravensguard and Ladies Subtle and Shard. Samuel DeClare, the very soul of song, looking fine and noble in his pure white robes, and only just a little disturbed, like a god who had come down to mix with men but could no longer quite remember why. And Christina Valdez, mostly hidden inside voluminous black robes, with the hood pulled well forward to hide her face. Constantly wringing her hands and never meeting anyone's gaze. Now and again, a tear would fall, to splash on the marble floor. And Damnation

Rue, wrapped in new robes that already appeared a little shabby, a sneaky, sleazy little rat of a man, picking nervously with one fingertip at the mind trap still firmly fixed to his brow. Still looking for a way out, the fool.

The Lords and Ladies of Old Earth were not cruel. They praised all three of them as though they were volunteers and promised them that their names would be remembered forever. Which was true enough.

"You will sing," Lord Ravensguard said to Samuel DeClare. "The greatest, most moving song you know."

"You will mourn," Lady Subtle said to Christina Valdez. "The most tragic, heartbreaking weeping of all time."

"And you will broadcast it all telepathically," Lady Shard said to Damnation Rue. "You will project it, across all the open reaches of Space."

"Just one song?" said the Man with the Golden Voice.

"I only have to mourn?" said La Llorona, the Weeping Woman.

"And after I've broadcast this, I get my money?" said the Rogue Mind.

"Yes and yes and yes," said the Lords and Ladies of Old Earth. Who were not cruel, but knew all there was to know about duty and responsibility.

The three of them were taken immediately to the landing pads on top of Siege Perilous, where the starship was waiting for them. Specially adapted, with powerful force shields and a preprogrammed AI pilot. The ship was called *Sundiver*. The three of them stepped aboard, all unknowing, and strapped themselves in, and the AI pilot threw the ship up off the pads and into the sky, and then away from Old Earth and straight into the heart of the Sun.

The three inside knew nothing of this. They couldn't see out, and the force shields protected them. The pilot told them that the time had come; and one of them sang, and one of them mourned, and one of them broadcast it all telepathically. It was a terribly sad song, reaching out from inside the heart of the Sun. Earth did not hear it. Humanity did not hear it; the Lords and Ladies saw to that. Because it really was an unbearably sad song. But the Medusae heard it. The telepathic broadcast shot out of the Sun and spread across the whole planetary system, to the outer ranges of Space where the Medusae heard it. That marvelous, telepathically broadcast, siren song.

The aliens moved forward, to investigate. The Fleet fell back on all sides, to let them pass. The Medusae came to the Sun, our Sun, Old Earth's Sun, drawn on by the siren song like so many moths to the flame. And then they plunged into the Sun, every last one of them, and it swallowed them all up without a murmur. Because as big as the swarm of the Medusae was, the Sun was so much bigger.

They never came out again.

The *Sundiver*'s force shields weren't strong enough to last long, in the terrible heat of the heart of the Sun, but they didn't have to. The ship also carried that ancient horror, the Time Hammer. The weapon that could break Time. The AI pilot set it to repeat one moment of Time, for all eternity. So that the siren song would never end. The Man with the Golden Voice sang, and the Weeping Woman mourned, and the Rogue Mind mixed them together and broadcast it, forever and ever and ever. They're in there now, deep in the heart of the Sun, and always will be.

We never saw the Medusae again. It could be that they died, that not even they could withstand the fierce fires of the Sun. Or it might be that they are still in there, still listening, to a song that will never end. Either way, we are safe, and we have had our revenge upon them, and that is all that matters.

That is the story. Afterward, we left Old Earth, that poor poisoned planet, our ancient home who could no longer support us. Humanity set forth in our marvelous Fleet of Dreadnaughts, looking for new worlds to settle, hopefully this time without alien masters. We keep looking. The last of Humanity, moving ever on through open Space, on the wings of a song, forever.

So Ian Watson asked me to write him a science fiction story: galactic space war, about five thousand words. Only one model suggested itself, and that was the incredible Cordwainer Smith. I've always loved his work and jumped at the chance to write something in that vein. Where you're looking back at the future from the far future, and history is turning into legend. Where the central truth of the story is all that really matters.

IT'S ALL ABOUT THE RENDERING

There is a House that stands on the border. Between here and there, between dreams and waking, between reality and fantasy. The House has been around for longer than anyone remembers, because it's necessary. Walk in through the front door, from the sane and everyday world, and everything you see will seem perfectly normal. Walk in through the back door, from any of the worlds of if and maybe, and a very different House will appear before you. The House stands on the border, linking two worlds, and providing Sanctuary for those who need it. A refuge, from everyone and everything. A safe place, from all the evils of all the worlds.

Needless to say, there are those who aren't too keen on this.

It all started in the kitchen, on a bright sunny day, just like any other day. Golden sunlight poured in through the open window, gleaming richly on the old-fashioned furniture and the modern fittings. Peter and Jubilee Caine, currently in charge of the House, were having breakfast together. At least, Peter was; Jubilee wasn't really a morning person. Jubilee would cheerfully throttle every last member of the dawn chorus in return for just another half-hour's lie-in.

Peter was busy making himself a full English breakfast: bacon and eggs, sausages and beans, and lots of fried bread. Of medium height and medium weight, Peter was a happy if vague sort, but a master of the frying pan. On the grounds that if you ever found something you couldn't cook in the pan, you could still use it to beat the animal to death. Peter moved happily back and forth, doing half a dozen difficult culinary things with calm and easy competence, while singing along to the Settlers' "Lightning Tree" on the radio.

Jubilee, tall and blonde and almost impossible graceful, usually, sat hunched at the kitchen table, clinging to a large mug of industrial-strength black coffee, like a shipwrecked mariner to a lifebelt. Her mug bore the legend *Worship Me Like the Goddess I Am or There Will Be Some Serious Smiting.* She glared darkly at Peter over the rim of her mug as though his every cheerful moment was a deliberate assault on her fragile early morning nerves.

"It should be made illegal, to be that cheerful in the morning," she announced, to no one in particular. "It's not natural. And I can't believe you're still preparing that Death by Cholesterol fry-up every morning. Things like this should be spelled out in detail on the marriage license. I can hear your arteries curdling from here, just from proximity to that much unhealthiness in one place."

"Start the day with a challenge, that's what I always say," said Peter. "If I can survive this, I can survive anything. Will any of our current Guests be joining us for breakfast?"

"I doubt it. Lee only comes out at night, and Johnny is a teenager, which means he doesn't even know what this hour of the morning looks like. Look, can we please have something else from the radio? Something less . . . enthusiastic?"

The music broke off immediately. "I heard that!" said the radio. "Today is sixties day! Because that's what I like. They had real music in those days, songs that would put hair on your chest, with tunes that stuck in your head whether you wanted them to or not. And no, I don't do Coldplay, so stop asking. Would you care to hear a Monkees medley?"

"Remember what happened to the toaster?" said Jubilee, dangerously.

There was a pause. "I do take requests," the radio said finally.

"Play something soothing," said Peter. "For those of us whose bodies might be up and about, but whose minds haven't officially joined in yet."

The radio played a selection from Grieg's *Peer Gynt*, while Peter cheerfully loaded up his plate with all manner of things that were bad for him. He laid it down carefully on the table and smiled over at Jubilee.

"You sure I can't tempt you to just a little of this yummy fried goodness, princess?"

Jubilee actually shuddered. "I'd rather inject hot fat directly into my veins. Get me some milk, sweetie."

Peter went over to the fridge. "Is this a whole or a part-skim day?"

"Give me the real deal. I've got a feeling it's going to be one of those days."

Peter opened the fridge door, and a long green warty arm came out, offering a bottle of milk. Peter accepted the bottle, while being very careful not to make contact with any of the lumpy bumpy fingers.

"Thank you, Walter," he said.

"Welcome, I'm sure," said a deep green warty voice from the back of the fridge. "You couldn't turn the thermostat down just a little more, could you?"

"Any lower, and you'll have icicles hanging off them," said Peter.

There was a rich green warty chuckle. "That's the way I like it, uh-huh, uh-huh . . ."

"No seventies!" shrieked the radio.

Peter shut the fridge door with great firmness and went back to join Jubilee at the kitchen table. He passed her the milk and sat down, and then he ate while she poured and then sipped, and the gentle strains of "Solveig's Song" wafted from the radio. It was all very civilized.

Peter glanced back at the fridge. "How long has Walter been staying here, princess?"

"He was here long before we arrived," said Jubilee. "According to the House records, Walter claims to be a refugee from the Martian Ice People, exiled to Earth for religious heresies and public unpleasantness. Hasn't left that fridge in years. Supposedly, because he's afraid of global warming; I think he's just more than usually agoraphobic."

Two small hairy things exploded through the inner door and ran around and around the kitchen at speed, calling excitedly to each other in high-pitched voices as they chased a brightly colored bouncing ball. They shot under the kitchen table at such speed that Peter and Jubilee barely had time to get their feet out of the way, just two hairy little blurs.

"Hey!" said Jubilee, trying hard to sound annoyed but unable to keep the fondness out of her voice. "No running in the House! And no ball games in the kitchen."

The two small hairy things stopped abruptly, revealing themselves to be barely three feet in height, most of it fur. Two sets of wide eyes blinked guiltily from the head region, while the ball bounced up and down between them.

"I don't mind," said the ball. "Really. I'm quite enjoying it."

"Then go enjoy it somewhere else," said Peter. "I have a lot of breakfast to get through, and I don't want my concentration interrupted. My digestion is a finely balanced thing and a wonder of nature."

"And stay out of the study," said Jubilee. "Remember: you break it, and your progenitors will pay for it."

"We'll be careful!" said a high, piping voice from somewhere under one set of fur.

The brightly colored ball bounced off out of the kitchen, followed by excitedly shouting hairy things. A blessed peace descended upon the kitchen as Peter and Jubilee breakfasted in their own accustomed ways and enjoyed each other's company. Outside the open window, birds were singing, the occasional traffic noise was comfortably far away, and all seemed well with the world. Eventually, Peter decided he'd enjoyed about as much of his breakfast as he could stand and got up to scrape the last vestiges off his plate and into the sink disposal. Which shouted, *Feed me! Feed me, Seymour!* until Peter threatened to shove another teaspoon down it. He washed his plate and cutlery with usual thoroughness, put them out to dry, and stretched unhurriedly.

"Big day ahead, princess," Peter said finally. "I have to fix the hot water system, clean out the gutters, make all the beds, and sort out the laundry."

"I have to redraw the protective wardings, recharge the enchantments in the night garden, clean up after the gargoyles, and refurbish the rainbow."

"I have to mow the lawns and rake the leaves."

"I have to clean out the moat."

Peter laughed. "All right, princess. You win. Want to swap?"

"Each to their own, sweetie. Be a dear and wash my mug."

"What did your last slave die of?"

"Not washing my mug properly. Be a dear, and there will be snuggles later."

"Ooh . . . Sweaty snuggles?"

"In this weather, almost certainly."

And that should have been it. Just another day begun, in the House on the border. But that . . . was when the front door bell rang. A loud, ominous ring. Peter and Jubilee looked at each other.

"I'm not expecting anyone," said Jubilee. "Are you?"

"No," said Peter. "I'm not."

The doorbell rang again, very firmly. One of those *I'm not going to go away so there's no point hiding behind the furniture pretending to be out* kind of rings. Peter went to answer it. He opened the front door and immediately stepped outside, forcing the visitor to step back a few paces. Peter shut the door very firmly behind him and had a quick look around, just to make sure that everything was as it should be. In the real world, the House was just an ordinary detached residence, a bit old-fashioned looking, set back a comfortable distance from the main road, with a neatly raked gravel path running between carefully maintained lawns. Flowers, here and there. The House was almost defiantly ordinary, with doors and windows in the right places and in the right proportions, tiles on the roof, and gutters that worked as often as they didn't. Nothing to look at, keep moving, forgetting you already.

Standing before Peter was a rather uptight middle-aged person in a tight-fitting suit, whose largely undistinguished features held the kind of tight-assed expression clearly designed to indicate that he was a man with an unpleasant duty to perform, which he intended to carry out with all the personal pleasure at his command.

"Is this number thirteen Daemon Street?" said the person, in the kind of voice used by people who already have the answer to their question but are hoping you're going to be stupid enough to argue about it.

"Yes," said Peter, firmly. He felt he was on safe enough ground there.

"I am Mr. Cuthbert. I represent the local Council." He paused a moment, so that Peter could be properly impressed.

"Damn," said Peter. "The *move along nothing to see here* avoidance field must be on the blink."

"What?"

"Nothing!" said Peter. "Do carry on. The local Council, eh? How interesting. Is it an interesting job? Why are you here, Mr. Cuthbert? I've been good. Mostly."

"It has come to our attention," said Mr. Cuthbert, just a little doggedly, "That you have not been maintaining the proper amenities of this residence to the required standards."

"But . . . it's our house," said Peter. "Not the Council's."

"There are still standards! Standards have to be met! All parts and parcels of every house in the district must come up to the required criteria. Regulations apply to everyone; it's a matter of Health and Safety." And having unleashed that unstoppable trump card, Mr. Cuthbert allowed himself a small smile. "I will have to make . . . an inspection."

"What?" said Peter. "Now?"

"Yes, now! I have all the necessary paperwork with me. . . ."

"I felt sure you would, Mr. Cuthbert," said Peter. "You look the type. Well, you'd better come on in and take a look around. You'll have to take us as you find us, though."

While Peter was having his close encounter with a supremely up its own ass denizen of the local Council, there was a hard, heavy, and even aristocratic knock at the back door. Jubilee went to answer it, frowning thoughtfully. Visitors to the House were rare enough, from either world. Two at once were almost unheard of. The back door to the House was a massive slab of ancient oak, deeply carved with long lines of runes and sigils. Jubilee snapped her fingers at the door as she approached, and the heavy door swung smoothly open before her. She stepped forcefully out into the cool moonlight of late evening, and her visitor was forced to retreat a few steps, despite himself. The door slammed very firmly shut behind her. Jubilee ostentatiously ignored her visitor for a few moments, glancing quickly around her to reassure herself that everything on the night side of the House was where it should be.

Here, the House was a sprawling Gothic mansion, with grotesquely carved stone and woodwork, latticed windows, cupolas, garrets, leering gargoyles peering down from the roof, and a tangle of twisted chimneys. Set out before the House, a delicate wicker bridge crossing the dark and murky waters of the moat, leading to a small zoo of animal shapes in greenery and deep purple lawns. Ancient trees with long, gnarled branches like clutching fingers stood guard over a garden whose flowers were famously as ferocious as they were stunning. The night sky was full of stars, spinning like Catherine wheels, and the full moon was a promising shade of blue.

Jubilee finally deigned to notice the personage standing before her. He didn't need to announce he was an Elven Prince of the Unseeli Court. He couldn't have been anything else. Tall and supernaturally slender, in silver-filigreed brass armor, he had pale colorless skin, cat-pupiled eyes, and pointed ears. Inhumanly handsome, insufferably graceful, and almost unbearably arrogant. Not because he was a Prince, you understand, but because he was an Elf. He bowed to Jubilee.

"Don't," Jubilee said immediately. "Just . . . don't. What do you want here, Prince Airgedlamh?"

"I come on moonfleet heels, faster than the winter winds or summer tides, walking the hidden ways to bear you words of great import and urgency. . . ."

"And you can cut that out, too. I don't have the patience," said Jubilee. "What do you want?"

"It has been made known to us," the Elven Prince said stiffly, "that many of the old magics, the pacts and agreements laid down when this House was first agreed on, are not being properly maintained. As required in that Place where all that matters is decided. I must make an inspection."

"Now?"

"Yes. I have the proper authority."

"Buttocks," said Jubilee, with more than ordinary force. "All right, you'd better come in. And wipe those armored boots properly. The floor gets very bad-tempered if you track mud over it."

Peter led Mr. Cuthbert around the House. Because the man from the local Council had entered the House from the everyday world, that was the aspect of the House he should see. So it always had been, and so it must always be, in the House that links the worlds, if only because most people can't cope with more than one world at a time. Mr. Cuthbert took his own sweet time looking around the kitchen, sniffing loudly to demonstrate his disapproval of absolutely everything, and then allowed Peter to lead him out into the main hall.

"How many rooms in this residence, Mr. Caine?" Mr. Cuthbert demanded, peering suspiciously about him.

Peter didn't like to say *It depends,* so he just guessed. "Nine?"

"Oh dear," Mr. Cuthbert said smugly, shaking his head happily. "Oh dear, oh dear, Mr. Caine . . . That doesn't agree with our information at all! I will have to make a note."

And he got out a notepad and pen, and took his own sweet time about making the note. Peter tried to lean in to see what he was writing, but Mr. Cuthbert immediately turned away so he couldn't.

"I haven't been here that long," said Peter. "The wife and I only moved in three years ago."

"You haven't got around to counting the number of rooms in your house in three years, Mr. Caine?"

"I've had a lot on my plate," said Peter.

"So, you don't actually own this desirable residence?" said Mr. Cuthbert.

"We hold it in trust," said Peter. "It's like the National Trust. Only more so. You'll find all the proper paperwork was submitted to the Council long ago. . . ."

Mr. Cuthbert sniffed loudly, to indicate he didn't believe that for one moment but would let it go for now. He was so busy with this little performance that he didn't notice all the faces in the portraits on the walls turning to look at him. Disapprovingly. Mr. Cuthbert wasn't supposed to notice anything of that nature, but with the avoidance spells malfunctioning, God alone knew what else might go wrong in the House. . . .

Two small hairy things chased their ball down the hall and then slammed to an abrupt halt to stare at Mr. Cuthbert.

"My nephews," Peter said quickly. "They're visiting."

"What a charming young boy and girl," said Mr. Cuthbert, just a bit vaguely. And to him, they probably were. Though given his expression, charming was probably pushing it a bit. He reached out to pat them on the head, but some last-minute self-preservation instinct made him realize this wasn't a good idea, and he pulled his hand back again. Peter hurried him past the hairy things and showed him the downstairs rooms. Mr. Cuthbert was, if anything, even less impressed than before, and made a number of notes in his little book. Finally, they went upstairs.

"We have two Guests staying with us at the moment," Peter said carefully. There were others, but none of them the kind that Mr. Cuthbert could usefully be introduced to. "In the first room we have a young lady called Lee, visiting from the Isle of Man. Next door is Johnny, a young man just down from London, for a while. Do we really need to disturb them this early in the day?"

"Early?" said Mr. Cuthbert. "I myself have been up for hours. I am not the sort to let the day pass me by when there is important work to be done. Oh no, I must see everything while I'm here. And everyone. My job requires it." He stopped suddenly and looked around. "What the hell was *that*?"

"The hot water boiler, up in the attic," Peter said quickly. "It's temperamental. Though you'll have to bring your own ladder, if you want to inspect it. We don't go up there."

"The boiler can be inspected on a future visit," Mr. Cuthbert conceded. "There must be something seriously wrong with it if it can make noises like that. Sounded very much like something . . . growling."

"Oh, you are such a joker, Mr. Cuthbert," said Peter. "Such a sense of humor."

Mr. Cuthbert headed for the Guest rooms. Peter glared up at the attic. "Keep a lid on it, Grandfather Grendel! We've got a visitor!"

He hurried after Mr. Cuthbert, who had stopped outside

the first Guest door. Peter moved quickly in and knocked very politely on the door.

"Lee? This is Peter. We have a caller from the local Council. Are you decent?"

"Close as I ever get, darling," said a rich sultry voice from inside the room. "Come on in, boys. The more the merrier, that's what I always say."

Peter swallowed hard, smiled meaninglessly at Mr. Cuthbert, and put all his trust in the House's special nature. Fortunately, when he and Mr. Cuthbert entered the room, it all seemed perfectly normal, if a bit gloomy. A slim and very pale teenage Goth girl was reclining on an unmade bed, dressed in dark jeans and a black T-shirt bearing the legend *I'm only wearing this till they come up with a darker color*. She also wore steel-studded black leather bracelets around her wrists and throat. Her unhealthily pale face boasted more dark eye makeup than a panda on the pull, and blood-red lips. The bedroom walls were covered with posters featuring *The Cure, The Mission,* and *Fields of the Nephilim.* The girl rose unhurriedly to her feet, every movement smooth and elegant and just that little bit disturbing, and then she smiled slowly at Mr. Cuthbert. Peter moved instinctively to put himself between Lee and the man from the Council.

"Just introducing Mr. Cuthbert to the Guests, Lee," he said quickly. "He can't stay long. He has to get back. Because people might notice if he went missing."

Lee pouted. "I don't know why you keep going on about that. It was just the one time."

"Are you . . . comfortable here?" said Mr. Cuthbert, apparently because he felt he should be saying something.

"Oh yes," said Lee. "Very comfortable." She smiled widely at Mr. Cuthbert, and there was a flash of very sharp teeth behind the dark lips.

Peter quickly manoeuvred Mr. Cuthbert back out into the corridor. The man from the Council was flustered enough that he let Peter do it, even if he didn't quite understand why.

"Does she pay rent?" he said vaguely.

"No," said Peter. "She's a Guest."

"I'll have to make a note," said Mr. Cuthbert. And he did.

The next door along opened as they approached it, and out stepped a quiet, nervous young man, in a blank white T-shirt and distressed blue jeans. He was handsome enough, in an unfinished sort of way. He put his hands in his pockets, because he didn't know what else to do with them, and looked mournfully at Mr. Cuthbert.

"Hello. You're not from the tabloids, are you?"

"No, Johnny," Peter said quickly. "He's from the local Council."

"Don't I know you from somewhere?" said Mr. Cuthbert, doubtfully. "I'm almost sure I've seen you somewhere before. . . ."

"I was on a television talent show," Johnny said reluctantly. "It all got a bit much, so I came here to . . . get away from it all for a while."

"Oh, I never watch those shows," Mr. Cuthbert said immediately, in much the same kind of voice as one might say *I never watch bear baiting*. He insisted on a good look around Johnny's room, found nothing of any interest whatsoever, made a note about that, and then trudged back down the stairs again. Peter hurried after him. Mr. Cuthbert strode back through the House, into the kitchen, and then stopped abruptly at the front door. He gave Peter a stern look, the kind meant to indicate *I am a man to be reckoned with and don't you forget it.*

"I can see there are a great many things that will have to be dealt with, to bring this property up to scratch, Mr. Caine. I will of course be sending in a full investigative team. Have all the floorboards up, to inspect the wiring. Might have to open up all the walls, rewire the entire House. And a residence this size, with Guests, should have proper central heating, not just some noisy old boiler in the attic. That will definitely have to be replaced. I'm sure I saw rising damp, the whole of the outside needs rendering, and what I can see of your roof is a disgrace! We'll have to put up scaffolding all around the property." He smiled thinly, his eyes full of quiet satisfaction. "I'm afraid this is all going to prove rather expensive for you, Mr. Caine, but regulations are regulations, and standards must be maintained. Good day to you. You'll be hearing from me again, very soon."

He left the house as importantly as he'd arrived, slamming the door behind him. Up in the attic, Grandfather Grendel made a very rude noise, and the House smelled briefly of rotting petunias.

Jubilee led the Elven Prince Airgedlamh around the House, though of course he saw a very different establishment. He strolled arrogantly down the hall, refusing to be hurried, remarking loudly on the substandard nature of the ambience, and the lack of proper protective magics. He did notice the portrait faces on the walls glaring at him with open disdain and met them all glare for glare. He was used to general disapproval. He was an Elf. Jubilee let him wander around the downstairs rooms, making haughty and occasionally downright rude remarks as the mood took him, before Jubilee was finally able to lead him upstairs to the Guest rooms. Grandfather Grendel made some more extremely rude noises.

"Be still, old creation," said the Elven Prince, without even looking up at the attic. "Don't make me have to come up there."

He pushed open the first door and strode right in, not giving Jubilee time to knock or even introduce him. Inside, the room was dark and clammy and subtly oppressive. The Elven Prince slammed to a halt in spite of himself, and Jubilee moved quickly in beside him. Lee might be just a teenage Goth in the day world, but here her true nature was unleashed. Leanan-Sidhe was a dark Muse, from the Isle of Man. Inspiration for artists of the macabre and the mysterious, those who dreamed of her often produced powerful and magnificent work, only to burn out fast and die young. Leanan-Sidhe was a harsh mistress and a debilitating Muse, and everyone knew what she fed on.

The Elven Prince bowed stiffly to her, again almost in spite of himself. The Muse's room was a dark cavern, with blood dripping slowly down the rough stone walls. Leanan-Sidhe reclined at her ease on the huge pulpy petals of a crimson rose, floating in a sea of tears. She was a dark presence, of overwhelming demeanor, more shadow than substance. Her ashen face floated in the darkness like a malignant moon on a very dark night. She had no eyes, only deep dark eye sockets, and her mouth was the color of dried blood. She smiled sweetly on Prince Airgedlamh, revealing rows of very sharp teeth, like a shark.

"Come on in, sweet prince, my very dear, and I'll show you what dreams are made of."

The Elven Prince wavered but stood firm. "Tempt me not, dark muse. . . ."

"But, darling," said Leanan-Sidhe, "that's what I do. . . ."

She laughed richly, and the Elven Prince couldn't get out of the room fast enough. Jubilee smiled sweetly at Leanan-Sidhe, who dropped her a brief wink, and then she went back out into the hall. With the door safely shut again, Prince Airgedlamh quickly regained his composure and insisted on moving on to the next room. Jubilee nodded, and again Johnny was there waiting for them.

"Hello," he said sadly. "I'm Johnny Jay, the voice of the suffering masses. Pop prince of show tunes. Simon Callow says I'm a genius."

"I do not know you," said Prince Airgedlamh.

Johnny Jay actually brightened up a little. "Really? Oh, that's wonderful! Such a relief to meet someone who doesn't want something from me. Even if it's only an autograph."

Prince Airgedlamh looked at Jubilee, who shrugged briefly. "Mortal stuff. He sings."

"Yes," said the Elven Prince. "I see the mark upon him. Send him to the Unseeli Court. The Fae have always had a fondness for human bards."

"I think he's got enough problems at the moment," said Jubilee.

But the Elven Prince had already lost interest and turned away. Johnny nodded glumly and went back into his room. Prince Airgedlamh stopped at the top of the stairs and looked up at the attic, where loud shifting noises suggested something very large was trampling down its bedding.

"What *is* that? I can sense its age, but its true nature is hidden from me."

"Oh, that's just Grandfather Grendel," said Jubilee. "He's been up in that attic for centuries, according to the House records. My husband and I inherited him when we moved in. As long as we throw him some raw meat once in a while and a handful of sugar mice, he's happy enough. Every now and again, he threatens to spin himself a cocoon and transmogrify into a whole new deity, but it hasn't happened yet. I think he's just bluffing. Of course it could just be a plea for attention."

"Guests are supposed to be strictly temporary," said the Elven Prince. "That is the point of a Guest, is it not?"

"Nothing in the rules," Jubilee said blithely. "Besides, who knows what temporary means, with a lifespan like Grandfather Grendel's?"

They went back down the stairs and had only just reached the bottom when two small hairy things came running down the hall, pursued by the bouncing ball. They stopped abruptly to stare at the Elven Prince and then snarled loudly at him. Huge mouths full of jagged teeth appeared in their fur.

"Vermin," said Prince Airgedlamh. "I will have to make a note."

"We are not in any way vermin!" snapped one of the hairy things. "We are scavengers! We keep the House free of pests. We're only supposed to eat small things. . . ."

"But we are perfectly prepared to make an exception in your case!" finished the other. "No one bullies Jubilee while we're around."

"Want me to do something appalling to Prince Scumbag here?" said the ball, bouncing threateningly in place.

"Everything's under control, thank you," said Jubilee, in her best calm and soothing voice. "You boys run along."

They did so, reluctantly. The Elven Prince did his best to pretend nothing had just happened. He sniffed coldly and looked down his long nose at Jubilee.

"I can see there is much here that will have to be done, to bring this House into line with all the relevant agreements. The gargoyles must be neutered, the moat must be dredged, and many of the old magics have been allowed to fade around the edges. They will all have to be renewed, with the appropriate blood sacrifices. Your garden is a disgrace, and where have all the mushrooms gone? This House has fallen far from what it should be, and much work will have to be done to put things to right. Appropriate payments will, of course, also have to be made."

He bowed quickly to Jubilee, before she could stop him, and then he strode back through the House and was out the back door and across the wicker bridge, heading off into the night. Jubilee closed the door thoughtfully after him and then walked back down the hall.

"All right! That's it! Everyone join me in the kitchen, right now! House meeting!"

In the kitchen, very soon afterward, Peter and Jubilee, Lee and Johnny sat around the table and looked at one another glumly. The radio was being quiet, thinking hard, trying to be useful. The fridge door had been left open, just in case Walter felt like contributing something useful. Up in the attic, Grandfather Grendel was being ominously silent.

"We can't let this happen," Peter said finally. "We just can't! Scaffolding from the Council, blood sacrifices for the Unseeli Court, all kind of interior work to satisfy both sides . . . there's bound to be an overlap! They couldn't help but interfere with each other, and cause all kinds of conflicts. This House is supposed to link the two worlds, not bang their heads together."

"It could mean the end of the House as a refuge," said Jubilee. "If no one feels safe and secure here, if we can't guarantee anonymity. . . . No more Sanctuary for anyone."

"I can't go back to the Isle of Man," Lee said firmly. "I have had it up to here with being a Muse. I do all the hard work and the artists take all the credit! I never even get a dedication. . . . And they're such a *needy* bunch! So clingy . . . All those bloody poets hanging around, demanding inspiration. . . . I haven't had a decent holiday in centuries! I never wanted to be dark and morbid anyway. . . . I should have been a sylph, like Mother wanted. . . ."

"I know what you mean," Johnny Jay said diffidently. "I won't go back to London. I just won't. Ever since I won that damned talent contest, the television people and the tabloids have been making my life a misery. I never wanted to be a national icon; I just wanted to sing and make people happy. The tabloids have been doorstopping all my family and friends, and anyone who ever spoke to me, looking for *interesting* stories; and when they don't find any, they just make some up! I've never even been to Spearmint Rhino!"

"I am not leaving!" said Leanan-Sidhe. "I have claimed Sanctuary, and I know my rights! I demand that you protect me from this unwelcome outside interference!"

Peter looked at Jubilee. "The rules of the House say we have to give Guests Sanctuary. No one ever said we had to like them."

"We can still give them a good slap," said Jubilee.

"Can I watch?" said Johnny Jay, brightening up a little.

"We have to do something," said Peter. "If the nature of the House is compromised, if the two worlds can no longer be kept separate . . . Could that actually happen, princess?"

"I don't think the matter has ever arisen before," said Jubilee, frowning thoughtfully. "The House exists in a state of spiritual grace, of perfect balance between the two worlds of being. Shift that balance too far either way, and this House could cease to function. A new House would have to be created somewhere else, with new management. We would not be considered. We would have failed our duty. After all these centuries, we would be the first to fail the House. . . ."

"It hasn't come to that yet, princess," said Peter, laying one hand comfortingly over hers. "Can the House really be threatened so easily? I thought the House was created and protected by Higher Powers?"

"We're supposed to solve our own problems," said Jubilee. "That's the job."

"Cuthbert might not know what he's doing," said Lee, "but you can bet that bloody Elf does. He must understand the implications of what he's saying."

"Of course he does!" said Jubilee. "He knows exactly what he's doing. Our usual avoidance fields didn't just happen to fail, revealing us to the normal world at exactly the same time as the Unseeli Court decides to take an interest in us. This was planned. I think somebody targeted us, set this all in motion for a reason."

"To destroy the House?" said Lee.

"Who would want to do that?" said Johnny Jay.

"Or . . . are they doing this to get at someone who thought they were safe, inside the House." Lee scowled, and something of her darker persona was briefly present in the kitchen with them. They all shuddered briefly. Lee politely pretended not to notice. "I thought anyone who claimed Sanctuary here was entitled to full privacy and protection? If any of those demanding little poets have followed me here to make trouble . . ."

"Your safety in all things is guaranteed, for as long as you care to stay here," Jubilee said coldly. "It isn't always about you, you know. I think . . . this is all about me and Peter. It's all about us."

"Your family never was that keen on our marriage, princess," Peter said carefully.

"It wasn't their place to say anything," said Jubilee. "It's the tradition, that the House's management should be a married couple, one from each world. I was happy to marry you and happy to come here; they should have been happy for me."

"I was never happier than when you joined your life to mine," said Peter. "You're everything I ever wanted. The House was just a wonderful bonus. But . . . if our marriage is threatening the House . . . I'm here because I wanted to be part of something greater, something important. I won't let that be threatened because of me. We can't let the House be destroyed because of us, princess. Not when it's in our power to save it."

"It's my family," Jubilee said grimly. "Has to be. My bloody family. They'd be perfectly ready to see this House destroyed, just to have me back where they think I belong. Because they can't bear to believe that they might be wrong about something. Maybe . . . If I was to go back, they might call this off. . . . But, no. No. . . . I could leave this House to protect it, but I couldn't leave you, Peter. My love."

"And they'd never accept me," said Peter. "You know that. I'd have to agree to leave you, before they'd take you back."

"Could you do that?" said Jubilee.

"The House is bigger than either of us," said Peter. "We've always known that, princess. I could not love thee half so much. . . ."

"Loved I not honor more," said Jubilee. "We both love this House, what it represents, and the freedoms it preserves."

"That's why we got the job," said Peter. "Because we'd do anything to protect this place. And now, that's being turned against us."

"I could leave," Lee said abruptly. "If I thought it would help. If only because you two clearly serve a Higher Power than me."

"Same here," said Johnny Jay.

"No!" Peter said flatly. "Either the House is Sanctuary for everyone, or it's Sanctuary for no one. You mustn't go, or everything we might do would be for nothing."

"And we can't go, either!" Jubilee slammed her hands down flat on the tabletop, her eyes alight with sudden understanding. "Because that's what they want! They're depending on our sense of duty and responsibility to outweigh our love for each other. That we'd be ready to break up, to preserve the House! I'm damned if I'll let my arrogant bloody family win! There has to be a way. . . ."

"It's not as though we're defenseless," said Lee, her blood-red mouth stretching wide, revealing far too many teeth for one mouth. "Let us lure them in here, and I will teach them all the horror that lurks in the dark."

"Do you sing, O muse of psychologically challenged poets?" said Johnny. "Because I'll wager good money that between us we could whip up a duet that would rattle the bones and trouble the soul of everyone who heard it, whatever world they came from."

"We will chase them, we will chase them, we will eat them up with spoons!" chanted the small furry things in the doorway, while the ball bounced excitedly up and down between them.

"I could throw things at people," Walter said diffidently from the fridge. "If they got close enough."

There was a low steady rumbling, from up in the attic, as Grandfather Grendel stirred. When he spoke, his words hammered on the air like storm clouds slamming together.

"Let all the worlds tremble, if I must come forth again. There have been many powers worse than elves, and I have slaughtered and feasted on them all, in my time."

"No!" Jubilee said sharply. "This House was created by the Greatest of Powers, to put an end to conflicts, to give hope and comfort to those who wanted only peace. If we defend the House with violence, we betray everything it stands for. There has to be another way."

"There is." Peter leaned forward across the table, taking both of Jubilee's hands in his. "The House exists . . . because it is necessary. It was brought into being, and is protected by, Powers far greater than your damned family, princess. Even your people wouldn't dare upset those Powers; so call their bluff! Tell them that if this House's function is destroyed because of them, we'll make sure everyone knows it's all their fault! Tell them; it's all about rendering unto Caesar. Let both sides perform whatever home improvements they feel necessary . . . as long as they don't interfere with each other, or the running of the House! Or else! Your family might have raised arrogance to an art form, but even they're not dumb enough to anger the Powers That Be."

"Peter, my love, you're brilliant!" said Jubilee. "I think this is why I love you most. Because you save me from my family."

"Any time, princess," said Peter.

The next day, bright and early, but not quite as early as the day before, there was a very polite knocking at the House's front door. When Peter went to open it, he found Mr. Cuthbert standing there, looking very grim. He nodded stiffly to Peter, or at the very least, in Peter's direction.

"It seems . . . there may have been a misunderstanding," he said reluctantly. "It has been decided in Council that this residence is exempt from all Health and Safety regulations, and obligatory improvements. Because it is a Listed and Protected building. No changes can be made without express permission from on high." Mr. Cuthbert glared impotently at Peter. "I should have known the likes of you would have friends in high places!"

"Oh yes," said Peter. "Really. You have no idea."

And he shut the door politely but very firmly in Mr. Cuthbert's face.

Meanwhile, at the back door, Jubilee was speaking with the Elven Prince Airgedlamh of the Unseeli Court.

"So it was you," she said.

"Yes," said the Elven Prince. "All things have been put right; no improvements will be necessary. The Unseeli Court has withdrawn its interest in this place. The House will endure as it always has, and so will you and so will we."

"Go back to the family," said Jubilee. "Tell them I'm happy here."

"Of course. But there are those of us who do miss you at Court," said the Elven Prince. "Good-bye, Princess."

I had the main idea for this story years ago: it was going to be a stage play about a house on the borderland, with doors to reality and fantasy and the people who found sanctuary there. But I could never find a story to suit it. Until now. I love the characters, and I keep meaning to go back to them.

FIND HEAVEN AND HELL IN THE SMALLEST THINGS

They threw me into Space and then dropped me into Hell, with just a dead woman's voice to comfort me. They should have known better. They should have known what would happen.

We sat in two rows, facing one another. Twelve people. Yes, call us people, because we certainly weren't men or women anymore. Twelve people from Old Earth, wearing the very latest hard suits. The new armor, built for strength and speed, cutting-edge science, and all the latest weapons. Along with a built-in AI to interface between the occupant and the armor . . . to speak soft soothing words to us, keep us human, and keep our minds off the perfect killing things we'd become. We sat in two rows, six hard suits staring at six hard suits, identical suits of faceless armor, except for the numbers One to Twelve stenciled on our chests.

I was Twelve. Looking at the suit opposite me was like looking at myself. Gleaming steel in the shape of a man, with a smooth featureless helm where a face should be. We couldn't look out, but it also meant the world couldn't look in and see us; and for that, we were grateful. We don't need faces. We see the world with new eyes, through the augmented senses of the hard suits.

We were all of us strapped in, very securely. To hold us steady. Or to keep us under strict restraint so we couldn't hurt anyone. Including ourselves. Just in case we were to go crazy. It does happen. After all, no sane person would allow himself to be put in a hard suit. The armor keeps us alive. The armor makes us strong and powerful. The armor is our life support and our life sentence, a prison we can never leave.

We don't use our names anymore. Just the numbers. The people we used to be are gone. We don't talk much. We never met one another, before they marched us aboard this ship at gunpoint. We've never seen one another outside our armor, and we don't want to. Pretty people don't get locked inside hard suits. Not handsome, whole people, with their whole lives ahead of them. They let me look in a mirror once, at the hospital, and then they had to pump a whole bunch of tranks into me to stop me screaming.

The ship's Captain spoke to us through the overhead speakers. His voice sounded human enough, but he was no more human than we were. Just a memory deposit, grafted onto the ship's AI. A computer haunted by an old man's memories, the ghost in the machine. A memory of a man, to run a starship, to take things like us to worlds where Humanity isn't welcome.

"This is the Captain of the *Duchess of Malfi*," said the human-sounding voice. "We'll be dropping into orbit around our destination anytime soon. The planet's official designation is Proxima IV. Everyone else calls it Abaddon. Why? Because it's just another name for Hell."

The Captain wears a ship the way we wear our armor. It occurred to me that might make him a little more sympathetic to our plight than most.

"What did you do, Captain?" I said through my suits' speakers. "What did you do, to be imprisoned in this ship?"

"Are you crazy?" said the Captain. He sounded genuinely amused. "I asked for this. Begged for it! Thirty years' service in the Fleet, running the space lanes, at play among the planets . . . and they took it all away from me. Just because I got old. And then they came to me and offered me my own ship and the freedom of space. Forever. Of course it wouldn't be me, as such, just the memory of me, but still . . . I jumped at the chance. I only thought I knew what captaining a ship was like. If you could only see the glories I see, through the ship's sensors. They say Space is empty, but they're wrong. They need to see it with better eyes. There are delicate forces and subtle energies out here that would put the brightest rainbow to shame. There are giants that walk among the stars, living shapes and concepts we don't even have names for. We are not alone, in the dark. . . ."

An awful lot of people go crazy when you take their humanity away and lock them inside a box. Even if it's a box as big as a ship. I tried again.

"Don't you miss being human, Captain?"

"Of course not! How could I miss being that small, that limited? Anyway, the real me is still human. Somewhere back on Old Earth, probably dreaming about me, out here . . . Look, whatever briefing they gave you about what you're doing, forget it. Abaddon isn't like anything you've ever encountered before. Here's the real deal: everything on the planet below is deadly to Humanity. The air, the gravity, the radiation, everything you might eat or drink, and anything you might happen to encounter. Very definitely including the extensive and murderous plant life. Once you're down there, you're at war with the whole world. Don't get distracted; you'll die. Don't let anything get too close to you; you'll die. Don't get lazy or sloppy; you'll die. Just . . . do your job, and try to survive."

"Are there any human people at the Base on Abaddon?" said Three. The voice that issued from his speakers was neither male nor female. All our voices were like that. Anything else would have been cruel.

"Hell no," said the Captain. "No people anywhere, on Abaddon. It's not a people place. That's why they've sent you to work on the terraforming equipment, because robots and androids can't operate under the extreme local conditions. Now brace yourselves; we're entering the atmosphere."

The whole cabin shook as the *Duchess of Malfi* dropped like a stone and gave every indication of hitting something that was doing its very best to hit back. I say cabin; cargo hold would probably be more accurate. No frills or fancies, just a holding space for twelve suits of armor. Turbulence shook us like a dog shakes a rat, slamming us all back and forth in our reinforced straps. Of course we didn't feel a thing. Feeling is one of the first things you learn to do without. The armors' servomechanisms whined loudly as they struggled to compensate for the sudden movements. My suit's AI flashed up status readouts on the inside of my helm to reassure me we were still operating well within the armor's specifications.

Any human being would have been killed by that fierce descent, but we were never in any danger. Hard suits are designed to insulate their occupants from any danger they might encounter. I could hear the wind howling outside the ship, screeching like a living thing, hating the new arrival that pierced its atmosphere like a knife. The Captain was right. We'd come to a world that hated us. Welcome to Hell.

"The landing pads are almost two miles from Base Three," said the Captain. "Once I've dropped you off, find the beacon and head straight for the Base. Don't let anything stop you. Or you won't get to Base Three."

"What happened to Base One and Base Two?" said Seven.

"They really didn't tell you anything, did they?" said the Captain. "How very wise of them. The whole planet is covered by one massive jungle, and everything in it hates you. Base One was entirely mechanical, drones and robots run by the Base AI. Planets overwhelmed the whole thing inside a week. You can't even see the Base anymore; it's buried so deep in vegetation. Base Two had a human crew; they lasted almost two months, before they stopped answering their comm. The rescue party found the Base completely deserted. Force shield down, main doors wide open, no trace of a living person anywhere. Not a clue anywhere as to what happened to them. Maybe you'll find out. Maybe you'll last longer."

A holo viewscreen snapped on, floating in midair between our two rows, showing remote sensor imaging of what was waiting for us down on Abaddon. At first, all I could see was the light, bright and vicious and overpowering. My suit's filters had to work hard to compensate, so I could see anything. The landing pads were still some distance below us, shining like three crystal coins dropped into an overgrown garden. In reality, each pad was almost half a mile wide, specially designed to absorb the destructive energies that accumulate from starship landings. The jungle came right up to the edges of the three pads, surrounding them with tall rustling stalks of threatening plant life.

"Why do they allow plants to grow so close to the landing pads?" said Nine.

"Base Three sends out drones to burn it all back, once every hour," said the Captain. "But the jungle grows back faster than the drones can suppress it. If it weren't for the pads' radiations, the jungle would have buried them, too. Base Three has its own force shield; nothing gets past that. Remember: once we land, watch yourselves. You've got no friends down there."

You'll be fine, Paul, said a warm, comforting female voice in my head. The hard suit's AI. *Just follow your training, and everything will be well. I'm right here with you.* I didn't say anything, but I shuddered in spite of myself.

The whole ship cried out as we slammed down onto the landing pad. The holo viewscreen disappeared, replaced by a flashing red light and an emergency siren. The Captain's voice rose over it. "Out! Out! Everybody out! I'm not staying here one moment longer than I have to!"

Our straps flew open, releasing us at last, and we all stood up. Guns and other weapons appeared and disappeared quickly, as we ran our system checks. Servomotors whined and whirred loudly as we checked our responses, like knights in armor off on a crusade. And then a hatch opened in the far wall, a ramp extended down to the landing pad, and we went slamming heavily down the steel walkway to meet what was waiting for us.

The light hit us hard, almost blinding us despite our suits' filters, but none of us hesitated. We just kept pressing forward, wanting to be well clear of the ship, before it took off again. The ramp disappeared the moment the last one of us stepped off, and the hatch slammed shut. We were down on Abaddon. We moved quickly to stand back to back, in squads, the way we'd been trained. The light was just about bearable now, but the air seemed . . . sour, spoiled. Two suns blazed fiercely in the sky, too fierce to look at directly. The sky was the crimson of fresh blood, the roiling clouds like dark masses of clotted blood, outlined by great flurries of discharging energies, from storm patterns higher up. A heavy wind blasted this way and that, howling and shrieking. Abaddon, just another name for Hell.

The jungle was all around us, unfamiliar plants a good ten, twelve, fourteen feet high in places. The colors were harsh and gaudy, primal and overpowering, clashing blatantly with one another in patterns that made no sense, in a manner openly upsetting and even disturbing to human aesthetics. There were things like trees, with dark purple trunks and massive spiked branches, weighed down with masses of serrated puke-yellow leaves. All of them bending and bowing at impossible angles, as though they wanted to slam their tall heads down on us. And all around them, every variation or type of plant you ever saw in your worst nightmares. Thrashing and flailing with endless hate and vitality, whipping long, barbed flails through the air, pushing and pressing forward as though they couldn't wait to get at us.

They'd seemed restless enough on the viewscreen, but once we appeared on the landing pad, they all went crazy, absolutely insane with rage and bloodlust. Every living thing strained toward us, churning and boiling like attack dogs let off the leash. I actually saw some of them rip their own roots up out of the dark wet earth and lurch forward on roots curled like claws. There were huge flowers with mouths full of grinding teeth, wild with eagerness to drag us down. Seedpods hurtled through the air to explode among us like grenades, razor-edged seeds clattering harmlessly against our armor.

It was as though the whole jungle was coming at us at once, struggling against one another in a vicious urge to get to us, with no sense of self-preservation at all. We stood together in our squads, taking it all in.

"There aren't any animals," said Three. "It's all . . . plants. But plants aren't supposed to act like this!"

"The Captain was right," said Seven. "The whole world hates us. How refreshingly honest."

"We are definitely not welcome here," said Four. "You think this world knows we're here to terraform it?"

"Don't anthropomorphize," said One. "Just deal with what's in front of you."

"We have to get to Base Three," I said. "Power up all weapon systems. Remember your training. And try not to shoot me in the back."

Well done, Paul, said my AI. *Take charge. You'll get through this okay. Paul? I wish you'd talk to me, Paul.*

We strode forward, off the landing pad and into the jungle, and opened up with everything we had. I had an energy weapon built into my left hand. I fired it, and a huge mass of seething vegetation just disappeared. Good weapon, very effective, but it took two minutes to recharge between shots. My right hand held a projectile weapon, firing explosive flechettes. I moved my hand back and forth, cutting through all the plants in front of me like an invisible scythe. But my armor only held so much ammunition. So I used both weapons to open up a trail, and then stepped forward into it and kept going.

Nine was right there beside me. He had a flamethrower working, burning the thrashing plants right back to the ground. Two moved in on my other side. He had a grenade launcher. Lots of noise and black smoke, and bits of dead plant flew through the air. We worked well together, opening up a wide path before us. My armor was locked onto Base Three's beacon, and all I had to do was head straight for it.

We all felt the shock as the *Duchess of Malfi* took off, throwing itself back up into the sky again, but none of us could spare the time to watch it go. We had to keep all our concentration on the plants trying so hard to kill us. They pressed in from every side, clawing and scraping and hammering at our armor, searching for weak spots, for a way in. The various fires we started never seemed to last long, and for every plant we killed, there were always more pressing forward to take their place. The jungle had already closed in behind us, cutting us off from the landing pads.

We moved slowly, steadily forward, all twelve of us together, an oasis of calm rational thought in a sea of violence, heading for Base Three. I'd tried contacting them on the open channel, but there was no reply. I remembered the Captain's voice, telling how Base Two had been found wide open and deserted. . . . But I couldn't think about that. Not when there were still so many plants to kill. With my ammunition reserves already running low, I had no choice but to shut down my guns and fall back on the amazing strength built into my armor. I grabbed striking plants with my steel hands, tore them apart as though they were made of paper, and threw them aside. Some twisted around my hands as I held them, still trying to get at me. A long, bristling creeper wrapped itself around my arm, constricting furiously, but I tore it loose with one easy gesture, crushing it in my hand. Thick and bloody pulp spurted through my fingers. It couldn't touch me. Nothing could touch me. And it felt good, so good, to be able to strike out at a world that so openly hated us.

Two was pulled down by a mass of lashing creepers. They just engulfed him in a moment, crushing him with implacable force. His armor cracked in a dozen places under the incredible pressure. The creepers broke the armored joints and pulled Two apart. He died quickly, the plants soaking up his spurting blood, before it even reached the ground. Seven ran out of ammunition, or his gun jammed. Either way, he just stood there looking at it, and the top of a tree came slamming down like a massive bludgeon and slammed him into the ground. All his joints ruptured at once, and blood flew out of his armor at a hundred points. He didn't even have time to scream. We never saw what happened to Ten. We just looked around, and he wasn't there anymore. We heard him screaming over the open channel for a while, and then he stopped.

The rest of us plowed on through the jungle, killing everything that came at us. It was only two miles to Base Three, but it seemed to last forever.

We finally burst out of the jungle and there was Base Three, right before us. Reassuringly solid, rising tall and majestic into the blood-red sky, untouched by the world it had come to change forever. There was a shimmering on the air around it, from the force shield. It made the Base look subtly unreal, as though we'd fought all this way just to find a mirage. But the energies the field generated were more than enough to hold the plants back, and we stumbled across a wide-open perimeter to reach the Base. The force shield had been programmed to let us through, and we strode through the shimmering presence like walking through a sparkling waterfall, out of danger and into safety.

A few plants got through the force shield by clinging stubbornly to our armor. We quickly ripped them away, tearing them apart and then trampled them underfoot until the pieces stopped moving. Some of the larger growths clung to our armor as though they were glued there; so we all washed one another with our flamethrowers, just to be sure. We didn't feel anything, inside the hard suits. When we were finished, we turned to face the main doors and found that gun barrels had appeared on either side of the doors, covering us. Possibly to assist us against invading plants, possibly to remind us that Base Three was ready to destroy any or all of us, should the need arise.

Because the armor made us too powerful to be trusted. And because everyone knew that if you weren't crazy before they put you in the suit. . . .

The main doors slid smoothly open, and those of us who'd made it through the jungle stamped heavily forward into Base Three. Tracked by guns all the way. Once we were all inside, the doors closed very firmly behind us. Human lighting, and a human setting, seemed strangely pale and wan after the extreme conditions of the planet's surface. The Base Commander's voice came to us through overhead speakers. Like the ship's Captain, he was just a memory deposit imprinted on the Base's AI. I doubted he was as happy about it as the Captain had been.

"Welcome to Base Three." A very male, very authoritative voice. Military to the core. Presumably intended to be the kind of voice we'd accept orders from. "Welcome to Abaddon. None of you can leave until the job here is completed. I have been assured that once the terraforming equipment has been assembled and tested, you will all be picked up and sent . . . somewhere more pleasant. You can believe that or not, as you please. I see nine of you. How many left the ship?"

"There were twelve of us," I said. "Three of us died just getting here."

"Get used to it," said the Base Commander. "Nine out of twelve is a lot better than the last crew they sent."

"How many crews have there been before us?" said One.

"That's classified," said the Commander. "But learn the lesson well. Now you know what to expect from Abaddon. Everything here hates you. Every living thing on this planet wants to kill you. The air is poison; the gravity is deadly; the radiation levels would fry your chromosomes. We are at war with the world."

"Will we be allowed access to information compiled by the previous crews?" I said.

"Of course," said the Commander. "Study the files all you want. Profit from their mistakes. But all you really need to know is that every other crew who came here is either dead, or missing presumed dead. So stay alert. And kill everything you see, before it kills you. Now, go to your quarters. Get what rest you can. You start work first thing in the morning."

We all had more questions, but he didn't want to talk to us anymore. Eventually, we gave up and followed the illuminated arrows set into the floor, guiding us to our private, separate quarters. We didn't want to be around one another. We had nothing in common, except what had been done to us, against our will. No one ever volunteers to be put into a hard suit. There was a common room, but we had no use for it. We had nothing to say to one another, didn't even want to look at one another. Too much like looking at ourselves.

My room was a steel box, with a basic bed to lie on. No comforts or luxuries, because those were human things. My AI opened up the front of my armor, and I fell out. Or what was left of me fell out. A mess of tubes and cables still attached me to the inside of the suit, delivering nutrition and fluids and taking away wastes, for recycling. I lay on my side on the bare bed, my back and all its attachments still stretching away into the suit standing upright in the middle of the room. Like a guard watching over me.

I breathed heavily, slowly, disturbed by how different the Base air seemed, after the familiar recycled air of my hard suit. Seemed was the best I could manage; I had no sense of smell or taste anymore. I didn't have much of anything anymore. No legs, and only one arm. Half my torso replaced by medtech holding me together and keeping me alive. No genitals. Half my face gone, replaced with smooth plastic. The rest of me was mostly whorled and raised scar tissue. I lay on my side on the bed, my eye squeezed shut, so I wouldn't have to see myself. I can't sleep inside the suit, or I'd never leave it. Never have to look at what they'd done to me, in the name of Science and Mercy.

Are you all right, Paul? The warm female voice of the suit's AI drifted through my mind. I was never free of her, even when I wasn't in the suit.

"I'm fine," I said. "Leave me alone. Please."

You know I hate to see you like this, Paul. It breaks my heart. Or it would, if I still had one. I wish I still had arms so I could hold you. But I'm still here, still with you. Even if all I can do is comfort and reassure you. Be the one sane voice left in your head. You might be a thing in a hard suit, and I might be just a memory_imprinted in silicon, but we're still man and wife. I'm still Alice, and you're still my Paul.

"You're the voice they put in my head to keep me from going psycho," I said. "Let me sleep. . . ."

Why are you so hard to talk to, Paul? We always used to be able to talk about everything.

"That was then; this is now. Please, let me sleep. I'm so tired. . . ."

Yes. Of course. I'm sure things will seem much better, in the morning. Just remember: whatever's out there, you don't have to face it alone. I'll be right there with you. Are you crying, Paul?

"Good night, Alice."

Good night, Paul.

They dragged me from the wreckage of the air car, more dead than alive. They saved my life, and then expected me to be grateful. They told me my wife was dead. Alice was dead. I was so badly injured they had to cut more than half of me away, and then they decided the only way to save me was to seal me into a hard suit. Only the really badly damaged go into hard suits, because the bond is forever. And the process is really expensive. But the

Empire has a desperate need for people in hard suits to do all the really dangerous work on truly hostile alien worlds, so they're always ready to cover the bill. And people who might have been allowed to die mercifully in their sleep wake up to find they've been sealed in a steel can, forever. Indentured for life, to cover the Empire's expenses.

Is it any wonder so many of us go crazy?

These days, every hard suit has its own built-in AI, to interface with the occupant. To talk with them and console them, encourage them in their work and keep them sane. To help with this, the AIs are programmed with the memories of someone close to the occupant, someone who cared about them. A wife or a husband, a father or a daughter. Anyone who could provide a memory deposit. Everyone is encouraged to make regular deposits at the Memory Bank, in case there's an accident, and the brain needs to be reinforced with old memories. The Empire doesn't tell you that they have the right to those deposits, once you're dead. They don't want you to know. It would only upset you.

They imprinted my dead wife's memories onto my suit AI. From a memory deposit made some years earlier. She always meant to update it, but somehow she never got around to it. She had no memory of dying in the car crash. She had no memory of the last three years. *You've changed,* she kept saying to me. *You haven't,* I said. And I cried myself to sleep every night, even as she tried to comfort me.

First thing in the morning turned out to mean 5:00 a.m. Base time, of course. With its two suns, Abaddon had a planetary cycle that would drive anyone crazy. The alarm drove me out of my bed and back into the armor, and then I followed the arrows in the floor to the transport ship kept inside the Base, where the plants couldn't get at it. The ship blasted up through the top of the Base, through the force shield, and out across Abaddon to the unfinished terraforming equipment we'd come to work on.

We sat in two rows, looking at one another, strapped firmly in place. No windows, no holo viewscreen, no sense of where we were or where we were going. It was, at least, a fairly smooth ride compared to the trip down. The transport ship dropped us off in a clearing full of crates and half-assembled machinery and shot off again the moment we'd all disembarked. The Commander didn't want to risk his ship. He'd have a hard time replacing his ship.

For a while we just stood there together, looking around us. Piles and piles of wooden crates, and something really high tech in the middle of the clearing, looking distinctly unfinished. It didn't look like something that would eventually transform the entire planet. Something that would tame the jungle and make Abaddon a place where people could live. Where plants would behave like plants.

At least we had a pretty large clearing to work in. The ground had been specially treated so nothing could grow on it. It was gray and dusty, and solid enough that even our heavy footsteps sounded dull. The jungle had grown right up to the edge of the perimeter, and once again, the moment we appeared everything went absolutely insane with rage. Every living thing strained forward, frantic to get at us.

I did ask why the terraforming equipment couldn't be surrounded by a force shield, like the Base, but apparently the field's energies would disrupt the delicate terraforming equipment. So it was up to us to defend it the hard way. Only three of us were scientists, specially trained to assemble the equipment; the rest of us were just grunts, trained to walk the perimeter and slap down the plants as they pressed forward. They couldn't survive long on the gray ground, but it didn't stop them making mad suicide rushes, to get at us and the equipment.

So the six of us divided up the perimeter and walked back and forth, each of us protecting our sector. The plants surged endlessly forward, as though just the sight of us drove them right out of their minds. We walked back and forth, shooting them and frying them, blowing them up and cutting them down, and still they kept coming. To preserve our ammunition, we quickly learned to meet them with the built-in strength and speed of our armor.

The plants lashed us with barbed flails, ground at us with bony teeth inside flower heads, tried to force their way in through our joints, or just crush us under coil after coil of constricting creepers. We tore them up and ripped them apart, and our armor ran thick with viscous sap and sticky juices. The violent colors and clashing shades didn't get any easier to deal with. The light was still painfully bright, and the wind slammed back and forth so viciously our armor had to fight to keep us upright. We set fire to the jungle, but it never lasted. We blasted the plants with heavy gunfire and ravening energies, and they just kept coming. We tore the plants up out of the ground, with their roots still twitching, and still they fought the hands that held them. As though just our presence on this planet was an offense beyond bearing.

There was a kind of sentience in the plants, in the jungle. I could sense it. They knew what they were doing. They hated us. The plants must have known they would die, that their continuing assault was suicide for every individual plant . . . but the jungle didn't care. We were the hated enemy. We had to be fought. The plants came at us again and again, their barbs and teeth and thorns clattering viciously against our armor with almost hysterical rage. And all the time they were keeping us occupied, other plants were trying to break through on some unguarded front, to get at the scientists and their equipment. As though the plants knew they were the real threat. The six of us worked the perimeter, killing everything we came into contact with. One, Three, Eight, Nine, Eleven, and me. We didn't talk to one another. We had nothing to say. Occasionally, we'd overhear the three scientists on the open channel, discussing some technical matter. It might as well have been machines talking.

There wasn't much left of my senses. Torn flesh and brain damage had seen to that. The armor replaced them with specially calibrated sensors, channeled through the suit AI. So I could see and hear for miles, and the pressure sensors built into my steel hands were sensitive, as well as strong. It wasn't touch, but it would do. I was isolated from the world, but I could still experience it. I missed taste and smell, but it's wasn't like I had any use for them anymore. It was all tubes, now.

My vision was sharp enough that I could see every detail, every color and shade and shape, of every plant I killed. I could hear every scream and howl they made as they pressed forward, all the sounds of rage and pain and horror. I wondered, briefly, how that was possible. Plants didn't have vocal chords. Wind blowing through seedpods, or reeds, perhaps . . . It didn't matter. I was here to kill the plants, not understand them.

And killing them did feel so very good. I was strong inside my suit, strong and powerful in my armor. Stalks and flails and creepers tore like paper in my steel hands, and I could rip apart the largest plant with no effort at all. I broke everything I hit and everything I stepped on died, and I smiled so very broadly behind my smooth, featureless helm. Another reason why people don't trust us. Because any one of us could do a hell of a lot of damage to people, if we ever lost control. Or threw it away . . .

Three cried out suddenly, and I looked around just in time to see his hard suit disappear under a mass of writhing blue and purple creepers. They wrapped right around him in a moment, burying him under layer upon layer, until he'd disappeared in a cocoon of pulsating vegetation, and then they just jerked him off his feet and hauled him away, into the thrashing jungle.

I ran forward and plowed into the jungle after him, forcing my way through the active plants by sheer strength. Nine was right there at my side. The others yelled for us to come back, that defending the terraforming equipment was far more important than rescuing one missing grunt. That we were all expendable. I knew that. So did Nine. That's why we went after Three. Because you have to hang on to some of your humanity or you really would go crazy.

Strangely, the plants had left a trail for us to follow. A ragged path between tall plants, from where they'd dragged Three away. The surrounding vegetation hadn't blocked or overgrown it, though they'd had plenty of time. So Nine and I pressed steadily on, the earth shaking under the heavy pounding of our steel feet. And the plants on either side of the trail . . . held back. It took us a while to realize they weren't attacking us anymore. And the further from the clearing we went, the quieter everything became, until we were just walking through a still and silent forest, with no need to kill anything. Nine and I looked at each other and kept going.

It could be a trap, Paul. But it doesn't feel like a trap. This is something else. Something new.

"Watch my back," I said to the AI on our private channel. "Full sensor scans. Don't let anything creep up on me."

Of course, Paul. I have Three's beacon. Straight ahead. He's not moving. He isn't answering my calls. Neither is his AI.

We finally found Three standing alone and very still, right in the middle of a small clearing. Or rather, what was left of Three. The hard suit was standing entirely motionless, and it only took me a moment to discover why. The armor was empty. It had opened itself, and there was no trace of the occupant anywhere. Just the broken ends of tubes and cables, hanging limply from the suit, from where Three had broken free of them. Nine and I looked around very carefully, but there was no sign of any body. No blood, no signs of violence. Nothing.

His AI is dead, Paul. Wiped clean. Suicided.

"Could Three still be alive here, somewhere?" said Nine.

"Without his tubes and cables?" I said. "Not for long. Why would he open his suit? The air alone would kill him."

"Could the plants have forced it open, from outside? There's no sign of violence on the front of the armor."

"The plants couldn't have reached him," I said. "He would have had to persuade his AI to open it for him."

"But why?" said Three. "Why has his AI suicided? Where's the body? None of this makes any sense!"

We searched the surrounding jungle, looked and listened with our sensors set to their fullest range, and found nothing, nothing at all. The jungle was still and quiet, and the plants made no attempt to interfere with our search. They just stood there, swaying this way and that under the urging of the gusting wind. Almost like normal plants. As though they weren't mad at us anymore. Or, perhaps, because they were satisfied with Three's death. Maybe even sated, if they'd eaten the body . . . And then I stopped dead where I was. I'd caught a glimpse of movement, right at the edge of my sensors. Human movement, not plant. Or at least, something very like human. I pointed it out to Nine, but he couldn't see anything. And now neither could I. I had my AI replay the sensor images and share them with Nine. Just a glimpse, of something that looked human but didn't move like anything human . . .

"Not Three," I said. "Whatever that was, it was a complete human figure. Not like us."

"Could it have been a survivor from Base Two?" said Nine.

"I don't see how," I said.

"We have to check this out."

"Yes. We need to be sure what that was."

We strode quickly through the jungle, and the plants let us pass. And soon enough, we came to another clearing, and in it, another hard suit. Standing still and silent and very empty. Its steel armor had been chaffed and smoothed by wind and weather, and the stenciled number on its open chest was Thirty-Two. Nine and I stood very still, studying it from a safe distance.

"It's an older model," I said. "This could have come from Base Two, I suppose."

"But you saw something moving," said Nine. "This thing hasn't moved in ages."

We eased forward, one careful step at a time, and peered into the hard suit's interior. The hanging tubes and cables had withered. The interior of the suit was full of flowers. Alive and flourishing. Blossoming with wild psychedelic colors.

"This . . . is getting seriously strange," said Nine. "Did the suit's occupant . . . turn into flowers?"

"I doubt it," I said. "He opened up his suit and left it, just like Three. Somehow they left their suits behind and went . . . somewhere else. Except there's nowhere for anything human to go, on Abaddon." I turned slowly around in a complete circle, studying the jungle. "Tell me, Nine, what's wrong with this picture?"

"The plants are quiet," said Nine. "Nothing's attacked us since we left the others to follow Three."

"Maybe they're not hungry anymore," I said. "After Three."

"I never got the feeling they wanted to eat us," said Nine. "Just kill us. They wanted us dead. Wanted us gone." He looked at me sharply. "We are gone. We left the clearing. We have to get back! This could all be a distraction, to lure us away while they launched an attack on the equipment!"

We raced back down the trail. The plants had kept it open. Nine had his guns at the ready and I had my flamethrower, but we didn't need them. The plants just watched us pass, misshapen multicolored heads bowing and bobbing in the wind. And when we finally burst back into the clearing, all was just as we had left it. The three scientists were still working on the terraforming equipment, while the others patiently patrolled the perimeter. They all looked around as we crashed back into the clearing and demanded to know where we'd been, and what had happened to Three. But Nine and I were too busy looking back at the jungle. The plants had gone mad again, straining forward with everything they had, desperate to get at us, and kill us. In the end, I just said, *The plants got Three.* And Nine said nothing at all.

We went back to guarding the perimeter. And the long hard day wore on.

Somehow the rest of us made it through to the end of the shift alive. Bone-deep weary and exhausted from fighting back the plants all day, but alive. The perimeter was heaped with torn apart, bullet-riddled and flame-blackened pieces of vegetation, some of them still twitching. We were all out of ammunition and power cells, reduced to fighting the jungle with brute force. The armor did all the heavy lifting, but we still had to work the armor. The real tiredness came from the unrelenting concentration, because you couldn't relax, couldn't let your guard down, even for a moment. Or you might end up like Three.

We were all searching the blood-red skies for the transport ship long before it was due to appear, and when it finally did touch down, we immediately turned our backs on the job and headed for our ride home. I looked back, just as I was about to climb aboard, and the plants had fallen still again. They were only violent when we were around to make them mad. . . .

I thought about that, all the way back to Base Three.

We sat in silence in our two rows, securely strapped in, facing one another. None of us had anything to say. I reported Three's death to the Base Commander. He didn't seem too surprised. Or upset. After we landed, and we were walking back to our quarters, it occurred to me to ask Four, one of the scientists, how long he thought it would take to finish assembling the terraforming equipment. *Unless we get a lot more help,* he said, *Three years, maybe four.* I tried to think of years like the day we'd just had and couldn't. Years of constant fighting, against an enemy that would never give up? Maybe the Captain was right. Maybe this was Hell, after all.

In my private quarters, lying on my bed on my side, so I could keep an eye on my tubes and cables and make sure they didn't get tangled, I remembered the crash again.

We were flying over the Rainbow Falls, my Alice and me, in our old air car. We were arguing. We were always arguing, back then. We had been so much in love, but it hadn't lasted. That was why I crashed the car. I drove it quite deliberately into the side of the mountain, at full speed. Alice was screaming, I was crying. I wanted to kill us both, because she said she was going to leave me, and I couldn't bear the thought of living without her. So I crashed the car, and she died, and I lived. They saved me, the bastards. And then they put me in a hard suit, and they put her voice in my head, forever. I couldn't bear to live without her, and now I couldn't bear to live with her. Because the memory deposit came from the time when she still loved me. She didn't remember the crash. She didn't remember the arguments, or not loving me. She thought we were still happy together, because we were when she made the deposit. She still thought we were in love, and I didn't have the heart to tell her.

They gave her to me as a kindness, but every kind word she said was a torment.

On the transport ship out, the next day, I told the Commander about the old, empty hard suit I'd found.

"I'm not supposed to talk about that," said the Commander's voice. "But you'd just dig it out of the old records anyway, if I didn't. The crew of Base Two were mostly hard suits. Like you. Their superiors were human, but they stayed inside the Base. Only the hard suits went out into Abaddon to work. And some of them . . . learned to love this world. This hateful, ugly world. They decided they didn't want to fight anymore. So they just walked out into the jungle and opened up their suits."

"But . . . what happened to the bodies?" I said. "Did the plants eat them?"

"There's never been any evidence that the plants here are carnivorous," said the Commander. "The hard suits' occupants just . . . disappeared. Now and again, some of the work crews would report seeing ghosts, moving through the jungle."

"Ghosts?" said Nine. I knew he was thinking of the moving human figure I'd seen.

"Illusions. Mirages," said the Commander. "It's just stress. This planet wears you down. If you see anything like that, don't go after them. You won't find anything. No one ever does. It's just something else the planet does, to distract you, so it can kill you while you're not looking."

"What happened to the human crew in Base Two?" I said. "Did they learn to love this world, too?"

The Commander had nothing else to say. We flew the rest of the way in silence.

Out in the jungle again, we walked the perimeter. Maddened raging plants pushed forward from all sides, and I ripped them out of the ground, crushed them to pulp in my terrible grip, and threw them aside. Or trampled the more persistent ones under my steel feet. I blasted them with fire and bullets and energy bolts, giving it everything I had, just to hold the line. The plants never fell back, never slowed down, never for one moment stopped trying to kill us. I thought of years of this, of endless killing, destroying living things that were only fighting to defend their home. Years . . . of living with my murdered wife's kind and loving voice in my head.

In the end, it only took a moment to decide. I hadn't gone native. I hadn't learned to love this ugly, vicious, vindictive world. It still looked like Hell to me. I was just so very tired of it all.

I stopped fighting, and walked out from the perimeter and into the jungle. The plants immediately stopped fighting me and actually seemed to fall back, opening up a path before me. I walked on through the jungle, the plants bobbing and nodding their heads to me, as though they'd been waiting for this. Even the wind seemed to have dropped. It was like walking through a garden on a calm summer's day. Part of me was thinking: *This is how they do it. This is how they get to you.* But I didn't care. I just kept walking. I could hear the others calling out to me, on the open channel, but I had nothing to say to them.

Paul? Why are you doing this?

"Because it's the right thing to do. Because I'm tired. Because . . . killing is wrong."

I don't understand, Paul. You know I could override your control. Walk you back to the perimeter.

"Are you going to?"

No. I was put here to help and comfort you. I know I'm not really Alice, but I'm sure she would want you to do the right thing.

I walked until I couldn't see the perimeter anymore, and then I just stopped and looked around me. Hideously colored, horribly shaped plants, for as far as the sensor could see. Under a sky of blood, with air that would poison me, and gravity that would crush me. Abaddon. Just another name for Hell. Where I belonged.

"Alice," I said. "You know what I want. You know what I need you to do for me."

I can't, said the warm, familiar voice that was all that was left of my dead wife. *I can't let you just die. Please, don't ask me to do this, Paul.*

"I can't go on like this," I said. "I want out. Just . . . open up the suit. I want this to be over. Open the suit, and let me out into this brave new world that has such ugly wonders in it. I don't want to live like this."

I can't do that, Paul. I can't. I love you.

"If you love me, let me go."

Like I should have let you go, I thought. I was still sane enough to see the bitter irony in that.

Paul? What is that? Who is that? Who are those people?

I looked around. Not far away, this time, not far away at all, the ghosts came walking through the jungle. Just vague human shapes at first, moving easily and unharmed among the plants, as though they were at home there. Not walking in a human way. They stopped, and one of them raised an overlong arm and beckoned to me. I plunged forward, and the plants really did fall back, encouraging me on. The ghostly figures retreated before me, one of them still beckoning, and I followed them deeper into the jungle, away from the terraforming equipment, away from Base Three, and all that was left of my old human life.

What are you doing, Paul? Where do you think you're going?

"I'm chasing a dream," I said. "Of a life when I still had hope, and options, and choices that meant something."

I could stop you.

"But you won't. Because you still love me."

She didn't stop me.

I followed the vague figures that were somehow always ahead of me, no matter how much I increased my pace. I stopped once, to look back. The trail had closed behind me. There was only the jungle. The plants watched, still and silent, to see what I would do. I turned my back on my old life and hurried on.

And finally, the ghosts stopped. One of them came back to meet me. It stepped out of the concealing jungle to stand right before me, and I took my time, looking it over. Not human. Humanoid, but not human. Taller than me, smoothly slender, different in every detail. Its basic shape was stretched out and distorted, the arms and legs had too many joints, and the face . . . had nothing I could recognize as features, let alone sense organs. Only yesterday I would have described it as hideous, alien, inhuman. But I was trying to see the world with better eyes. And anyway, compared to the broken half thing inside my hard suit, I was in no position to throw stones. I nodded to the shape before me, and to my surprise it nodded back, in a very human way.

"You're not a ghost," I said. Just to be saying something.

"No," it said. Complex mouthparts at the base of its head moved, producing something very like a human voice. "Not ghosts. But we are dead men. Technically speaking. We are the surviving crew of Base Two. Made over, made new, made to walk freely in this best of all possible worlds. We came here in armored suits, just like you, but we have found a better way. If you want answers, if you want a way out of that suit and your old life, come with me. Come with us to the Cave of Creation, and be born anew."

I didn't even have to think about it. "Does this Cave of yours have a can opener?"

"Something like that, yes."

I went with them, walking through a calm and peaceful garden, with humanoid things that only remembered being human. They bobbed and bounced around me, as though their bones were made of rubber, as though the heavy gravity was no concern of theirs. And I trudged along inside my steel can, and dreamed of freedom. The jungle suddenly fell back on all sides, to reveal a larger than usual clearing, with a great earth mound at its center. You only had to look at it to know it was no natural thing. The dark earth had been raised up by conscious intent, given shape and form and meaning. There was a large dark hole in its side. My guides led me forward across the clearing, right up to the earth mound, and then the one who'd spoken to me strode easily up a set of steps cut into the earth mound, heading for the opening. The others stood and looked at me. I didn't hesitate, but I had to go slowly, carefully, so the earth steps wouldn't collapse under my weight.

By the time I reached the dark opening, my guide had already gone through. I stepped into the darkness after him, and a great light sprang up, blinding me for a moment. When I could see again, I was standing on an earth ledge, looking down into a great cavern that seemed to fall away forever, packed full of strange alien technology. I had no idea at all what I was looking at. Shapes so strange, so utterly other, that my merely human mind couldn't make sense of any of it. Even with my armor's sophisticated sensors. My thoughts whirled at forces and functions without obvious meaning, or perhaps too much meaning. Parts and sections that seemed to twist and turn through more than three physical dimensions at once. Wonders and marvels, intimidating and terrifying. Heaven and Hell, all at once.

My guide stood beside me, waiting patiently for me to come to terms with what it had brought me to see.

"We were not the first to find this world," it said finally. "Another species came here, long ago, determined to change this world and remake it in their image. And this is the machine they built, to do that. Except . . . they learned to love this world. And they decided: Why change the planet when you can change the people? So that's what they did. They reprogrammed the machine to remake them, and when it was done, they went out into the world and lived in it. The machine still works. It can change you and make you a part of this world, like us. It's a good world, when it's not fighting for its own survival. Join me. Become like us. Hell can be Heaven, if you look at it with the right eyes."

"Do you think it's telling the truth?" I said to Alice on my private comm channel. "I want to believe . . . but I could be wrong."

I don't know. I can't tell. Is this really what you want, Paul?

"You know it is, Alice."

Then do it. Because . . . I'm not real. I'm not really Alice. Just a memory, a ghost, imprinted on silicon. I'm the past, and this is the future. I know about the crash,_Paul. I know you crashed us deliberately. I'm a computer. I have access to records. Why did you try to kill us both, Paul?

"Because . . . you changed, and I didn't. You didn't love me anymore. You were going to leave me."

And now you've changed . . . and you want to leave me.

"Yes. You have to be better than me, Alice. You have to let me go."

*Of course I will, Paul.*_She laughed softly, briefly. *Memories shouldn't linger. Time for both of us . . . to move on.*

She opened up the front of the hard suit, and I fell out onto the hard-packed earth of the ledge. A small, crippled, dying thing. I cried out, once, as I felt the AI shut itself down, forever, and then all my umbilical tubes and cables jerked out of my back, no longer connecting me to the armor. The great alien machine blazed bright as the sun . . . and when I could see again, I was something else.

Outside the earth mound, everything was different. I moved easily, freely, marveling at the world I found myself in. The plants were beautiful, the jungle was magnificent, the sky was astounding and the sunshine was just right. But more than that, the whole world was *alive*; the jungle and everything in it was singing a song, a great and joyous song that never ended, and I was part of that song now.

I could remember being human, but that seemed such a small and limited thing now. I was whole and free, at last. I knelt down and studied a small flower at my feet. I put out a hand to touch it, and the flower reached up and caressed my hand.

If there's a model for this one, it's probably the work of Roger Zelazny, one of my all-time heroes. The editor for this one wanted stories about soldiers wearing futuristic battle suits. I started thinking about what kind of man would allow himself to be sealed into such a thing. Only someone with nothing left to lose, and penance still to do.

JESUS AND SATAN GO JOGGING IN THE DESERT

So, I came up out of Hell, and I am here to tell you that after the Pit and the sulfur and the screams of the damned, the desert made a really nice change. Like a breath of fresh air. Don't ask me which desert; the Holy Land was lousy with unwanted and uncared-for beachless property in those days. Just sand and rocks for as far as the eye could see, with a few lizards thrown in here and there to break up the monotony. I allowed myself a little time out, to enjoy the peace and quiet, and then I went looking for Jesus.

He wasn't hard to find. Anyone else would have been sheltering in the shade, away from the fierce heat of the sun. Only the Son of God would be ambling along, caught between the heat and a hard place, just because God told him to. I followed him for a while, careful to maintain a respectful distance, wondering how best to break the ice, so to speak. He really didn't look good. Forty days and forty nights fasting in the desert had darkened his skin, made a mess of his hair, blackened his lips, and stripped all the fat off him. Still, he strode along easily enough, back straight and head held high. He stopped suddenly.

"Well, Satan? Are you going to follow me all day, or should we get on with it?"

He looked back at me, grinning as he saw he'd caught me off guard. Don't ask me how he knew I was there. I nodded quickly and hurried to catch him up. His face was all skin and bone, but the smile on his cracked lips was real enough, and his eyes were full of a quiet mischief. Don't let anyone tell you the Son of God didn't have a sense of humor. We stood for a while and looked each other over. It had been a long time. . . .

"So," Jesus said finally. "Satan, look at you! All dressed in white and shining like a star!"

"Well," I said, "I always was the most beautiful. I like what you've done with the loincloth. Really stresses the humility."

"How is that you're out of Hell?" said Jesus. Not accusing, you'll note, just genuinely interested.

"I'm allowed out, now and again," I said. "When He's got a point He wants to make. But He always keeps me on a tight leash. Sometimes I think He only lets me out so Hell will seem that much worse, when I have to go back."

"No," said Jesus. "That's not how He works. Our Father is many things, but He's not petty."

I shrugged. "You know Him better than I do, these days. Anyway, I've been called up here to tempt you. To test your strength of will for what's to come."

Jesus gave me a hard look. "Forty days and forty nights, boiling by day and freezing by night, and only bloody lizards for company, and that's not enough of a test of willpower?"

I shrugged again. "Don't look at me. I don't make the rules. Our Father moves in mysterious ways."

Jesus sniffed loudly. "Aren't you supposed to be out and about, tempting mankind into sin?"

"Don't you believe it," I said. "They don't need me. Most men sin like they breathe. Some of them actually get up early, just so they can fit in more sins before the end of the day. I don't have to tempt men into falling; I have to beat them off with a stick at the Gates of Hell, just to get them to form an orderly line."

"Boasting again," said Jesus. "You are a proud and arrogant creature, and the Truth is not in you. But you do tell a good tale."

"All right, maybe I do indulge in a little tempting now and again," I said. "Mostly for the ones too dumb to know a good opportunity when they see one. But . . . Just look at the world He gave them! A paradise, a beautiful land under a magnificent sky, food and water ready to hand; all right, not here, but I think He threw in the deserts just so they'd appreciate the rest of it."

"Even the desert is beautiful," said Jesus. And even after forty days and nights of suffering he could still say that and mean it. You could tell. "It's calm here," he said. "Serene, peaceful, untroubled. Everything in its place. There is beauty here, for those with the eyes to see it."

"You're just glad to get away from all the noise," I said knowingly. "All the voices, all the crowds and their demands, all the pressure . . . Go on; admit it!"

"All right, I admit it," he said easily. "I'm only human . . . some of the time. I came to this world to spread my teachings, not amuse the crowds with miracles. But you have to get their attention first. . . ."

"I have to ask," I said. "Why do you bother? All they ever do is whine and squabble and fight over things they could just as easily share. They don't need me . . . pathetic bunch of losers. I do love to see them fall, because every failed life and lost soul is just another proof that I was right about them, all along."

Jesus looked at me sadly. "All this time and you still don't get it. All right, let's get on with the temptations. What are you going to offer me first? Riches? Power? A nice new loincloth? I have all I need, and all I want."

"I'm here to show you all the things you could have, and all the things you could be," I said as earnestly as I knew how. "The things you're throwing away because your vision's so narrow."

He was already shaking his head. "You're talking about earthly things. Why are you doing this, Satan? You must know you won't succeed."

"Hey," I said. "It's the job. And never say never. I have to try . . . to make you see the light."

"Why?" said Jesus. "So that if I fall . . . you won't feel so alone?"

"Look at you," I said, honestly angry for a moment. "You're a mess. You could be King of the Jews, King of the World; and here you are, wandering around in the backside of nowhere, burned and blackened, and stinking so bad even the lizards won't come anywhere near you. You're better than this. You deserve better than this! Come on, after forty days and nights of fasting, your stomach must think your throat's been cut. Turn some of these stones into loaves of bread and take the edge off, so we can talk properly. Enough is enough."

"Man shall not live by bread alone," said Jesus, "but by every word God utters. Faith will restore you, long after bread is gone."

"Is this another of those bloody parables?" I said suspiciously.

He sighed. "I can't help feeling one of us is missing the point here."

I looked out across the desert. Blank and empty, hard and unyielding. "Why did you agree to come out into this awful place? You couldn't have fasted at home?"

"Too many interruptions," he said. "Too many distractions. Too many people wanting this and needing that. I'm out here to think, to meditate, to understand where I'm going and why."

I snapped my fingers, and just like that we were transported to the holy city. Don't ask which one; believe me when I tell you none of the cities were much to talk about, back then. I apparated to right at the top of the pinnacle of the temple. A long way up. And down. We both clung tightly to the pinnacle, with both hands. There was a strong wind blowing. Jesus glared at me.

"What are we doing here? How am I supposed to meditate all the way up here? Take me back to the desert!"

"Tempting first," I said. "You want people to look up to you, don't you? You said yourself, you have to do the miracles to get their attention. So: throw yourself down from here. All the way down . . . and God will send his angels to catch you and lower you safely to the ground. Now that would be a real showstopper of a miracle. No one would doubt you really are who you say you are, after that."

He clung tightly to the pinnacle, with a surprising amount of dignity, carefully not looking down. The wind blew his long messy hair into his face, but he still met my gaze firmly. "You don't put God to the test. It's all about faith."

"But He wouldn't really let you get hurt, would he?"

"He doesn't interfere directly in the world, not even for me. Because if he did, that would be the end of free will, right there and then."

"Free will," I said. I felt like spitting, but the wind was blowing right at me. "Wasted on mankind. But all right, on with the tempting. We've got better places to be."

Another snap of the fingers, and we were standing on the top of the highest mountain in the Holy Land. Which wasn't much, as mountains go, but still, a nice view whichever way you looked. I had to jazz it up a bit, because I had a point to make. I gestured grandly about us.

"See! All the kingdoms of the world, laid out before you! All of this I will give to you, to do with as you wish. Protect the people, care for them, raise them up, make them worthy! I will make you King of all the World, including a whole bunch of places you don't even know exist yet, if you'll just bow down and worship me. Instead of Him."

He looked out over the world for a long moment. "Can you really do that?" he said, not looking at me.

"Yes," I said. "I have been given special dispensation, from on high. The temptation has to be real, or it wouldn't mean anything."

Jesus laughed quietly, and turned his back on the world. "Worship God, and serve only Him. Because only He is worthy of it. What . . . is all the world against Heaven?"

I sighed, and nodded, and took us back to the desert. I didn't snap my fingers. Couldn't summon up the enthusiasm. I pulled up a rock and sat down. Jesus did have a point about the peace and quiet of the desert. He sat down on another rock, facing me.

"Is that it?"

"Pretty much," I said. "I've covered all the bases He wanted covered and got the answers He expected. I've a few things of my own left to try, before I go back. But I'm starting to wonder if there's any point."

"You don't have to go straight back," said Jesus. "We can sit here and talk, if you like."

"There are things we should talk about," I said as seriously as I knew how. "We could talk about Our Father, Brother."

He looked at me consideringly. "We're . . . brothers? How did that happen?"

"Brothers in every way that matters," I said. "Think about it! He's as much my Father as yours. I was the first thing He created, the first angel. Made perfect and most beautiful. He put me in charge of everything else He created . . . and then objected when I used the authority He gave me! I didn't fall; I was pushed! I failed Him, so He's trying again with you. Both of us created specifically of His will, to serve His purposes. Come on, you know what I'm talking about. It's not been easy for either of us, has it? Living our lives in the shadow of such a demanding Father. Trying to please Him, when it isn't always clear what He wants. He always expects so much of both of us. . . ." I looked at him squarely. "Don't you fail him, Jesus, or you could end up like me. . . ."

"You always were the dumbest one," said Jesus. "You didn't fail Him. You failed yourself. You weren't punished for using your authority, but for abusing it. That's why you had to leave Heaven. And you know very well that you can leave Hell anytime you choose; all you have to do is repent."

"What?" I said. "Say I'm sorry? To Him! I'm not sorry! I'm not sorry because I've done nothing to be sorry for! I did nothing wrong! I was His first creation; He loved me first! What did He need other angels for? He had me! I did everything for Him. Everything. If He had to have other playthings, angels, or humans, it was only right I should be in charge of them. I was the first. I was the oldest. I knew best!"

"No, you didn't," said Jesus. "That's the point. You always did miss the point. Hell isn't eternal and was never meant to be."

"The guilty must be punished," I said stiffly. "Just like me."

"No," Jesus said patiently. "The guilty must be redeemed. They must be made to understand the nature of their sin, so they can properly repent of it. Hell is an asylum for the morally insane. God's last attempt to get your attention. Hell was never meant to be forever. Do you really think I'd put up with a private torture chamber in the hereafter? The fires are there to burn away sin, so all the lost sheep can come home. Eventually . . . all Hell will be empty, its job done. And every soul will be in Heaven, where they belong."

"I'll never say I'm sorry," I said, not looking at him. "He can't make me say it. I'll never give in, even if I'm the only one left in Hell."

"If you were, I'd come down and stay with you," said Jesus. "To keep you company. Until you were ready to leave."

I looked at him then. "You really would, wouldn't you?"

He looked at me thoughtfully. "Be honest, Satan. What would you do, if I did say yes to you? If I was to turn away from our Father, what then?"

"What couldn't we do together?" I said, leaning forward eagerly. "We could fight to overthrow the Great Tyrant, and be free of Him! Free to do what we wanted, instead of what He wanted. Take control of our own lives! We could set the whole world free! No more laws, no more rules, no more stupid restrictions. Everyone free to do whatever they wanted, free to pursue everything they'd ever desired or dreamed of . . . No more guilt, no more repressed feelings; just life, lived to the hilt! Wouldn't that . . . be Heaven on Earth?"

"If there was no law, no right or wrong," said Jesus, "how could there be Good and Evil?"

"There wouldn't!" I said. "You see, you're getting it! My point exactly!"

But Jesus was already shaking his head. "What about all the innocents who would suffer at the hands of those who could only be happy by hurting others?"

"What about them?" I said. "What have the meek ever contributed? What have the weak ever done, except hold us back? Survival of the fittest! Stamp out the weak, so that generations to come will be stronger still!"

"No," said Jesus. "I've never had any time for bullies. As long as one innocent suffers, I'll be there for him."

"Why?" I said. Honestly baffled.

"Because it's the right thing to do."

He still wasn't listening to me, so I decided to try one of my own special temptations. Not one of the official ones, probably because it was a bit basic, but it hadn't been officially excluded, so . . . I called up the most beautiful woman I knew and had her appear before us. Tall and wonderful, smiling and stark naked. I've never seen a better body, and I've been around. She smiled sweetly at Jesus, and he smiled cheerfully back at her.

"Hello, Lil," he said. "It's been a while, hasn't it? How's tricks?"

"Oh, you know," said Lilith, in her rich sultry voice. "Going back and forth in the world and walking up and down in it, and sleeping with everything that breathes. Giving birth to monsters to plague mankind. Play to your strengths, that's what I always say."

"You two know each other?" I said just a bit numbly.

"Oh sure," said Jesus. "Lilith herself, Adam's first wife in the Garden of Eden, thrown out because she refused to accept Adam's authority. Or, to be more exact, because she wouldn't accept any authority over her. And we all know where that leads. You got your punishment, Satan, and Lilith got hers. And just like you, she can put down her burden and walk away the moment she's ready to repent."

Lilith laughed. "What makes you think it's a burden? Come on, Jesus, how about it? You look like you could use some tender loving care. See what you're missing! How can you really understand mankind, if you don't do as they do? Do everything they do?"

But he was already shaking his head again. "No," said Jesus. "I made up my mind about that long ago. I can't afford to be distracted by the pleasures of the world. I have a mission. Home and hearth, woman and children, are not for me. I have to follow my higher calling. Because so much depends on it."

"Oh yes?" said Lilith. "And what about you and Mary Magdalene?"

He smiled. "We're just good friends."

Lilith laughed. "From you, I believe it." She looked at me and shrugged in a quite delightful way. "Sorry, Satan, I did my best, but you just can't help some people."

I nodded and sent her on her way. Her scent still hung around, long after she was gone. Jesus and I sat together for a while, both of us thinking our separate thoughts.

"Come on," I said finally. "Your forty days and nights are up. Time to go back. I'll walk along with you for a while. Just to keep you company."

"Thank you," he said. "I'd like that."

So we got up and headed back to civilization, or what passed for it back in those days.

"Sorry I had to do the whole temptation thing," I said. "But . . . it's the job."

"That's all right," said Jesus. "I forgive you. That's my job."

I looked at him. "You know one of your own is going to betray you?"

"Yes," said Jesus. "I've always known."

"They'll blame it on me, but it's just him. Do you want to know who it will be?"

"No," he said. "I've always known. I try so hard not to treat him any differently from the others. He means well, in his way. And I keep hoping . . . that I can find some way to reach him. And perhaps . . . save both of us. They're good sorts, the disciples. Best friends I ever had."

"You know how the story's going to end," I said roughly. "You can't change it. Can you?"

"Perhaps," he said. "I could be tempted . . . but I won't. It's just too important."

"You must know what they're going to do to you!" I said. "They're going to nail you to a fucking cross! Like a criminal! Like an animal!"

"Yes. I know."

"It's not right," I said. I was so angry, I was shaking so hard, I could hardly get the words out. "It's not right! Not you . . . Just say the word, Jesus, and I swear I'll come and rescue you! I'll take you down off that cross and kill anyone who tries to get in our way! I'd fight my way up out of Hell to rescue you!"

"You would, wouldn't you?" said Jesus. "But you mustn't. I have to do this, Brother."

"But why?" I said miserably.

"To redeem mankind," said Jesus. "Because . . . I have faith in them."

We walked for a while in quiet company.

"Come on, Jesus," I said. "We'll never get there at this rate."

So we went jogging across the desert, side by side, two sons of a very demanding Father, who might have faced the world together if only things had been just a bit different.

"Come on, Satan," said Jesus, grinning. "Put some effort into it. Go for the burn."

I had to laugh. Typical Jesus. He always has to have the last Word.

Okay, I had the main idea for this one years and years ago. Jesus is fasting in the desert for forty days and nights, tempted by the Devil, told in the style of the Odd Couple. Some ideas just move into your head and won't leave you alone. But I couldn't think of anyone who would buy it. And then Christopher Golden came along, wanting stories written from the point of view of the Bad Guy. And I shouted YES! punched the air, and wrote the whole thing in under two hours. I think the material is actually quite respectful to the original. It's all how you look at these things.

FOOD OF THE GODS

We are what we eat. No. Wait. That's not quite right.

I wake up, and I don't know where I am. Red room, red room, dark shadows all around and a single, bare red bulb, swinging back and forth, coating the room with bloody light. I'm sitting on the floor with my back pressed against the wall, and I can't seem to remember how I got here. And set on the floor before me, like a gift or an offering, on a plain white china plate, is a severed human head.

I'm sure I know the face, but I can't put a name to it.

I can't think clearly. Something's wrong. Something has happened, something important, but I can't think what. And the severed head stares at me accusingly, as though this is all my fault. I can't seem to look away from the head, but there isn't much else to look at. Bare walls, bare floorboards, a single closed door just to my left. And the blood-red light rising and falling as the bulb swings slowly back and forth. I don't want to be here. This is a bad place. How did I end up in a place like this?

The name's James Eddow. Reporter. Investigative reporter, for one of the dailies. Feeding the public appetite for all the things it's not supposed to know. I went looking for a story, and I think I found one. Yes, I remember. There were rumors of a man who ate only the finest food, prepared in the finest ways. A man who wouldn't lower himself to eat the kind of things other people eat. The Epicure. He lived in the shadows, avoiding all publicity, but everyone who mattered had heard of him, and it was said . . . that if you could find him, and if you could convince him you were worthy, he would make you the greatest meal of your life. Food to die for.

It had been a long time since I'd handed in a really good story. My editor was getting impatient. I needed something new, something now, something really tasty. So I went looking for the Epicure.

I went walking through the night side of the city, buying drinks for familiar faces in bars and clubs and members-only establishments, talking casually with people in the know, dropping a little folding money here and there, and finally found myself a native guide. Mr. Fetch. There's always someone like him, in every scene. The facilitator, always happy to put like-minded souls together, at entirely reasonable rates. He can lay his hands on anything, or knows someone who can, and he knew the Epicure, oh yes, though he gave me the strangest look when I said I just had to meet him. Actually had the nerve to turn up his nose and tell me to run along home. That I didn't know what I was getting into. But money talks, in a loud and persuasive voice, and Mr. Fetch put aside his scruples, just for me.

Why can't I move? I don't feel drugged, or paralyzed. But I just sit here, with my hands folded neatly in my lap, while the face on the severed head stares sadly back at me. I know that face. I'm sure I do. Why am I not shocked, or horrified? Why can't I look away? I know that face. The name's on the tip of my tongue.

Mr. Fetch took me to a faded hole-in-the-wall restaurant, in the shabbier end of the city. No one looked at us as we marched through the dining area. The diners concentrated on their meals, while the waiters stared into space. A door at the back led through into an entirely ordinary kitchen, and there, sitting at an empty table, was the Epicure. Not much to look at. Average size, average face, fever bright eyes. His presence seemed to fill the whole kitchen. He smiled on me and gestured for me to sit down opposite him. Mr. Fetch couldn't wait to get his money and depart at speed. He wouldn't even look at the Epicure.

The great man looked me over, nodded slowly, and immediately identified me as a journalist. I just nodded. This wasn't the kind of man you could lie to. He laughed, briefly, and then started talking, before I'd even got my tape recorder set up. As though he'd been waiting for someone he could tell his story to. Someone who'd appreciate it.

I can smell the hunger on you, he said in his soft rich voice.

Tell me, I said. *Tell me everything.*

I eat only the finest food, said the Epicure, *made from the finest ingredients. The food of the gods. I have a meal waiting, already prepared. Would you care to join me?*

Of course, I said. *I'd be honored.*

It was excellent. Delicious. Good beyond words. I asked him what was in it, and he smiled a slow satisfied smile.

The last journalist who came looking for me.

I was too angry, too disappointed, to be shocked. I laughed, right in his face.

That's it? That's your great secret? You claim you're a cannibal?

Oh no, he said. *There's far more to it than that.*

Still sitting in the red room. Still staring at the neatly severed head. There's a sense of threat in the room now, a feeling of menace and imminent danger. I've got to get out of here, before something bad happens. But still I don't move, or rather, it's more that somehow I don't want to move. Something bad, something really bad, has already happened. Have I . . . done something bad?

Memories surge through me, jumbled, flaring up in bright splashes of good times and bad, a rushing kaleidoscope of my past, my life.

I remember being young, and small, and rolling down endless grassy slopes, with the smell of grass and earth and trees almost unbearably rich in my head. The sun was so bright, the air so warm on my bare arms and legs, comforting as a mother's arms. I remember walking along a sandy beach, with Emily's arm thrust possessively through mine, both of us smiling and laughing and telling each other things we'd never told anyone before. To be young and in love, happiness building and building inside me till I thought I'd explode through sheer joy. And then . . .

I remembered Emily walking away from me, her shoulders hunched against the cold night air, and the pleas I was yelling after her. I'd tried to talk to her, but she wouldn't listen, her reasons just excuses to justify a decision she'd already made. I remembered standing at my parents' grave, after the car accident, and feeling a cold empty numbness that was worse than tears.

And the worst memory of all, realizing long before my editor told me, that I just wasn't good enough to be the kind of reporter I wanted to be.

Memories, memories, good and bad and everything in between, things I hadn't let myself think of in years, rushing by me faster and faster, sharp and vivid and yet somehow strangely distant.

The Epicure continued eating as he lectured me on traditional cannibal beliefs. How certain ancient peoples believed that eating a brave man's heart would give you courage, or eating a big man's muscles would make you strong. How recent medical science had both proved and extended these beliefs. Take a planarian worm and teach it to run a maze. Then chop up the worm and feed it to other planarian worms. And they will run the maze perfectly, even though they've never seen it before. Meat is memory. Eat a man's mind, and you can gain access to all his most precious memories. For a while.

He laughed then, as the drug he'd put in my food finally took effect, and I lost consciousness.

I finally recognize the face on the severed head. Of course I know that face. It's mine. Because I'm not who I think I am. I'm somebody else, remembering me. The Epicure doesn't care about the meat, he eats minds so he can savor the memories. All my most precious moments, all my triumphs and despairs, all the things that made me who I am . . . reduced to a meal, to satisfying another man's appetite. I want to cry at what I've lost, at what has been taken from me, but they aren't my eyes. Already my memories are fading, my thoughts are fading, as he comes rising up inside me, like a great shark in some bloody sea, eating up what's left of me so he can be himself again.

There's a rich, happy, satisfied smile on my lips.

You are who you eat. But not for long.

A wonderful example of You're not reading the story you think you're reading—one in which the big reveal comes right at the very end and makes you see everything in a completely new light. I once wrote a story where the big surprise was in the very last word of the very last sentence; and I was unbearably smug for days. . . .

HE SAID, LAUGHING.

I wanted a mission, and for my sins, they gave me one.

Vietnam is another world; they do things differently here. It's like going back into the Past, into a more primitive place. That's what I thought when I got here. It only took me a few months to learn the darker truth, below the surface. Being sent to fight in Vietnam in 1970 is like being thrown down into Hell, while all the time knowing that Heaven is only a plane trip away.

It's hot as Hell, even when it isn't trying. The humidity is inhuman; it's like trying to breathe underwater. Your clothes are always soaked with sweat, and rain, and blood. If you're lucky, that's just from broken blisters. Even worse than the heat is the knowledge that you're always being watched. You can't trust anyone. Not the South Vietnamese army, not the civilians, not even your own people. Eyes, everywhere. Waiting to see you die. Is it any wonder I went a little crazy?

They kept me hanging about in Saigon for weeks, and then

the CIA man sent for me. He had a nice little air-conditioned office, and I didn't care how long he kept me waiting. When I finally got to see him, he sat behind a nice little desk with papers all in order. He didn't get up when I came in, just waved for me to sit opposite him.

"Captain Marlowe," he said. "I'm CIA. You don't need to know my name."

"Then what do I call you?" I said, as though I cared.

"You call me sir." He smiled briefly. I didn't bother. He was CIA. That meant he was probably part of the Phoenix group. Kill teams, operating without restraints, and sometimes without orders. He could do anything he wanted with me.

He pretended to study the file before him. My file.

"You have been a bad little soldier, haven't you, Captain? Civilian massacre. Whole village wiped out, on your orders, with your active participation. One hundred and seventeen men, women, and children. Why, Captain?"

"Because it was there," I said. "I've already said all I'm going to say. When do we get to the court-martial?"

He considered me for a moment. "Doesn't have to be one, Captain. We have a . . . sensitive mission, for you. Carry it out successfully, and I make everything in the folder disappear. You go home with an honorable discharge."

"If I don't?"

"Then you get a dishonorable discharge, first class. I take you out the back of this building and put two bullets in your head."

I surprised him by actually thinking about it. I wasn't sure I wanted to go home, after everything I'd seen, and done. I didn't think I was safe to send home, among defenseless civilians. But I wasn't ready to die, not quite yet.

"Who do I have to kill, sir?"

He opened another, thicker file, and skimmed a photo across the table to me.

"That is General Kurtz. He's gone missing, deep in country. Gone native. He's been left alone for some time, because of his excellent kill ratios, but now . . . seems he's sending his people after anything that moves. Killing everyone, ours and theirs. You are to go up the river, to his compound, find out what he's doing, and if necessary put a stop to it."

"I get to kill a general?"

"If his methods are found to be . . . unsound, yes. Blow his stupid brains out."

"And I get this mission because . . . ?"

"Because you are completely and utterly expendable, Captain. If you fail, we'll just find another psycho in a uniform and send him. And keep on sending people like you, until one of them does the job."

"I kill him, and I can go home? What's the catch?"

"The catch is, he'll probably kill you like he's killed everyone else. You want this mission, or not?"

"I'll go," I said. "Save your bullets for Charlie."

They gave me a boat, a run-down piece of shit called the *Suzie Q*. Crew of three to run it, and take me up river, following what maps we had. I didn't ask their names. Didn't want to know. They were just grunts. They didn't matter to me, except to get me where I was going. They were even more expendable than I was.

One by one, they died, going up the river. In country, into the jungle, into those parts of the world where man was never meant to live, because you can't survive there if you insist on being a man. You need animal instincts, animal drives, and a complete willingness to kill everything else that moves.

I saw all kinds of action along the way, action and firefights and killing, but I let the crew do that. I didn't want to get involved. Partly because my mission was too important for me to endanger myself, but mostly because I was afraid that if I started shooting, started killing, I wouldn't be able to stop.

One by one they were killed, and by the time I got to the end of the river, it was just me, on the *Suzie Q*, chugging slowly through the dark waters, with dark green forest on either side, the trees leaning forward to make a canopy to blot out the sun. There was no day, anymore, just an endless twilight.

I knew I was getting closer to Kurtz's compound when I saw lights up ahead. Bright flaring yellow lights, like will-o'-the-wisps dancing on the air. They were torches, held in unmoving hands by a small army of natives, lined up on the bank at the end of the river. Huge muddy banks rose up to either side of me, casting a dark shadow across the river. The natives watched me ease my boat to a halt. None of them said anything. They wore rags and tatters of clothing. Some North uniforms, some South, most just rotting fragments of cloth. All standing perfectly, unnaturally still. The whole area was completely silent. Not even any of the normal jungle noises, of beast and bird and insect. I looked around me. There was no sign of any compound, or buildings, or any kind of civilization. Just great dark holes in the muddy banks, like caves. Or eyes.

There was a small natural docking area ahead, just a flattened-off sandbank. I stepped off the boat, and two natives came forward to greet me. The smell hit me first. A terrible smell, of death and rotting flesh. They stopped before me. Their eyes didn't blink, and they didn't breathe, and there were patches of decaying flesh all over their naked gray bodies. They were dead. They were dead, and they moved.

I'd only thought I knew what Hell was.

They took me with them, into one of the dark caves. Turned out that General Kurtz had dug his compound out of the earth itself. Long tunnels led from the riverbanks into the ground beneath the jungle. I shouldn't have been surprised. Charlie's always had a fondness for tunnels. The warren was huge, extensive, tunnels crisscrossing. There were no signs anywhere, but my guides knew where they were going. The tunnel ceilings slowly lowered, till we had to walk bent over, moving through the dark, wet, muddy passages like worms in the earth. The smell got worse and worse. A terrible stench of death and decay. And finally, in the heart of that torchlit maze, I was brought into the awful court of General Kurtz.

It was almost shockingly normal, even civilized. A table, and chairs, and books on shelves in the walls. Kurtz himself was stick thin, with sharp aesthetic features, restless with never-ending nervous energy. His general's uniform flapped about him, as though he'd once been a much larger man. It was spotlessly clean. The stench was just as appalling, though. All the smells of death, and not one scent of living things. Kurtz clearly couldn't smell it. He lived in it every day.

I stood before the man I'd been sent to kill and nodded to him. I didn't have any weapons. The native guides had taken my gun and my knife. I didn't care. I'd been trained to kill with my bare hands, if need be. And even in this awful place, before this strange, unsettling man, I had no doubt I could kill him, if need be. I wouldn't get out alive, of course, but it had been a long time since I'd given much thought to that. General Kurtz gestured for me to sit down. The same kind of casual order I'd seen from the CIA man. The gesture of a man who has power. I sat down.

Kurtz smiled briefly. "Yes," he said. "They're dead. The men who brought you here. Dead men walking, torn from their graves, and set to work by me. They're all dead here, except me. All my troops, all my armies: dead men. Zombies. Old voodoo magic, from the Deep South of America. Don't worry; they won't try to eat you, like in that film. They don't eat, any more than they drink or piss or sweat. They're beyond such earthly needs. They have no appetites, no desires; there is nothing they want. The bodies may move, but there's no one home. Left to themselves, they would just stand beside their empty graves, until they rotted and fell apart. I give them orders, and they obey. I give them order and purpose. For as long as they last. They are my warriors of the night, my army of the unliving.

"War is far too important to be left to the living."

"Dead soldiers," I said numbly. "They don't get tired, and they don't get hurt, and they'll follow any order you give them, because nothing matters to them."

"Exactly. The perfect fighting force. I just point them in the right direction, and they swarm over everything in their path. Like army ants. And if I lose a few, through too much damage, I can always replace them with the fallen enemy dead. You're not shocked, Captain. How refreshing."

"Why this is Hell, nor am I out of it," I said. "I've always known this was a bad place, a dark place, that I had come among mad people. Zombies aren't the worst thing I've seen in country."

"No. This isn't like any other war we've ever fought. The only way to win, to survive, is to be willing to do even worse things than the enemy. To encourage the darkness in our minds, in our souls. This is a dark place, and the only way to deal with that darkness is to come to terms with it. To embrace it, to make it your own. Give it shape and purpose and meaning. I have done . . . awful, unforgivable things, Captain, but for the first time . . . I am making progress. Taking and holding territory. Driving the enemy back.

"I will win this war, that people are saying cannot be won. I tried everything else first, but this is the only thing that works. Sometimes . . . I wonder what it must be like, to be dead, and not to have to feel anymore. To have no needs, or fears, or conscience. To be just the perfect killing machine. I held this territory with living men for some time. Growing more desperate, more extreme with every fruitless *victory.* The things I did, the things I had to do . . . You feel less and less. When you have power, you can do anything, everything, because nothing matters. You end up driving yourself to extremes, just to feel . . . something. There is comfort in death.

"But I'm not ready to die yet. After I've won the war here, the war they sent me to win knowing it could not be won . . . then I will go home. I will bring my dead people with me, and I will bring the war home. I will give them a taste of the Hell they sent us all into, and make our country a charnel house just like this."

He looked at me. "You won't kill me, Captain. Because that's not what you really want. I can see the same darkness in your eyes that I have come to know. Stay here with me. I will kill you, and then raise you up, and take all your cares away. No more pain, no more bad dreams, no more conscience. I will take you home with me, and we will show those fat, sheltered civilians the true cost of war.

"There will be blood and suffering and death all across America when Johnny comes marching home. Revenge is a dish best served cold.

"The horror! The horror!" he said, laughing.

Once again, they come to me for a zombie story, and I think . . . what hasn't been done? So I turned to one of my old favorites: Apocalypse Now. The original short novel—Heart of Darkness—is such a wonderful model you can hang pretty much anything on it and it still works. I once used it in my science fiction novel Deathstalker War, where I stopped the whole plot dead for two hundred pages just so I could write a version of Heart of Darkness featuring the Muppets. Really. I'm not kidding. And here I go again . . . because the real horror in this story isn't the risen dead; it's the darkness in the hearts of men.

SOLDIER, SOLDIER

I shot the kid in the belly, spreading his guts across a wall. One kid is worth two women; one woman is worth two men. That's what they drum into each and every one of us, till you scream it in your sleep.

Just me and Matt, stalking the smoking ruins. The silence is unnerving: no shots, no crackling fires, no voices yelling or cursing or screaming. Matt walks slowly down the other side of the deserted street, his rifle in his hands. I keep mine slung over my shoulder. It's heavy, and under the midday sun, it's growing heavier. The air's hot and sticky and my feet hurt. A cool beer would be great, but there isn't any. I reach into my rucksack and pull out a Coke, smashing the glass bottle open against a wall. The sickly lukewarm drink is better than nothing.

Matt stops and listens, and then I hear it, too: footsteps approaching. Matt slides into a dark doorway as I unsling my rifle with the ease of long practice. I throw off the safety and wait. A figure springs into view at the end of the street, and even against the sun I can see the dark gray uniform. The bastard's one of ours.

I hear Matt curse quietly as he steps back into the light, rifle hanging disappointedly at his side.

I put up my rifle and take another gulp of Coke. It slides down nice and easy. Matt asks the newcomer what he wants. He jumps to attention under Matt's tone and swings a snappy salute. The way he tells it, the captain said we're to take out a sniper's nest at the end of the next street. Matt and I look at each other and shrug. What the hell.

We take it out.

We blast and frag the house, and shoot them down as they crawl out. There are three bodies, and only one is recognizably human. The others are hamburger.

Back at the camp, we stand to attention while the captain talks. They know we're in the city. The radio reports a bloody massacre of soldiers and civilians by an unknown guerrilla force. Both sides are unanimous in condemning the atrocities. Both sides blame the other. Matt doesn't smile, but then he never does unless his rifle is bucking at his hip. Then he smiles kind of dreamy, far away. But his eyes don't miss a thing.

The captain commends us both, but his voice doesn't have the fire it used to. His voice is tired, like his face. Too many wars, too many not-wars, too much fighting. Getting punchy.

Has it only been five years since the aliens first built that missile base on the moon? Seems longer. What was I doing five years ago, before I got volunteered for this new kind of army? I don't remember, and somehow it doesn't seem too important anyway. All that matters is that the aliens are sitting up there, building something big and nasty on the dark side of the moon. Can't let the people know, they'd just panic. But when we're ready, we'll go up there and take them out. And then we'll go looking for whoever sent them.

Till then, we just sneak in on all the little wars and not-wars, to train ourselves for the Big One. Learning not just how to kill, but how to do it good. A kid is worth two women, a woman is worth two men. That was the captain's idea. Keep the wars going as long as possible, teach us to fight mean. We've got to defend the human race.

You're doing a fine job, the captain says, not looking at us; keep it up and you'll get a crack at the aliens, and then we can get back to real life again.

Sure, we say politely, sure.

He mumbles on for a bit, but we aren't listening. In my mind's eye, I can see the kid's face as I splash his guts across the wall. I lick my lips. Wish I had that nice cold beer. Or even my nice lukewarm Coke.

The captain winds down at last, and we salute and leave. He means well, but he isn't seeing too clearly anymore. Maybe he and his kind never did. The war goes on as usual, only now it's a three-sided war.

Does it matter? No. Time to get out and kill some more. Feel that rifle bucking in your hands, the ground shake as the bomb explodes, watch their faces as they get it. A kid is worth two women; a woman is worth two men.

Yeah.

Starting here, these are my earliest stories, those that appeared back in the late seventies, early eighties, when I was just starting out. This one was the first thing I wrote to actually appear in print, in a British fanzine, Tangent. I got the idea from watching a news report about insurrection in a foreign land, where the reporter said he couldn't even be sure how many sides there were in this war. Which started me thinking about governments who might decide to get involved for their own purposes. I was still developing my own voice at this point, but I think the story works.

MANSLAYER

In the deeps, in his tomb, dreams Manslayer. Around the many layers of eroded stone, cold waters stir sluggishly, but no shivers twitch his bulk. In the icy dark, Manslayer waits patiently for the day he will be called forth to live his task again. Darkness within, darkness without. Manslayer dreams blood. . . .

I.

Brand twisted and withdrew his blade in one easy movement, gracefully sidestepping as his opponent sank to his knees, clutching with desperate hands at the crimson rip in his gut. Blood welled between the fingers and spilled onto the dirty floor. The man toppled forward and was still.

Brand hefted his sword lightly and glanced casually around the tavern at the watching, hostile faces. Satisfied that there were no challenges, he knelt beside the dead man, jerking free the neckcloth to clean his blade. The tavern bedlam resumed around him as he sheathed his sword and then methodically robbed the corpse.

He sank into his chair with a satisfied grunt and tossed a bulging purse onto the table before his companion. She raised a painted eyebrow as a single gold coin rolled free and settled quickly with a faint shimmer. She reached for the purse, and Brand's dagger was suddenly in his hand. The girl hesitated only slightly, before moving smoothly on to raise her goblet and silently toast Brand. The dagger disappeared.

"You fight well."

Brand nodded his acceptance of the fact, sipped slowly at his own wine.

"It's what I do."

"My master has work for you at the Great Reefs."

Brand's curiosity stirred. "I'm no diver. Why me?"

An elegant shrug was his only answer. Brand studied her openly, eyes tracing her supple figure, mouth smiling appreciation. This one hadn't been slave long; the thick, coarse wool of her tunic contrasted strongly with the obvious breeding of her delicate beauty and poise. She'd lose both quickly, he mused bitterly, under the lash and never-ending work. The depth of his bitterness surprised him, and he stopped it short, gulping down more wine. She was none of his business.

"How much will your *master* pay me?" he asked softly.

A dull anger stirred behind her eyes, quickly suppressed

"I haven't yet decided you're the man I was sent to find."

Brand shrugged. "You asked for the best bravo in Ithliel; you found him."

"You're the only bravo in Ithliel!"

"Thereby proving my point."

She hesitated, then leaned forward conspiratorially.

"Out beyond the Great Reefs are the richest pearl beds in the Known Kingdoms; my master's family have been harvesting them for nearly two centuries, and still they stretch on. A newly opened bed has proved the richest of all. But of late . . ." she hesitated, drank from her goblet. "There have been accidents; divers have been lost, never returning to the surface. Others have returned without their minds, lost somewhere in the Deeps.

"The sorcerer my master keeps to protect his divers has been tormented by nightmares that drive him screaming from his rest, and he is close to madness. His only advice has been to hire a man like you, a hero, a man to dive down to the Far Reefs and destroy the evil that lurks there."

Brand chuckled. "I'm no hero, girl."

"There's more." She reached into a pouch at her waist and handed a small amulet to Brand. He studied it dubiously, turning it over and over in his hands.

"What is it?"

"One of our divers brought it to the surface a month ago."

Brand studied it more closely. On one side, strange sigils were etched deep into the metal, presumably by acid. On the obverse, a hazy design of some kind of monster. Brand found it vaguely disturbing and quickly handed it back.

"The sorcerer Gerrandes called it the Beast Out of Time."

Brand shrugged.

"It is an old legend, of a demon that has always been with us, and always will, whose only reason for existence is the death of man. A demon of blood and darkness."

Brand felt the hackles rising on the back of his neck and stirred uneasily in his seat.

"It's only a legend, girl, nothing more."

"Perhaps. My master has been sacrificing to it ever since this was found, but to no avail."

"Sacrifice? You mean people?"

"Only slaves."

Brand stirred again. "The task sounds intriguing. How much?"

"You're still willing to help after all I've told you?"

"Maybe. I'm a mercenary; my sword is for hire because that's my only skill. I'll fight anything for a price. How much?"

"Three black pearls."

Brand spilled what was left of his wine. The black pearl was so rare as to be almost literally priceless. The Emperor of the North had one in his crown . . . to be offered three . . .

"When do we start?"

She smiled, revealing a single gold-capped incisor, and rose gracefully to her feet. Brand pushed back his chair and took her gently by the arm.

"You haven't told me your name yet."

Her eyes hardened. "I am slave; I have no name."

Brand suddenly twisted her arm back to reveal the raw slaver's brand on the inside of her wrist, and then held up his own arm to show a twin brand.

"I was once slave," he said softly, releasing her arm. "I never forgot my name, though I no longer use it."

She wouldn't meet his eyes, sullenly rubbing her bruised arm.

"Do you have a room here?"

She nodded reluctantly.

"Then should we go there, two slaves together, and share the only pleasure two slaves may?"

She searched his face for a long moment, and then one side of her mouth twitched in what might have been a smile.

"My name is Mareem."

2.

The icy water lapped at his sides as Brand grimly clung to the side of the rocking boat, panting air back into his raw lungs.

"Three minutes; you're doing better."

Mareem handed him a steaming draft and Brand nodded his thanks. Warmth pulsed slowly through him, fighting back the ocean cold.

"How much longer before I can stay down the full seven

minutes of a diver?" he asked, more to make conversation than because he really cared. Mareem chuckled.

"Another few months ought to do it."

Brand uttered a convincing groan, though the drink's pleasant warmth was welling softly through him.

"Feeling better, hero?"

Brand snorted. "Some hero. Lord Vallar hates me, the Court ignores me, and the sorcerer Gerrandes has the unsettling habit of looking at me, shrugging, and turning quickly away."

Mareem laughed. "Finished with that goblet? Then drink this." She took away the empty goblet and handed him a crude wooden cup half filled with an oily blue liquid.

"What is it?"

"If I told you, you wouldn't drink it. Gerrandes said it would help you. Now do as you're told."

Brand grinned and gulped it down, lips thinning away from the bitter taste.

"What does it do?"

"Helps you stay underwater indefinitely."

Brand stared at her.

"Try it."

He handed back the cup and breathed deeply for long moments, hyperventilating his blood, before ducking under the surface. The light faded slowly away as he sank back to the seabed, urged ever down by the iron weights at his waist. The thick salt stung his eyes, but he had become used to that. With the drink inside him, he no longer felt the cold, though he knew that long exposure to it would kill him as surely as lack of air.

Down he drifted into the murky darkness, till finally his feet scuffed sand. He grew bored waiting for the dull ache in his chest, before realizing that his air was still good. He started to laugh and nearly choked as water filled his mouth. He swallowed quickly and was easy again. He pushed himself toward the surface.

A fish as long as his arm swam up to him and stared curiously with goggle eyes. Brand stared impassively back. A flick of the tail and it was gone. He shrugged and resumed the long upward swim.

Another fish flashed past him, this time without pausing, and then another, and another. He paused in his ascent as fish swarmed past him in ever-increasing numbers. He glared into the murk but could see no reason for the panic.

The light faded and was gone. Blind, he clawed at his eyes and the water was suddenly cold around him. It tasted of blood. . . .

Water spilled into his slack mouth as he floated gently just beneath the surface.

3.

Vallar glared petulantly at Brand, who stood dripping on the polished marble floor.

"So the fish were excited, and you panicked. I see no reason for postponing the dive."

Wrapped in a thick blanket, Brand gratefully accepted another goblet of wine from the sorcerer Gerrandes. The honeyed wine soothed his raw throat as he glared around the packed Court, taking in the gloomy nobles in their multicolored silks. Heavily armed guardsmen lined the ancient stone walls, their weapons gleaming dully under the flickering oil torches.

The Court ostentatiously ignored Brand, muttering in small groups on the edge of his vision. None dared speak openly against him, but Brand knew well that only their fear of the evil beyond the Reefs kept them in check. Once that was finished, he would do well to shield his back from daggers and his cup from poison.

Nothing scares a slaver more than an ex-slave.

Brand grinned wolfishly and tipped his goblet in a sardonic toast.

"But, my lord," Gerrandes protested, "Both the bravo and I have now shared a deathly dream of blood and darkness; surely this proves there must be Something out beyond the Far Reefs. . . ."

"If there is, he's being paid more than enough to kill it." Lord Vallar's voice was testy, despite the soothing ministrations of his body slaves, who plied him with wine, fed him sweetmeats, and massaged his neck and shoulders. "Every day, our divers bring back fewer pearls. This must be stopped ere we are ruined." Noble hands flapped in a petulant gesture, momentarily upsetting his slaves, one of whom wasn't quick enough in dodging the waving hands. There was a solid sounding thump, though the slave hardly swayed, being used to the more painful disciplines of the overseers. Vallar let out a muffled scream and waved his bruised hand wildly before him.

"Guards! Guards! Take this slave away and kill it! No, kill it here, now, were we can see it done!"

The slave's face whitened as two burly guardsmen took him by the shoulders and forcibly knelt him before Vallar's throne. One raised a sword on high and then suddenly collapsed in a heap, to be joined shortly by his groaning companion.

Brand grinned, and his dagger disappeared again. Vallar's mouth flapped silently open and shut, reminding Brand irresistibly of the fish that stared at him just before the panic.

"By what right . . ."

Brand shut him up by the simple expedient of grabbing a handful of loose robes and shaking Vallar violently.

"I was once slave, Vallar. My last master was somewhat like you. He's dead now, which is why I'm no longer slave."

He dropped Vallar and stalked back to Gerrandes, who quickly offered him a freshly filled goblet of wine.

"It . . . it is obvious to us that you are still suffering from the effects of your narrow escape this morning, and we will therefore overlook this . . . this . . ." Vallar stumbled to a halt under Brand's sardonic gaze.

"Most kind of you, my lord," said Gerrandes, bowing low. Brand grinned.

Vallar gestured for four slaves to remove the dead guardsmen, and the reprieved slave hastily followed them out, not daring to do more than bob a quick nod of thanks to Brand. Vallar settled himself comfortably on his throne, and the remaining body slaves took up their soothing ministrations again.

Brand emptied his goblet and wiped the back of his hand across his mouth. Vallar shuddered fastidiously.

"You, bravo. The dive will take place tomorrow, as arranged."

"But my lord, he was nearly killed today, surely . . ."

"Be still, Gerrandes! I won't hear another word. Oh, if it'll make you any happier, I'll sacrifice another slave to quiet It . . . Be still! The audience is ended."

Vallar, Lord of the Great Reefs, Protector of Ishtrome, rose awkwardly to his feet and hobbled slowly out of his Court. Brand watched him go and Gerrandes shuddered at the dark gleam in the bravo's eyes. Then Brand shivered and huddled into his blanket, holding out an empty goblet for more wine. Gerrandes's fingers writhed briefly, and the goblet was full again. Brand blinked and sipped suspiciously, before smiling approval.

"My thanks. Tell me, Gerrandes, how ancient is that old goat anyway? With a prize as rich as the pearl beds I'm surprised one of his sons hasn't slid his throat long ago."

The sorcerer laughed tiredly. "Only he knows the exact locations of the master beds, mapped by his grandsire almost two centuries ago; as long as they stay a secret in his head, he's safe and he knows it."

"But what about the divers?"

"Dumb, all of them. Vallar cut their tongues out. It's an old family tradition."

"What was that about a slave sacrifice?" Brand's tone was casual, but the darkness was back in his eyes.

"Vallar has been sacrificing a young girl slave every day for the past two months, trying to appease whatever waits beyond the Reefs. It's done no good that I can see; if anything, our troubles are worse than before."

Brand shrugged. "They're only slaves."

"Exactly." Gerrandes knew better than to refer to Brand's earlier defense of Vallar's body slave. "Now, if you'll excuse me . . ." He bustled out. Brand nodded, and stood brooding for a moment while the Court pointedly ignored him. Then he slowly made his way back to his pokey little room in the draft East Wing; Vallar wasn't all the host he might have been.

He sank wearily onto the one good chair and clutched his blanket around him. The bed looked warm and inviting, but he was too tired to make the effort of getting into it.

"You look tired."

Brand started as a pile of bedclothes resolved itself into a girl under the sheets. He grinned, and the dagger in his hand disappeared.

"Mareem, how did you get in here?"

"Gerrandes arranged it."

Brand laughed and levered himself out of his chair. He threw aside his blanket and climbed quickly under the sheets. They lay side by side for a while, neither moving.

"The dive is tomorrow, isn't it?"

"Yes."

"It'll be dangerous."

"That's what I'm paid for."

"Aren't you afraid?"

"Of course. But three black pearls . . . I'd lead an army into Hell for that."

Mareem stirred beside him. "Are you really tired?"

"Yes."

"Oh."

"But not that tired."

4.

Brand sank slowly into the murky dark, pulled steadily down by the leather thong around his ankle, from which hung the lead ingot the divers used to jelp them reach the Very Deeps beyond the Reefs. No normal man could survive for long in the Deeps, and even Gerrandes's help was limited. The sword at his side was a comforting weight, and his left hand rested on the pommel.

The light faded slowly behind him as he sank into the murk, and Brand's respect for the regular divers grew; men who would daily undergo this experience to gather pearls for Vallar were brave indeed. Vallar . . . Brand's lips curled involuntarily, letting in a little water. Just before he left, Gerrandes had told him that a slave had already been sacrificed. Brand hadn't liked the answer to his question, "How?" The girl had been dropped into the depths with a lead weight chained to her ankles and left to drown. The similarity to his own situation did not escape him.

His feet hit bottom, and he reached slowly down to pull his foot free from the leather loop, trusting to his weighted belt to counteract his buoyancy

He was blind again . . . the sea salt was blood in his mouth . . . fear welled through him . . .

He fought it back and his mind cleared, though deep inside something screamed for him to flee. He concentrated on the feeling and found it strongest when he faced one direction. He gritted his teeth and swam steadily into it.

His progress was slow, and in his near-blind state, he was hard put to avoid rocky outcroppings from the Reefs. His head jarred painfully against a low overhead, and his hands waved aimlessly for a secure hold. His fingers brushed an uneven surface, and closer inspection found intricate carvings etched deep into the stone. Questing fingertips found the shapes eroded and coral-crusted into illegibility, but discovered ledges above and below the carvings, and to both sides. His imagination staggered at the thought of the wall made of such bricks as this, fully ten feet square. . . .

His inner fear was suddenly gone, and with it his bearings. He had no idea how far he'd swam, or how long. He shrugged, feeling carefully along the coral-crusted ledges; there had to be an opening somewhere . . . a lever. Buried under coral, but discernibly a lever. He tugged, but it was obstinate. He wrapped both hands around it, placed both feet firmly against the wall, and pulled. Muscles writhed and bulged for long agonizing moments, before the lever finally grated forward, throwing him off balance.

His flailing arms now found space instead of stone. He swam cautiously into the new opening, which rapidly proved to be a tunnel. He swam warily on. The path twisted and turned, then slanted sharply upward. He followed its path and was surprised when his head suddenly broke water into air. Misty and sickly sweet, but nonetheless welcome for that. Feeling cautiously around, Brand found himself to be in a pool of some kind. He pulled himself out onto cold stone floor. All was pitch-black and silence.

The air was unnaturally thick and heavy, and Brand found it as hard to move in as the water he'd swum through. He reached into the waterproof pouch at his waist and pulled out his tinderbox. A questing hand found a length of smooth wood, and he wadded oil-soaked rag around it. It would make a good torch. He struck sparks and ignited it.

Light flared up, illuminating a vast cavern fully a hundred yards in length and breadth. But Brand had no eyes for its size, for sprawled before him lay Manslayer.

5.

Deep within Manslayer, a heart beats once, pauses and beats again. Blood pulses sluggishly and shivers shake the slimy bulk. Rudely cast from his bloody dreams, Manslayer wakes, hurting and hating. He has no mind that men might understand, but in his own way, he hates. Thus was he created, the Beast Out of Time, the Manslayer, last weapon of the long vanished Daun in their war against Man. Manslayer, his name and reason for existence.

Hating, Manslayer opens an eye.

Brand bit back a scream as the single pale eyelid crawled open, revealing a blood-red eye. His sword was quickly in his hand, but as quickly drooped, forgotten, as Brand stood overwhelmed by the physical reality of legend. Manslayer sprawled before him, thirty feet of blubbery white, its flowing white hair draped around the mockery of a face which declared to all the gods that were and may be that no man had a hand in its making.

Brand's choked cry echoed through the Tomb as the Beast lurched unsteadily upright on its forearms, the long claws gouging furrows from the sold stone floor. Ponderously, the arm nearest Brand swept toward him, and he ducked more through instinct than design. Claws split the air above him, and his sword chopped deeply into the rippling flesh. A thick purple ichor spattered the floor. Manslayer slobbered and gurgled, swinging again, its speed dulled by its recent awakening from long sleep.

Sobbing in terror, Brand threw his torch to one side and hacked again and again at the monster, till the ichor drenched him from head to foot, till he could take no more. Absently, he noted that his torch still burned, though what he had taken to be a length of wood was in fact a human thighbone. Other human bones lay scattered across the vast stone floor. He stared wildly about; Manslayer was quickly awakening and would shortly crush him as easily as a man would a persistent louse. As both man and Beast paused to stare at each other in mutual hate, reason returned to Brand, and he raised his sword as though to stab again at the probing arm, then threw it directly into the single staring eye.

The slit pupil split still further under the urging steel, and Manslayer screamed, a ghastly ululation that clapped Brand's hands to his ears as he staggered backward. Manslayer clawed in futile fury at his pain, lacerating his eye further, and then he lunged at Brand, who fell backward into the entry pool.

The cold waters closed over his head, and his senses returned as he struck out strongly along the tunnel that led to the open sea. A disturbance in the water behind him jerked his head around. Even in the dim murk, he could make out a darker shadow following him. Manslayer. Fear gave Brand strength as he sped for the saving ocean.

He burst from the tunnel mouth and suddenly something slammed into his arms. He fought hysterically for long seconds, before realizing it wasn't fighting back. A shudder rang through him as he found it to be the corpse of the slave girl set out as sacrifice. He threw it to one side and sped surfaceward. He glanced back in time to see Manslayer throw itself onto the corpse and tear the body to bloody ruins. Brand shuddered and pulled himself on, throwing wild thanks to a number of gods for the start this gave him. He jerked the weighted belt from around his waist, striving for more speed.

And behind came Manslayer.

Higher and higher they swam, the light growing around them. Then there came a time when Brand looked back to find the Beast no longer pursued him. Instead, it shook its gargantuan bulk as though puzzled, and then twisted in sudden agony, limbs and tentacles writhing and thrashing wildly. The thickly haired abdomen suddenly bulged and distended to twice its normal size and as Brand watched, it burst, staining the waters a vivid purple. The head swelled, the single bloody eye bulged forth and fell away, as the head itself seemed to stretch and bend. As Brand stared, Manslayer fell apart and fell back into the dark depths that succoured it. The waters slowly cleared away the staining ichor, and the darkness of the deeps hid Manslayer's remains. Brand waited for a while, watching, but there was no more. He swam slowly upward, away from the monster-haunted dark, toward the blessed light of the surface.

6.

Gerrandes smiled, shaking his head as he gently smoothed ointment onto Brand's scarred back.

"You really should have known better than to ask Vallar for three black pearls."

"That was the price he offered, and I had thought nobles to be an honest people in the Southern Kingdoms."

Gentle laughter was his only answer.

Brand growled and waited stoically till Gerrandes was finished. He sat up gingerly, wincing at the dull ache in his back. The sorcerer handed him a cup, but he waved it aside.

"You should take it; you need strength."

"It's not the first time I've been whipped, nor likely to be the last. I'll survive. I'd better leave soon; Vallar will send men after me once he learns you cut me down."

"Why should he?"

"Because I know where the master pearl beds are. Or he thinks I do."

"And do you?"

Brand grinned, pulling his tunic carefully over his head. He winced as the rough cloth rasped along his tender back and then turned slowly to Gerrandes.

"What happened to the Beast? It seemed almost to fall apart . . . ?"

Gerrandes smiled. "In the Deeps, the Very Deeps, the sheer weight of the water would crush a man without the protection my sorceries give him. Manslayer had lived so long at the depths that his body had adapted to that weight. Thus, when he strove to follow you to the surface, the internal pressure of his own misshapen body burst him asunder."

Brand struggled with this answer.

"Then Manslayer is finally dead?"

The sorcerer frowned. "I think not; such Beasts are easier to create than destroy. They were created to be living weapons, to survive where no normal creature could."

"Then it sleeps again."

"Yes. Till its wounds are healed, and some fool such as Vallar wakes it with human sacrifice."

Brand shivered despite the warmth of the room, and with Gerrandes's help staggered to the door, where two slaves helped him onto his horse.

"I wonder who the last sacrifice was," Brand mused. "For in a way she helped save my life."

Gerrandes shrugged. "She was only a slave . . . her name was Mareem."

Brand's hands gripped hard on the reigns, and his eyes squeezed shut.

"Only a slave . . ."

Gerrandes stumbled back at the agonized rage in the words, and in that moment, Brand spurred his horse savagely and was gone, riding as though Hell itself pursued him.

In the deeps, in his tomb, Manslayer dreams blood. . . .

This was the first story I ever sold for actual money. In 1976, to an Irish semi-prozine, Airgedlamh. A good solid swords-and-sorcery story with a neat practical twist.

CASCADE

Her name was Cascade, and I think I killed her. I hope so. But still the rains fall, still the waters rise . . .

The dream first came a month ago, a dim and ugly mixture of scenes and sounds that culminated in a hazy image of Jenny, smiling, that threw me screaming awake. Jenny was dead, two days dead.

The dream came again the next night, and the next, till at last I was afraid to sleep, afraid to close my eyes and see that smiling face. At first, I thought the dreams only natural for a man whose girlfriend drowned herself in the river below his house, but when the song came, I knew that this was no thing of nature. And I knew that the woman who called me night after night was not my love, but my enemy.

The dreams continued, though I could no longer be sure why Jenny's smiling face inspired such terror in me, and often I awoke to the fading echoes of a lonely song on the dawn's cold wind.

Then came the night when I could stand it no more and

answered her call. I stood on the riverbank, staring down into the murk, knowing that deep down, among the choking weeds, she was staring back. Waiting.

I remembered Jenny's gentle sea-green eyes, staring at me almost in warning over that fixed, terrifying smile, and I knew that she would not, could not, rest till I had answered whoever called with her name and her face. As I stood at the water's edge a soft voice sang sweetly in my ears, and I knew my enemy's name: Cascade. She called, and I came, but with a witch knife in my hand.

I stripped down to my underwear and hefted the iron dagger in my hand. It was a comforting weight. The driving rain was cold against my body. I took a tentative step into the icy waters, wincing as the thick mud gave under my foot.

I eased further into the river and shivered as the waters crept up my ribs, the cold shuddering through me. Gradually, the waters rose up around me, until I leaned forward into the murk and they closed over my head. Somewhere, I could hear her singing.

She was the last, she sang, the last of a race that lived before man, and with man, and will survive after man. She was Cascade, the last of the water elementals, the undines and sirens. Pollution murdered her kith and kin, but she had made a pact with the wind-walkers for a long rain that would swell her watery domain till it overran the dirt that was our home, and all mankind would drown to rise again as servants in her calm and unchanging watery world. *Come,* she sang, *come and join me, first among my lovers,* and a lonely ache filled my heart till I thought it would burst. But still I clutched my knife.

I glared blearily through the murk among the waving weeds that choked the riverbed, and eventually I found what I suppose I had always known I would find. A grinning skull, the eyes glowing with green fire. The skull of my dead love, wooed and betrayed by the siren song, now containing a mind old and evil from before the time of man. I swayed before it as the song burst through my mind again, almost overpowering in its intensity. *Come join me, rule with me, I have been alone so long; open your mouth, let in the soothing waters that bring peace and comfort, and our cold lips will never part.*

I raised the dagger with heavy arm, wavered, and then swung it savagely down. The skull split cleanly in two, the eyes falling away from each other as the eerie corpse glow winked out. And I knew my dead love was free from the undine's grasp.

The waters pulsed around me, and a howling scream of rage tore through my mind, shaking me till I dropped the knife among the waving weeds, which no longer swayed aimlessly but now writhed and reached for me, tangling my legs and wrapping around my flailing arms. I watched a small stream of bubbles rise from my nose and knew my air was almost gone. I struggled wildly, clawing and ripping at the weeds till I broke free, and then pulled myself hand over hand for the surface. I burst into the air and hauled myself out onto the bank, throat burning, lungs jerking heavily, gasping down the damp dawn air.

I pulled myself to my feet, and staggering over to the garage, I seized the can of oil some impulse (Jenny?) had prompted me to buy the day before. The river waters writhed and boiled, ripples spreading from a frothing disturbance I dared not look at too closely. Instead, I watched the oil pour sluggishly onto the water, forming a dark layer that smothered the ripples. I fumbled in my discarded coat for a box of matches, my fingers numb and awkward from the icy waters. Grinning harshly, I struck a match, watched it flare for a moment, and then dropped it. A sheet of flame sprang up, spreading even as I watched, and deep in my mind something screamed in a terrible agony. I laughed loud and long, trying to drown out the screams, and then sat down on the bank and sobbed quietly to myself. The screams died away, until finally I sat dry-eyed, listening to the silence.

That was a week ago. The dreams no longer come, nor the

lonely songs that rang so sweetly on the early morning air. But still the long rain falls, still the waters rise, still the waters rise. . . .

This was specially written, to accompany someone else's art folio. A mood piece, inspired by a song from the group Camel. Very dark, very sad, very mournful. I was very young at the time. I think I'm right in saying that the payment was a quarter of a penny a word, and that it cost me more in postage to send in the story than I was paid.

SOULHUNTER

I was back down in the sewers, and let me tell you the stink was pretty bad. I waded quickly through the scummy waters to reach the junction marked on my memory, and then pulled myself up onto a crumbling stone ledge half covered with slime.

I reached into my haversack and taking out the fetus in its glass case, I placed it gently down beside me. The huge head and goggle eyes made a vivid picture of the midway point between life and death, human and abhuman. It was hard to think of a thing like that having a soul, but that was why I was here.

The Hags have a thing about sewers. Whether it's the darkness, the stench, or simply the claustrophobia, I don't know, but that's the way it is.

The Hags, in case you never heard of them, are what sit in the stars and eat souls. Reaching down through the long night, they specialize in souls from stillborn or aborted babies, souls without egos. Without an awareness of yourself as a separate and distinct entity, the soul's edges are what you might call hazy, not so well pinned down. And then it's up for grabs.

Now the Dragons (sluggish dark things that squat in the deep down caves), they'll eat anything: man soul, woman soul, child soul. But the Dragons are few and far between these days, and they sleep a lot. A few more centuries and they'll be extinct.

The Wolves (fat and furry, haunt the forest with fang and claw), they'll have a tear at anything that passes, but we're slowly weeding them out. Wolfsbane and holy water help.

The Hags are something different. We're not too sure what they are, though our espers say they live Out There somewhere, basking in suns you can't always see. But they have their hungers, and what they want is souls. Being so far away, they can't just reach out and take them like a Dragon or a Wolf, but a stillborn or aborted child soul hasn't any real defenses. A snap of the fingers, and there goes another baby screaming into Hell.

The main problem with Hags is getting in touch in the first place. There's no way I can fly out to a star I've never even seen, but all the Hags have a place somewhere that's their individual hold on Earth, that tells them where it is all the time they can't see it. Dragons like caves, Wolves like forests; Hags like sewers.

I'm a Soulhunter, first class. What I do is go after the Demons (Hags or Wolves or Dragons) and recover the lost souls. Or die trying.

The soul's center is a darkly insane place, where in an endless night owls flutter in a deserted barn and childhood horrors peer from shadowed corners. I know; I've been there. When as Demon rips through to your soul's center, there are no more locked doors to hide behind, and all your nightmares come swarming out. That's how a Demon feeds.

Of course they aren't really Dragons, or Wolves, or Hags. That's just the way my mind sees them. Scarecrow, an old friend of mine till a Wolf chewed on him, called them Snakes, Rats, and Spiders.

To each his own Nightmare.

I stared into the fetus's goggle eyes and let my mind drift up and out, searching. From star to star, I swam, spreading thinner and thinner over the empty dark, and finally I returned, shivering, to my body. It's cold out there. I shook the frost aside and tried again, throwing my net wider. The Hag screamed and slavered, and something red and sharp sliced into me, before I could break contact. I fell back into my body and clutched at the foot-long rip down my arm. The attack was purely mental, but my body's stupid; it can't tell the difference. Psychosomatic stigmata.

I'd found my Hag. Back in the old days, they called places like this genius loci. Of course that was back before espers and Soulhunters. Makes me shiver when I think of all those people without any kind of protection, not knowing about all those hungry soul-thieves hanging around them.

As I tightened a bandage around my arm, I could feel the Hag easing into its foci; my earthly surroundings. The stench was suddenly worse, and I emptied my gut in two quick heaves, like I'd been taught. Cobwebs formed on the walls, hanging down from the ceiling in long strands. (I know why Scarecrow called them Spiders.) The water turned blood red and swirled sluggishly up around my ledge. I drew my feet back from the edge as something curled sinuously through the water toward me. Mortar trickling onto my shoulder alerted me to the falling bricks, and I blasted them aside with a quick PK bolt. On the edge of my mind, I could hear a howling, a screaming, a hunger . . .

The cobwebs were thicker now, long, ropy strands that hung in twisted creepers and tattered shrouds through all the tunnels as far as I could see. Streamers brushed against my face, though no wind blew. My electric lamp sputtered and went out. Didn't bother me; I can see in the dark, like a cat. Only clearer. The thickening cobwebs hid the curved walls and trailed into the murky waters. Directly across from me, something stirred under the scum. As I watched, a rubbery tentacle writhed up out of the water, waving lazily back and forth on the stinking air, searching for me.

I threw myself forward as jaws snapped shut behind me, only just hanging onto the narrow ledge I was perched on. Behind me, the stone wall had split into a pair of ugly blackened lips and jagged teeth. As I watched, the lips writhed in a grimace that was smile and scowl and petulant sneer, and then it was just a wall again. Something tapped me on the shoulder, and I threw myself at the wall this time, but the tentacle snagged me anyway. I must be getting old. It was fat and blubbery, without much muscle to it (that's why they prefer child souls; can't fight back), and I broke free with only a few bruises.

I opened my mind again, to give the Hag a taste of my own strength, when fat, furry fangs and claws ripped into me like a knife through butter. I screamed and fell back into my body. Pain shook through me as blood soaked my back and shoulders.

There was a Wolf down here somewhere.

I'd heard tales of Demons so badly hit by Soulhunters that they hunted prey together, but I'd never believed it possible till now. Vicious cold shivered through me, as I drew my silver dagger from its sheath. If the Demons were teaming up, we were in for some interesting times.

(Old Chinese curse: May you live in interesting times.)

I pulled myself together in time to cut at a probing tentacle. It jerked spasmodically as flesh ripped under my blade, and then recoiled beneath the murky waters with a faint slurping sound. And then something nasty boiled up out of the water, big and hairy with white shiny fangs and clawed hands. (See why Wolf to me, Rat to Scarecrow?) I yelled and sprang at it, my knife seeking its throat, and then we were rolling back and forth on the narrow ledge. I slid half a foot of silver into its throat, and elbowed the kicking corpse back into the water.

I sat back and waited. Things were getting rough.

Of course that last bit didn't really happen. Wolves have no real physical existence on Earth, any more than a Hag or a Dragon; I'd just killed an image it created out of my surroundings. I'd hurt it, but it wasn't dead. Not yet. I reached into my haversack and pulled out a jar of wolfsbane.

(That's one part herb of the name, one part holy water, one part human blood.)

I rubbed the thick gunk over my hands and dagger, and waited patiently for the next sending, batting the probing tentacles away as they slithered up out of the water, reaching for me. The Hag was getting impatient.

A bubble formed on the scummy water, swelling up to some seven feet wide, and I could see something fat and dark huddled inside it. I didn't wait for the bubble to burst, just jumped it, slashed through with my dagger, and wrestled with something dark and slimy. Had an eye that looked at me. Fangs and claws. But it screamed and screamed when it felt wolfsbane on my hands and blade.

I stabbed and hacked, feeling it writhing under me in pain and fear. I was hurting pretty badly myself, but I concentrated on cutting deeper, until it suddenly convulsed and threw me back into the reeking waters. I staggered back to the ledge and hauled myself out of what was now a waist-high bloody soup. I huddled up in a ball, sobbing as much from fear as pain. I didn't know if I could take another sending. Finally, I quietened and looked out on the water. The bubble was gone with its creature, and I knew that Wolf was running with its tail between its legs. But it would soon be back. I had to rip the Hag to pieces and recover the lost soul, before the Wolf returned, or it would be over for both of us.

I glared at the bigheaded embryo in its glass case. Mother too old to bear the kid safely, Doctor had to abort it: no choice. Result, one soul up for grabs. Call in the Soulhunter. It still gives me the shivers, to think of all those babies neverborn in the old days, aborted for convenience. No wonder the Demons grew fat again, just like in the days of blood sacrifices.

I scowled at the embryo and then at my watch. Time was running out on me. I had to snag that Hag and rip it. But if the Wolf was still around, opening up my mind was death. Souldeath, too, maybe. My mind raced wildly as I smeared fresh wolfsbane on my blade, and then I had an idea. If it worked, no more Hag or Wolf; if it didn't, there wouldn't be enough left of me to bury. I shuddered once, quickly.

I'm a Soulhunter. It's what I do.

I gathered my remaining strength and sent my mind soaring. The Hag howled, and long claws reached for me. I lay still, mind blanked, as the Hag sliced into me again and again, the pain gnawing at my barriers.

And then long, lean, and deadly slammed into the Hag, Wolf images of blood and fear mixed with killlust and a maddening hunger. The Hag screamed and lashed out with a terrible fury, but the Wolf hung on, rending and tearing, hunger driving it even against its ally. I'd guessed right: helpless prey was the one thing neither Demon had expected, and faced with a soul for the taking, there was only the endless hunger that drove them.

I closed my mind against the whirling kaleidoscope of alien savagery, riding out the storm. When it was over, there was only the Hag. It tittered, ripping through my mental barriers like cloth, and I felt a coldness in my soul, like the first ice of a deadly winter. I screamed, bloodlust roaring in me as I threw my alternative self at the Hag's throat. My mind image isn't human; it's big and scaly, with fangs and claws and berserker rage. It's an image I have of myself as a fighter, and I threw it screaming and slavering at the Hag, which gibbered and clawed in terror, and then was gone. Maybe dead, maybe not. Hell, don't even know if it's alive in the first place. But it left behind a soul.

Don't ask me what it looks like, or how I know it's a soul. If you aren't a Soulhunter, you aren't ever going to know or understand. I touched it gently for a moment, and then we were both back in our bodies—me on that damn stone ledge, it in its glass case. I teleported it back to Base, where they'd hook it up to a synthetic womb till it was ready to birth, and then I sank wearily back against the rough stone wall.

No cobwebs, no scum on bloody waters, no nightmare things stirring under the waters, or in the shadows, or in the walls. Smelled pretty much the same, though. I slipped down into the water and made my way slowly back to the empty street above.

And let me tell you, that homely old sun hanging on the sky looked damn good to me.

This appeared in a semi-prozine called Fantasy Macabre, after being rejected many times. Probably the closest I've come to being controversial, but I can see my authorial voice starting to emerge.

AWAKE, AWAKE YE NORTHERN WINDS

Moonlight slides down marble walls as distant laughter spills from brightly lit taverns, and beacons blaze in tall minarets. A single fountain gurgles lazily in the early evening's heat. Shadows fill the alleyways. Above, blackbirds whirl silently on the night winds as drunken laughter erupts into screams that echo back from an unresponsive night, slowly dying away to an eerie silence broken only by the soft shuffling of shadowy figures as they leave the blood-soaked streets behind them. For this was how the night ghouls danced in Ravensbrook.

I.

The *Revenge* lay at anchor off Ravensbrook, called by some Port Blood. The fat moon hung heavy on the night, and a cool breeze murmured in the slack sails. Varles stalked his cabin like a caged mountain lion, head down, shoulders hunched. A hesitant knock interrupted his brooding, and he glowered at his first mate, Jarryl, for a moment, before raising one eyebrow in query. She nodded curtly, and Varles cursed under his breath, before following her up on deck.

The cold night air was fresh on his cheeks as he stared past the rigging at the shadow-strewn jungle that hid Port Blood. The sullen darkness threw back his gaze as an enemy's shield turns aside an arrow. And yet past that cloak of darkness lay the treasure that had haunted his dreams for so many nights. Varles pondered a long moment in silence, before a gentle voice broke into his reverie.

"Captain . . ."

"Aye?"

He turned to find Jarryl at his shoulder, moonlight shining in her long blonde hair held loosely in place by a hastily knotted bandanna.

"Captain, you can't trust Shade."

Varles nodded briefly in answer, turning back to the enigmatic jungle. After a moment, she left him. Varles smiled slightly. The wind swelled for a moment and a bird's silhouette hung outlined against the moon and then was gone. The gentle sounds of the night ocean were comforting, and almost hid the approaching footsteps that stopped just behind him. Varles did not turn.

"A cool night, Captain." The man's light voice was calm, assured.

"Aye."

"How long before ye'll be needing me, do ye think?"

"A few hours more." Varles nodded at the sky. "It lacks a while yet of dawn."

"Ye never had a taste for the sorceries of night, did ye?"

"The sorceries of day are perilous enough for me. The ghouls of Ravensbrook sleep but lightly; only a fool disturbs their rest without need."

Low laughter echoed quietly for a moment, but when Varles turned, there was no one there. He snarled, right hand dropping to the scimitar at his side, and tensed as a slender figure loomed out of the aft shadows. He half-smiled and relaxed as his first mate strode into the light.

"Any orders, Captain?"

Varles nodded. "At first light, we take a landing party ashore. Post a double guard before we leave. I trust the waters of Port Blood no more than the city I know to be cursed."

"Aye, sir."

She padded away into the darkness, and Varles stared out across the moon-flecked waters, leaning heavily on the massive bridgework, looted in its entirety from an old Falconian ship, before he sent it to the bottom. Hewn from the wood of a tree that had not grown naturally for centuries, it was studded with gold scrollwork and precious jewels from a dozen lands. It took Varles's weight with only the faintest of groans as he stared hungrily into the near impenetrable jungle shadows, letting his eyes adjust to the night. In and out of the trees, moonlight splashed across the odd patch of marble wall, sad remnants of what was once the pirate base Ravensbrook. In those days, many a proud ship sailed from her docks laden with spices and copra, musk and fruit, having left in payment loot from a dozen ships and as many countries. And then came the curse of Lord Ravensbrook, and one night when the pirate bands were at feast, there came a company of ghouls that left a trail of blood in their wake and only a few crazed souls to tell of their passing. Since that day, the Brotherhood had chosen other ports for their drinking and wenching, other islands for burying their booty.

Alone and abandoned, the marble walls of Ravensbrook fell prey to the ever-moving jungle. Insects crawled where men once lay, the cry of birds replacing the chatter of men. The very name Ravensbrook was struck from the sea charts, replaced with the name that night had earned it: Port Blood.

Varles had first heard the name and its legend from a drunken navigator in Raddorahn, and then again from the bloody lips of a dying man in Meligarr. And there were always the whispers, in as many tongues as there were versions, of the lost treasure of Port Blood, of the hordes that many a bold captain had amassed in his looting trail of blood and destruction, of the treasure left to the jungle on the night ghouls stalked the gleaming marble streets of Ravensbrook.

At first, Varles could not believe and then would not. The Brotherhood had few rules, but they were harshly enforced, often at the end of a sword or a gibbet. After so many had tried and failed, with none come back to tell the why of it, it was decided in Council that Port Blood was to be left to its memories, treasure or no treasure. But Varles's dreams had been stirred, and he knew that rules had been broken before by those with the guts to sail against the wind. He gathered his crew slowly, one by one, and then he waited. Waited for the one man who could give him his edge, his chance of succeeding where so many had failed.

He found the man called Shade awaiting execution in a prison at Mhule. They struck a bargain: Shade would serve with Varles in return for his freedom. The condemned man was in no position to refuse, and a few days and three murders later, the *Revenge* sailed hastily forth with a full crew and a strong wind at her back.

Varles took a last look at the murky jungle that crept almost to the foot of the tide-swept shore and growled once, deep in his throat, before retiring to his cabin for what little rest he could find before dawn.

2.

The rising sun splashed blood across the sky as the longboat was lowered into the water. The creaking of rope and wood and pulley echoed loudly on the still morning air, mixed with the muttered curses and chants of the crew as they labored. Varles sat in the longboat's prow and waited patiently for them to settle. His fingers idly toyed with a tiny dagger no more than five inches long, cast from pure silver.

"I've never understood what you see in that toy."

"Good morning, Jarryl." Varles nodded amicably to his first mate. "It's served me well enough in its way, and no doubt will again. It is no ordinary knife." Varles glanced up as he slipped the dagger into his flowing sleeve. Jarryl stood grinning before him, the gold of her hair ruddy in the early morning light. She sank down beside him as he made room and nodded at the grim shoreline ahead of them.

"You've long looked forward to this moment, have you not? In all the years I've served with you, after all the ports we've sacked, Port Blood still fascinates you in a way I never could. Do you even know why?"

Varles chuckled. "Mayhap. I'll know for sure when this day is over whether the dreams I had were worth all this. But if half the tales are true . . ."

"If half the tales told in taverns were true, you and I would have been rich a dozen times over." The longboat lurched as the ropes released and the oars dipped into the water. Jarryl threw a glance at the stern, where a spindly figure sat silhouetted against the rising sun. "Why in Mannanon's name did you bring him along?"

"Shade? He has his uses."

Jarryl waited a moment, before realizing she'd heard all Varles was going to tell her. She sniffed and turned back to watch the shore pull steadily closer with each stroke of the straining oars. The sea was calm, and the longboat slid smoothly through the water till it jarred on the last reef, and crewmen splashed through shallow surf to haul it up the beach.

Jarryl jumped down onto the muddy sand, disregarding Varles's offered arm, and looked across the short stretch of beach into the jungle. It was unnaturally quiet; no cries of animals hunting their prey or being hunted, no birds singing . . . the air was still and dry. Varles stood beside her, eyes narrowed at the gnarled and misshapen trees that blocked their path. Jarryl shook her head.

"Do we have to cut our way through that? It'll take hours to reach the city proper. Why couldn't we sail right into the port itself?"

"Ye are brave indeed to risk wakening the ghouls of Ravensbrook."

Jarryl jumped back a pace as the quiet voice sounded beside her. Her hand dropped to her swordhilt. Her lips pulled back in a snarl momentarily, and when she spoke, her voice was soft, calm, and very dangerous.

"Sneak up behind me again, Shade, and I'll cut ye down where ye stand."

Shade paused a moment, taking in her lithe musculature and ready fighter's stance, before nodding amicably. "I hear ye, lady. I will remember."

Jarryl nodded stiffly and turned back to Varles for instructions. He gestured at the crew lounging patiently by the beached longboat.

"Take half the men and your women and scout further up the beach; there ought to be a path not far from here." Jarryl nodded, but Varles stopped her with an upraised hand. "Keep alert; on this cursed isle, distrust even your own shadow."

Jarryl grinned, shot a last glance at Shade, and led her party up the beach. Varles turned to Shade, who was patiently studying the jungle. "Do ye feel any danger here?"

Shade shook his head. "On Port Blood, ye should expect to find nothing else, Captain. But I can say I feel no immediate threat, if that is any use to ye."

Varles stared into Shade's mocking gray eyes, so at odds with his courteous use of the formal *ye*, and then looked him slowly up and down. Dressed in a tunic of gray wool topped with a vest of brass mail and a thick white kerchief at his throat, he made a dowdy figure next to the captain's flashing silks and blood-colored cloak. But sun-bleached hair and gray eyes gave Shade a dignity and air of assurance that far surpassed his simple dress.

Many tales were whispered of Shade, the man who walked in shadows.

His father was a god, they said, or perhaps a demon. Or mayhap even one of the Elder races that sank with the rise of Man. Wherever you heard the story, the details changed. One truth they all whispered, with eyes a-flicker for unprivileged ears: Shade knew magics no other knew, or would care to. Certainly, his powers were far greater than Varles's, who knew only the simple spells of the sea that any mariner knows: the arts of wind calling and fair-weather sailing. From what Varles had seen of a sorcerer's life, he'd stick to his sword and his ship and leave the spell casting to those with a taste for it. He wondered fleetingly what Shade thought of him and his life. He shrugged. He cared not. There was a cry in the distance, and he raised a flounced-silk arm in answer.

Jarryl was standing alone some way up the beach, pointing into the jungle. As Varles watched, a crewman appeared as though from the air itself, followed quickly by another. Shade raised an eyebrow, and Varles hid a grin. Jarryl knew tracking better than any mate he'd ever had, though of course it would never do to tell her so. He set off up the beach with Shade and the others straggling behind him.

The path Jarryl had found was long neglected and overgrown, but it was undeniably a path. With swinging swords and machetes, they slowly cut their way through drooping creepers and heavy vine-strewn branches. Varles and Jarryl struggled side by side, the sweat dripping from their aching arms onto the dusty ground they trod. It seemed as though the very jungle itself was their enemy, intent on keeping them from their goal. They scowled, chewed their tongues to keep their mouths wet, and trudged slowly on. Shade strode unhurriedly at the rear of the party, making no attempt to help.

"What's the matter?" snarled Jarryl, during one of their infrequent halts. "The work too hard for your dainty hands?"

Shade shook his head. "My talents lie in other directions."

Jarryl laughed coarsely. "Aye, I've no doubt ye'd make a fine addition to a lady's bedchamber, pretty boy."

Shade smiled politely.

Varles called for the party to move on, and the slow march continued.

3.

"Baran! Will ye look at that. . . ."

Jarryl's voice died away as she stared out over the wreck of what had once been a thriving city. The burly sailor at her side shook a clinging creeper from his blade and followed her gaze. Stretched out before them the ruins of a proud city lay sprawled in the morning sun. The lofty walls were cracked and creeper-strewn, and the rusty iron gates lay lichen-pitted among tall grass. Tall watchtowers were holed and scarred by long rains, while weeds and foliage of a dozen varieties choked the narrow streets.

"This was a beautiful city, once," breathed Jarryl, eyes entranced at the sight of so much marble.

"Aye. But always remember why it fell." Baran's voice was low, and he gestured nervously at the sky with a scarred three-fingered hand. Jarryl glanced up at the handful of blackbirds circling over the fallen city and felt her hackles rise.

"The raves still glide over Ravensbrook," sighed a quiet voice immediately behind her, and she spun sword in hand to face Shade. She spat on the ground between her feet and then his. Shade's brow wrinkled in polite puzzlement.

"I warned ye not to sneak up behind me again." Jarryl's voice shook a little with rage and humiliation at being caught napping twice. "I give ye challenge; put forward your blade."

Shade chuckled and spread his empty hands. "I carry no blade, nor have I need of one."

He gestured with a slender-fingered hand and creepers fell from the surrounding trees to cover Jarryl in fold after fold of clinging greenery. She cursed and struggled as the sheer weight forced her to her knees. Remorselessly, the vines wrapped around her, squeezing tighter, ever tighter. Her vision blurred as her sword slipped from numb fingers. . . .

"Hold!" Varles pushed his way through the watching crew and took in the scene. "Shade, release her."

Shade smiled slowly, gray eyes narrowed. "She gave challenge to me."

Varles drew the silver dagger from his sleeve and set the point under Shade's chin. "By the terms of our bargain. obey me."

He applied a gentle pressure, and a single drop of blood trickled down Shade's throat to stain the white kerchief at his neck. The gray eyes never wavered, but the creepers slowly relaxed their hold till Jarryl was able to struggle free. Baran helped her stagger to her feet and recover her sword. She leaned on him for a moment, and then threw herself at Shade, her sword seeking his heart. Varles plucked her out of midair and threw her to one side. The crew murmured quietly at the captain's casual display of his strength, but none laughed as Jarryl rolled quickly to her feet and dropped into a fighting crouch, her sword flickering back and forth before her like a serpent's tongue. Varles made no move to threaten her, his blue eyes calm and watchful. The silver dagger had disappeared back into his sleeve again, but his right hand hovered near his scimitar. He was under no illusions that Jarryl's feelings for him would stay her for a moment if she felt her honor threatened.

Shade glanced from one to the other, taking in the rage heating Jarryl's face and coursing through her sword arm in bunching muscles, comparing it with Varles's relaxed stance, his sleepy blue eyes at odds with the wide shoulders and scarred arms wherein his strength lay coiled like a sleeping mountain lion.

The tableau held for a moment, and then the mood was shattered by a shrill scream. They all whirled in time to see Baran slump to his knees and fall on his face in the dirt. Blood rilled from two gashes across his back, which dripped a curious muddy green slime. Jarryl flailed wildly about her as Varles barked orders the crew jumped to obey, splitting into pairs, before darting into the jungle darkness. Shade knelt by the body and fumbled inside his tunic, before producing a paste amulet to mutter over. Varles and Jarryl stood back to back beside him, swords at the ready.

"We settle our differences later, agreed?" Varles's voice was still calm, though his eyes scanned the concealing jungle ceaselessly.

"Agreed." Jarryl warily eyed the city walls gleaming palely in the sun. "This is no place for quarrels; Port Blood's reputation seems to have been well earned."

Shade tucked away the amulet and then fingered the slime drenching Baran's back, before fastidiously wiping his fingers on the dead man's sleeve. He shook his head.

"What killed him?" Varles didn't take his eyes off the jungle.

Shade shrugged. "Sword in his back. It's the slime that interests me; it's like nothing I've seen before, yet strangely familiar for all that." He got to his feet and smiled condescendingly at their ready swords. "Ye won't need those. We are in no danger."

Varles glanced around suspiciously one more time and sheathed his blade. Jarryl relaxed but stubbornly hung on to her sword.

"Might there be others after the treasure?" she growled.

Varles frowned. "Possible but unlikely; there are few who'd risk the Brotherhood's anger, even for the treasure of Port Blood. And had there been another such voyage as mine, I'd surely have heard." He glanced down at Baran's body. "Are ye sure those are sword wounds, Shade?"

Shade raised an eyebrow. "To the best of my knowledge, Captain, but I am not infallible."

Jarryl sniggered and swung her sword lazily before her. Shade took no notice. Their heads snapped around as one as a shocked scream rent the air, followed by others till the air echoed with agony. Jarryl glared at Shade.

"No danger, ye said?" She started into the darkness.

Varles caught her by an arm. "If they couldn't cope together, we can't help them." He had to shout to be heard over the screams. "Rush in there alone, and you'd be picked off for sure."

"Then what do ye suggest, Captain?"

Varles glanced at Shade suspiciously, before gesturing at the city below them. "We'll have to entrust ourselves to the tender mercies of Port Blood. At least there we can fight with a wall at our backs."

Jarryl nodded and darted along the overgrown path that led down into the city. Varles and Shade followed her. The last scream died away in a sudden liquid gurgle. Silence held dominion over the jungle again, as though it had never been disturbed.

4.

Jarryl ran a callused hand caressingly over the smooth marble wall. In the cold lands of her people, marble was so rare as to command twice its weight in gold, and though she had seen many wonders in her rovings as a pirate, she could not hide her admiration for an entire city hewn from the pale-veined stone.

"Have you ever seen anything like it?" she demanded of Varles as he emerged from yet another derelict house, this time with a cup of wine in his hand. He shook his head and offered her the cup. She took it gratefully and studied the cup's acid-etched scrollwork for a moment, before gulping at the sticky wine. "Where did you find this?"

"In there. There was an empty bottle on the table, and another still sealed beside it."

"You mean this wine has been here since the city fell? How many years is that?"

Varles shrugged. "Must be a good vintage by now."

"Any wine that doesn't throw up your food is a good vintage after so many months at sea." She drained the cup and threw it back to Varles. He snatched it out of the air and tossed it carelessly back through the house's gaping door. Shade emerged from an alley's shadows and strolled over to join them.

"Did ye find anything?"

"No, Captain. It's strange: goblets and platters set out as though for a meal but newly abandoned. Signs of many a fierce struggle, but . . ." He shook his head. "Where are the bodies? The stories tell of a great slaughter among the unsuspecting revelers, but not even a bloodstain remains to mark their deaths."

He frowned, and reaching into a leather pouch at his waist, drew out a handful of blue chalk dust, which he muttered over and then tossed into the still air. Before Varles's and Jarryl's startled gaze, the dust spiraled madly on the air before them as though stirred by an unseen hand, before dropping slowly to the ground.

"Interesting." Shade scuffed the chalk dust into the ground with his boot.

"What does it mean?"

"Damned if I know, Captain. But I'll show ye another puzzle: Where are the birds that circled above the city? The ravens of Ravensbrook?"

They stared up at the sky. There were no birds, nor even insects. Varles shivered, despite the heat of the morning sun. "Mayhap they've gone to tell their master we're here."

Shade grinned sardonically. "Aye. Mayhap."

Jarryl scowled. "Have ye no better answer, pretty boy?"

Shade turned his disquieting gray eyes on her. "Aye. I have. Whatever magic first called the ghouls to Ravensbrook is still operating here, and I for one have no intention of being here when night falls."

He glanced around, and then started quickly down the street. Varles and Jarryl looked at each other, shrugged, and followed him, swords in hand.

Shade led them through a maze of narrow interconnecting alleyways, pausing now and then to throw his chalk dust upon the air and carefully scuffing it into the dirt, before continuing. He finally came to a stop before an old building whose walls loomed far above the highest of the city, with slit windows fully twenty feet above their heads and the roof as far beyond again. The huge wooden door was barred with bands of beaten steel whose ends were buried within the surrounding marble wall. Varles stared hungrily at the night-dark wood and caressed it lightly with his fingertips.

"Just as it was described to me, those many years ago in Meligarr. The storehouse of the Old Brotherhood, in the days before women were admitted to the Charter. Here lies the horde of a dozen master pirates! Loot from a hundred ports and countries that no longer squat on any map. Gold and jewels, spices and potions; enough wealth to make us rich beyond our most feverish dreams."

"Mayhap. My dreams arise from no mere fever." Jarryl sounded distinctly unimpressed. Varles chuckled and shook his head.

"I know you like to think the Brotherhood was nothing till women sailed the seas as well, but we'll know soon enough. Shade, this is your moment."

"I thank ye, Captain. If ye will allow me . . ."

Varles stepped back to give the man room. The sun was high in the sky, and the heat beat down unmercifully. As Shade studied the thick steel bands and the surrounding marble, Varles mopped at his face with a silk rag and took a slow pull of water from his canteen. He handed it to Jarryl, who nodded her thanks, before sucking greedily at the lukewarm water. The air was dry and still, the silence oppressive. No insects crawled in the dirt of the vine- and wood-strewn street, and still no bird flew. Varles glanced fleetingly up at the jungle beyond the city walls and promised himself a vengeance on whoever had taken his crew. Or whatever . . .

Jarryl reluctantly lowered the canteen and brushed gently at her dry and cracked lips with the back of her hand. Her palms were hot and sticky, and her sword hung heavy in her grip. She glanced at Varles, who was staring out at the jungle, eyes dark and brooding. Something like compassion moved within her for a moment, as she considered the letdown the breaching of the treasure house would bring. But until Varles saw for himself that it was just another tale spun from too many drinks on a quiet night, his dreams would never be free. Jarryl switched her attention to Shade, who was swinging a bone amulet on a chain before the barred wooden door. She curled a dry lip. Magic; she would have spat, had her mouth been wet enough. She preferred the simple honesty of a good blade and an enemy she could face. Taking a last gulp of water, she handed the leather canteen back to Varles.

Shade put away his amulet and threw up his arms in the stance of summoning.

"Hear me, ye shades of the light that is darkness, and the darkness that is light! Hear me, ye shadow demons, for I am Shade, to whom each shadow is every shadow! Hear ye the Hanged Man, the Walker in Shadows!"

His voice deepened and rang harshly on the still air while Varles and Jarryl watched slack-mouthed a man they had only thought they knew. His face was hidden in shadow though he wore no hood, and as they watched, he ripped away the kerchief from his neck to reveal a raw scar that circled his throat, the mark of the hangman's noose.

Jarryl could feel her hackles rising, and the air was suddenly cool on her cheeks. This was the man she had challenged. . . . She gripped her sword firmly. As she and Varles watched, Shade stepped slowly forward into the door's shadow and was gone. Varles nodded. Shade: the man who entered locked rooms but not through the door; who walked between light and darkness, life and death; the master thief of the Known Kingdoms.

Shade was suddenly walking toward them out of the door's shadow, and Jarryl bit back a startled curse.

"Well?" Varles's mouth was suddenly dry again with anticipation. Shade grinned.

"More treasure than all our dreams put together."

Jarryl hugged Varles and throwing back her head, howled with barbaric glee, glad that his dreams had not been betrayed. Her own dreams now stirred within her. Varles grinned at the fierceness of her embrace as his triumphant laughter echoed back from the walls. He clapped Shade on the shoulder and then spun Jarryl clean off her feet and threw her into the air, catching her easily as she yelled in mock anger. Their mirth rang clearly on the quiet, though Shade did not join them. They finally staggered to a halt, wiping tears of laughter from their eyes and clutching aching ribs. Shade was studying the door.

"What now?" Varles gasped, struggling to regain his calm. "Do ye have any spells to warp those steel bands and get us in?"

Shade shook his head. "No, Captain, but I have something else that may help." He opened a hand to show them a small glass ball filled with an amber liquid. He hefted it gently and then threw it at the steel band highest on the door. The ball shattered and amber liquid smoked and hissed on the dull-gleaming metal. Varles nodded.

"Acid. How much do ye have?"

Shade produced more of the glass balls, which he carefully applied to the steel bands. Metal boiled like water, steaming in the air. Shade cautiously wiped the bands clean with a rag he then quickly discarded.

"And now, Captain, we must use our brawn and sweat; one by one, the metal bands must be bent back and torn from their settings. It will be a long job."

Varles shrugged. "The sooner we start, the sooner we'll finish. I've not come this far to be balked by steel bands on a wooden door."

They labored long into the afternoon, levering the steel bands free from their settings, using their swords as crowbars and Varles's strength to bend the bands back upon themselves. Shade labored tirelessly beside them, his slender frame glistening with sweat. When the last band reluctantly fell into the street with an echoing thud, the sun was already sliding down the sky toward evening. Jarryl sank onto her haunches, head hanging, breath rasping in her parched throat. The sweat was running off her in rivulets, and her back ached unmercifully. Used as she was to the heavy work common to all who sail the seas, this had taxed her to her limits. Varles dropped a heavy hand on her shoulder, and she looked up with a faint smile. Stripped to the waist, he stood smiling down at her, breathing no less harshly.

"Well, we did it," he said slowly, as though having trouble convincing himself. His eyes stared past her, dwelling on his dreams of what lay behind the treasure house door.

"Aye, Captain," Jarryl smiled back. "We did it."

She rose to her feet and stood beside him as he gazed at the defenseless wooden door. She hoped for his dream. She glanced across at Shade, who had pulled his tunic back on and was adjusting the brass mail so that it fell comfortably. Jarryl frowned; it must be devilishly hot, but he insisted on wearing it. Did he perhaps know something they did not? She shrugged, and let her hand rest comfortably near her swordhilt. Shade leaned on the door and nodded to Varles.

"There's no lock; it's just warped shut by the heat, I imagine. One good blow from your shoulder . . ."

He darted lithely aside as Varles put his full weight to the door. It groaned and gave a good six inches. He rammed it again, and the door slid reluctantly back another foot. Another blow, and Varles forced his bulk through the gap, widening it again in the process. Jarryl slipped through after him. Shade glanced around at the deserted street and followed them in.

5.

Varles gasped. In the meager light from the doorway, pile upon pile of precious stones glowed dully. A wall of stacked gold bars gleamed to his left, and another of silver to his right. And everywhere, jewels: some naked, others still in gold and silver settings. Strings of pearls and necklaces of faceted and polished stones. Rings, bracelets, coronets, and amulets—the loot of an age!

Jarryl sank to her knees and reaching into the nearest pile held up a handful of multicolored fire. She turned a glowing face to Varles.

He grinned. "What think you of my dreams now?"

Jarryl chuckled and plunged both hands into the sparkling pile before her. She held up another batch of brilliant dazzle, and then threw them aside to grab a handful of gold coins and toss them into the air, followed by another and another.

"It's raining gold!" Her laughter rolled back and forth in the dimly lit room. Varles smiled, but made no move to examine any of the wealth stacked about him. Shade moved to his side.

"Beautiful it is, Captain, but how are we to get it back to the ship? With your crew gone, and their killers still out there waiting for us . . ." He shook his head.

Varles frowned, then nodded at a large wooden chest half full of gold coins.

"We fill that with the choicest jewels; we can manage the weight between us. I'm more concerned with what we'll use for weapons; swords were not made for use as levers."

He drew his scimitar; even in the sparse light it was a sorry sight, seeming more a butcher's blade than a fighting man's weapon. Shade chuckled quietly.

"Take your pick, Captain."

Varles followed Shade's sweeping gesture and grinned at the heap of jewel-encrusted swords and daggers lying in a corner. He threw aside his battered and notched blade, and rooting through the pile came up with a long curving scimitar that he tossed to Jarryl. She stopped draping strings of semiprecious stones around her neck long enough to snatch it deftly out of the air and test its balance. With a quick nod of approval, she sheathed it in place of her discarded sword. Varles rejected a short sword with a diamond-studded hilt in favor of a broad double-edged sword unadorned save for a single polished emerald set at the cross-piece. He hefted the blade, admired the superb balance, and then glanced across at Shade, who had made no move to examine the treasure or the weapons.

"Will ye not take something for yourself?"

"No thank ye, Captain. I do not carry weapons; I have no need of them."

Varles shrugged and started loading gold and jewels into the solid oak chest, scooping out the less valuable coins as he did so. Jarryl helped him and the chest was soon full. Varles slipped a few gold and silver bangles as far up his arms as they would go, and then glanced around one last time.

"We'd best leave it at that. Any more and we'll be too loaded down to fight." Her glanced at Jarryl and had to hide a smile. Her arms were buried under bracelets, and her fingers blazed with jeweled rings.

"And how are you going to wield a sword with all that junk in the way?"

She glared at him and reluctantly stripped off a few rings. Varles shook his head and took the weight of the chest. Jarryl took the other end when it became clear that Shade had no intention of doing so.

"Ready?"

Jarryl nodded, a dozen necklaces jangling accompaniment. They lifted. Staggeringly slowly out into the street, they were astonished to see the sun already sinking into the sea. Shade frowned.

"We'd best hurry. It's risky enough to use the sorceries of day in this cursed city; I have no wish to try the sorceries of night in such a place."

"But we can't use the jungle path back to the ship," Jarryl protested, taking the chest's weight on one thigh. "Those bastards could still be waiting for us."

"Aye, they could. Do ye know any other way out of the city?"

Jarryl scowled and shook her head.

"Then we have no choice," Shade said flatly. "It's either that or cut a new path, and we have not the time."

"We take the path," Varles decided. He signaled to Jarryl, and they lifted the chest again as Shade started down the street. Jarryl growled a curse, and they moved slowly after him. Far above the city, a lone raven soared in silence.

6.

In the jungle, they made slow progress. Shade had to use Varles's sword to cut back foliage that had already fallen back across the path since they last used it. Though its miraculously keen edge made the job easy, he soon tired of it, and during one of their frequent rest stops he muttered a spell that had the creepers and hanging vines crawl aside as they approached. Varles and Jarryl exchanged a glance but made no comment. They staggered grimly on. Despite all their efforts to make haste, night fell before they reached the coast.

The longboat was still there, though only just out of reach of the rising tide. Varles inspected it thoroughly, before helping launch it into the chill waters. His shoulder blades crawled every time he turned his back on the murky jungle, and he knew he would not rest easy till the *Revenge* was pulling away from Port Blood with a hold full of treasure and sails full of wind.

The longboat made its way slowly toward the ship, with Varles and Jarryl at the oars. The full moon was half masked behind clouds and the *Revenge* was no more than a patch of darkness against the skyline. Varles abruptly stopped rowing and signaled for Jarryl to ship her oar. He studied the ship's silhouette. Where were the nightlights and lookouts? He gestured for the others to lean close; there was no telling how far voices might carry on the still night.

"The ship is too quiet; something's wrong."

"You think the crew might have been attacked here as well?"

"It's possible, Jarryl. If another band had come for the treasure, they'd want no rivals to follow their wake."

"Perhaps they grew tired of waiting and came ashore themselves?"

"Not my crew, Shade."

Varles and Jarryl improvised muffles for their oars and rowed the remaining distance in silence. Varles pulled himself up the rigging and swung agilely onto the bridge. The lookout was not at his post, and the night-light's wick was cold. Jarryl swung over the side and stood beside him, her new sword swinging lazily before her. Shade joined them silently a moment later. They stared about them.

Apart from the soft creaking of the rigging, the ship was quiet. The wheel spun freely back and forth as currents moved the rudder. Varles gestured for the others to check belowdecks while he searched topside. From the crew's quarters, where empty hammocks dangled unstrung; to the galley, where an evening's meal lay half prepared; to the bridge, where Varles paced frowning alone: the ship was deserted.

They met again with grim faces. Whatever had taken their companions in the jungle had also struck aboard the *Revenge.*

"What now?" Jarryl swept her sword back and forth before her is frustration.

"We get out of these cursed waters," Varles answered curtly, eyeing the rigging with a calculating eye.

"And leave the treasure?" Jarryl turned incredulous eyes on him.

"Treasure's no use to a dead man. With what we brought out in the chest, we can buy a new crew to come back for the rest, enough to stage a full-scale war if need be."

"Quite right, Captain. We only invite danger by remaining." Shade's calm voice was at odds with his darkly frowning eyes.

"So, we sail on the morning tide. The three of us can manage her long enough to reach one of the main shipping lanes, and we've more than enough to bribe passage on whatever ship first comes along. Jarryl, you stand first watch; wake me in three hours, and I'll take the next."

"Aye, Captain."

They slept on deck together, side by side. Jarryl sat guard with knees drawn up to her chest and her sword on the deck beside her. The ship's familiar creakings were a comfort after the eerie silence of Port Blood and its surrounding jungle. The waves lapping against the sides of the ship were soothing, and she had to keep shaking herself to avoid falling asleep after the day's hard labor. The ship's rigging hung silhouetted against the sky. It trembled as the wind shook it. Jarryl's hackles rose. There was no wind. . . .

She shook Varles's shoulder and he came quickly awake, dagger in hand. She gestured at the shaking rigging and he nodded, rousing Shade with a cautionary hand over his mouth. Shade came awake with a start, and the three stood facing the trembling ropes. Varles silently offered Shade the silver dagger; he took it without comment.

A shadow appeared against the skyline. All three gaped as a crimson moon swam out from behind the clouds to reveal a thing that had once been a man but was no longer. Half rotten and covered with the slime found on decks of ships long sunk, it stood swaying silently before them with eyes of phosphorescent fire, a battered and corroded scimitar in its bony grasp. More of the foul creatures swarmed over the side as Varles remembered the slime on Baran's back. He stepped forward and his sword spun a deadly pattern before him, wreaking havoc among the silent invaders, though no blood spurted. The corpses fell if the heads were severed, but even then they made no cry, and their fellows lumbered closer, ever closer.

Varles and Jarryl fought savagely side by side, blades gleaming in the sparse light. Shade was squatting behind them, mixing powders in a small brass urn and muttering arcane runes under his breath. With Varles's silver dagger, he made a small cut in his wrist, so that a stream of blood ran down to mix with the powders in the urn. Before him, the fight raged back and forth in the cramped space, and for every corpse that fell another took its place. Already exhausted after the day's work and little sleep, Varles was gradually slowing, though his massive strength was still enough to send corpses flying clean over the side whenever a solid blow connected. Jarryl hacked her way through the crowding attackers, but even her vitality was flickering as the day's fatigue grew in her anew. And still they spun and danced, their swords licking out to reap a deadly harvest.

Then Varles's heart lurched as over the side of his ship clambered what was left of his crew. Dripping wet and with their death wounds still bloody, they stumbled forward to die again, taking their vengeance on those who dared the curse of Lord Ravensbrook.

Above the ship, the skies were full of soaring ravens, screeching triumphantly on the night air.

Even as he fought, one part of Varles's mind began to understand what had happened in Port Blood those many centuries ago, when all who had drowned or been buried in the port's bay had been summoned up to slay those who offended Lord Ravensbrook. Those who died then were dragged in turn back to the sea to become more slaves at his command. Thus came the legend of the ghouls of Ravensbrook.

Somewhere back in the city must lie a signal that called them forth to live again, Varles mused as he struck down the dead man who had once been his third mate and threw the headless body over the side with one sweep of an aching arm. Far above, the hoarse screams of the ravens grew fiercer, and Varles's lips stretched in a bloody grin. The ravens. When they were disturbed, the corpses walked. The old Lord must have had a sense of humor, after all. Varles fought on, sword swinging heavily back and forth, and Jarryl staggered on at his side. Familiar faces loomed before them, but still they hacked and cut, though they seemed to strike down friend as often as foe. Behind them Shade suddenly cried out, his harsh voice rising easily above the sounds of the battle and the screams of the ravens.

"Awake, awake, ye Northern Winds. . . . Gather ye thunders and lightnings, and send us a wind to carry us from these tainted waters. . . . Awake, awake, ye Northern Winds!"

Blood rilled down his arm as he stood erect in the stance of summoning, holding Varles's silver dagger above his head so that it blazed in the moonlight. Still Varles battled on with Jarryl striving wearily at his side, blood dripping from their wounds till the deck grew slippery beneath their feet.

Then the ship's creakings stirred into a new pattern as the deck lurched under their feet. The sails billowed out and filled as thunder rolled overhead and the first rain began to fall. Lightning split the sky and cracked down to strike the dagger Shade held aloft. He screamed once in agony but held the stance of summoning, though both his tunic and hair were afire. The ship lurched again as the wind rose and the blue glow of stormfire crawled along the ship's mast. The *Revenge* began to pick up speed under the wind's urging, and the things that were once men could no longer climb the ship's sides. Varles and Jarryl quickly cut down those remaining on board and leaped to Shade's side. Varles swung a blanket about his shoulders, smothering the flames, and together they lowered him to the deck.

Varles's questing hand found a beating heart, though Shade's body was covered in burns, and much of the sun-bleached hair was gone. As Jarryl watched, the gray eyes snapped open, questioning. She nodded and watched amazed as the blistered lips curled in a sardonic grin. She grinned savagely back.

The *Revenge* flew on before the rising storm, out to sea, flying to a cleaner setting and a more hospitable shore.

This was my first proper professional sale, to Andy Offutt for the anthology Swords Against Darkness, Volume 5, in 1979. I was watching an old pirate film on late-night television, full of fighting in the rigging, and ships blasting each other with cannon, and sword duels on the beach at dawn . . . and as soon as it was finished, I rushed upstairs and wrote this story. I'm still very proud of it, and just recently got around to writing a sequel: a novella called The Pit of Despair, which has just appeared from PS Publishing. I do love a good pirate story.

IN THE LABYRINTH

Shade lay shackled in the dungeons under Mhule. Silver chains led from ankles, wrists, and throat to a single iron loop deeply embedded in the damp stone wall. His eyes were blindfolded though neither torch nor lamp lit his windowless cell. The heavily armed guard who pushed a bowl of bread and slop through the door's revolving section shuddered nonetheless; for in the condemned cell, Shade was chuckling quietly, and there was murder in that laugh.

Captain Varles of the pirate ship *Revenge*, together with his first mate, Jarryl, stalked uneasily along the curving stone passage lit only by flickering oil lamps set high on the walls at irregular intervals and the blazing brands they carried. Damp collected on the low ceiling, sliding down pitted walls to collect in scummy puddles on the cracked stone floor. Straggly lichen and fungi pale as dead man's flesh lay clumped where wall met floor.

In the dungeons under Mhule, all was silent, and Varles and

Jarryl became convinced they were the only living things remaining. Jarryl took to peering into odd cells at random and once, when Varles thought he heard giggling in a dark cell, they held their torches to the window, but there was no one there. They strode on, passing deeper into the Labyrinth of Mhule.

When Varles last walked this route, it had been lit by brightly flaring torches, and a brace of well-bribed guides strode at his side. They had guarded his back while he made his deal with the man called Shade, who lay awaiting execution in Mhule's deepest dungeon. Varles smiled grimly. Shade, master thief of the Known Kingdoms. The man who walked in shadows. Little good his titles had done him since he slew the King's son. Now he waited only for the King's torturers to ready themselves for his prolonged execution. Unless of course Varles should free him first.

The two guards now lay dead at the top of the long, winding stairway that led down from the guardhouse, because they would take no more bribes and had threatened to betray him rather than enter the catacombs at night. Varles frowned uneasily. Dark tales were told of the Labyrinth of Mhule, muttered in taverns as the night wore on, and shutters were slammed shut against an evil all the city seemed reluctant to discuss. After an evening's wine, an old soldier, once a guard in the catacombs by day, had talked blearily to Varles and Jarryl of shadows with no man to carry them and paintings that stared with hostile eyes.

Varles's hand rested on the hilt of his scimitar. He needed Shade if he was to take the lost treasure of Ravensbrook, called by some Port Blood. Any risk was worth it that would bring him one step nearer the treasure he had dreamed of for so long. He stopped suddenly and scowled. Jarryl followed his gaze, and her sword whispered from its scabbard as she took in the blood-splashed cell door half torn from its setting. She knelt and tested the blood with her free hand as Varles glared into the gloom about them, his scimitar at the ready. Jarryl glanced into the cell, but like the others before, it was empty.

“The blood’s freshly spilled, Captain, but there doesn’t seem to be a body.”

“Aye.” Varles stooped and picked up something half-hidden in the shadow of the cell door. Jarryl hissed softly. It was a human jawbone, with strings of bloody meat still hanging from it. Varles tossed it back into the shadows.

“It would appear we are not alone in the Labyrinth, Jarryl.”

They exchanged a glance and made their way deeper into the darkness, swords at the ready. Some time later, they came to an iron portcullis lowered against them. Varles growled a curse. His bribed guards had told him nothing of this, though in their defense it could be said that never had they entered the Labyrinth at night. No King, they insisted with hands atremble, could pay them enough to walk the catacombs while night lay across the land. Varles studied the heavy iron grating and sheathed his sword, handing his torch to Jarryl. He took firm hold of the chill metal and slowly took the strain. Ropes of muscle corded across his broad shoulders as the ironwork groaned and shifted, and then he snarled triumphantly as, with a tortured squeal, the gate lifted a few inches from the floor. He grabbed desperately at the sweat-slippery metal, his muscles standing out in sharp relief as the portcullis rose another inch and another.

Jarryl squeezed as far into the narrow gasp as she could, eyes smarting from the smoking torches she carried, and waited patiently, knowing that should Varles slip, the massive ironwork would surely crush her, but trusting him nonetheless. The gate lifted still further, and with some small cuts and much muttered cursing, Jarryl finally wriggled through. There was a dull thud as the portcullis tore itself from Varles’s grip, and Jarryl nodded soberly as the crude barbs at its base dug hungrily into the soft stone floor. She quickly wound up the portcullis with much complaining of its rusty chains. Varles ducked past the grating, and Jarryl let it fall again.

Together they inspected the flight of rough-hewn steps that led down to the last level of the Labyrinth. Worn dangerously smooth by the passing of many feet, they stretched away into an unrelieved darkness neither Varles nor Jarryl could plumb. Jarryl handed Varles his torch, and side by side they padded down into the gloom.

At the foot of the steps, they stopped and glared quickly about, for lying in a pool of blood were the two guards Varles had slain but an hour past up in the guardhouse. He studied the vilely mutilated bodies as Jarryl guarded his back with drawn sword.

"Strange," he said slowly. "They insisted there was but one entrance to the Labyrinth, yet if that were true, how were they brought here without passing us?"

Jarryl shrugged lightly, eyes darting from shadow to shadow. "Have they any valuables on them, Captain? 'Twould be a shame to leave any sweets pickings for the morning's guards."

Varles nodded solemnly. "Aye, but it seems to me I took what little they had when I disposed of their services earlier this evening." He shared a brief grin with Jarryl, before turning back to the guardsmen. "How came they to be ripped apart, from throat to crotch? I give a clean kill, always."

Jarryl glanced at the mutilated corpses and shrugged uncomfortably, remembering the casually discarded jawbone. "Mauled by some animal, mayhap?"

"Aye." Varles sounded unconvinced. "Have you noticed how clammy the air is down here?"

Jarryl nodded. "I've heard the Labyrinth extends far out under the harbor. There's even some kind of mist down here."

She gestured with her torch at a few wisps that dissipated into the dank air even as they watched.

They made their way further into the catacombs, passing cells obviously long abandoned, their dull metal doors scarred with the rust and filth of long neglect. Their attention was caught by paintings on the walls, which, starting at the foot of the stairs, depicted in marvelous hues a legend of the long ago, when Others stalked the Earth along with Man. Heroes vied with monsters, both so vividly presented Jarryl was hard-pressed not to reach out a hand and prove them real. There was a war, and in it battles and treacheries, foulness and great deeds, for this was a war between Man and those who ruled before him.

Varles studied the walls curiously, for though they were dripping with a brackish water, the dyes seemed strangely unaffected, as though soaked into the stone itself. They walked slowly on, torches held close to the walls that they might more clearly see the long story unfold. There were many heroes, most of whom died unpleasant deaths, but strangely only one demon, which recurred again and again until the story ended, so suddenly as to be surely unfinished. The final painting, just as the first, showed the demon wrapped in chains, striving to reach a crowned man who threatened it with a blazing brand.

"A strange history indeed," Varles said slowly. "But I know this last man by his profile, Harak, first King of Mhule these centuries past. His head still marks their coins."

"And the demon?" Jarryl asked, glancing at the wall and as quickly away again.

Varles frowned. "It seems to me there was a similar painting on the door leading down from the guardhouse, half-hidden under the grime of years. When I commented on it, the guards talked hastily of something else." He shook his head and strode quickly on. Jarryl hurried after him.

The narrowing corridors led still downward, the cracked stone floor became ever more treacherous. Varles was no longer sure of his way, and more than once had to stop and retrace his steps. But finally, the torches revealed a featureless iron door set into the wall, with only a small revolving section to pass food through. Varles grinned, relieved his memory had not played him entirely false. He rapped on the door.

"Shade! Can ye hear me?"

"Aye! Get the door open and free me from these cursed chains!"

Varles sheathed his scimitar, took the ring of keys from his belt and began the slow process of trying them in turn. He soon found the right key and struggled with the obstinate lock.

"Captain Varles!" Shade's voice floated through the gloom so clearly Jarryl would have sworn he stood beside her rather than the other side of a thick iron door.

"Aye, Shade, I'm still here. What is it ye want that can't wait the few minutes it'll take to free ye?"

"I have to know, Captain, is it day or night?"

Jarryl glanced at Varles, who shrugged.

"Night, Shade, when else might we come a-calling?"

He pushed the door open and by the light of the flickering torches Jarryl studied the beaten and manacled figure who lay in the far corner of the condemned cell. Long and lean with sun-bleached hair, he wore only a filthy bloodstained tunic and a dirty rag at his throat. Half-healed wounds showed clearly on his wiry frame, and blood dripped from ankles, wrists, and throat where the chains chafed him. Jarryl's eyes widened; with no window, and no chance of release till his dying day, it was no wonder Shade had lost all track of time, but for what mad reason had the guards blindfolded a man kept in a completely dark cell?

As Varles entered the cell Jarryl heard a faint scuffling behind her. She spun, sword at the ready. Back down the corridor, something tittered in the darkness. She gripped her sword firmly and padded silently back down the passage.

Varles slipped his torch into a battered iron holder and busied himself with the deeply embedded iron loop, but this time the key was not easily to hand, and he began to doubt it was even on the ring. He paused, eyeing the wall dubiously. If all else failed, he could perhaps tug the iron ring far enough from the wall to saw at it with his scimitar.

"Captain, why are ye taking so long?" Shade's patient voice jerked Varles from his reverie. "If this be night, we face certain danger here. In nights past, I have heard something scuffling outside my cell that from its sound I'd not face through choice, something only the cold iron of my door kept at bay. If I must use the sorceries of night in such a place as this, I'll not answer for the consequences."

Varles repressed a shiver at Shade's calm and measured tone. He bent again to his task, and then spun suddenly around as Jarryl's shocked scream echoed faintly in the distance.

On leaving Varles with Shade, Jarryl had quickly made her way back down the passage, sword held out before her. She knew the tales city dwellers told of this place, but her contempt for all who walked the land instead of a ship's deck had led her to discount such fears till now. She felt sure something moved in the darkness ahead, though ever and again she rounded a corner with torch held high to find nothing but dancing shadows and the hint of a mocking titter. Whatever she was chasing seemed always to retreat before her, leading her back to the steps that ascended from this last level of the Labyrinth.

Jarryl sprang around the far corner in fighting stance to face an apparently empty corridor, but she knew better than to relax her vigilance. Whatever she pursued, she had not given it time to scurry far. She held her flickering torch a little higher, glanced down the corridor and gasped; the dead guards no longer sprawled at the foot of the stairs. Only a wide pool of blood remained to mark where they had lain.

A flicker of movement spun Jarryl around to face the wall at her right. She stared at the opening painting of the chained demon, uncertain as to what had caught her eye, and then her heart jumped as it slowly turned its awful head to look at her.

Swirling mists curled up around its misshapen body as the chains fell away, the painting coming horribly alive as she watched. A few strands of mist drifted out of the painting toward her, and then a thick fog boiled from the stone, filling the corridor. Jarryl backed away as the tittering sounded suddenly close and then screamed as something impossibly large loomed out of the fog. She dropped her torch and flailed out wildly with her sword, feeling something give under the keen blade's urging. High-pitched chattering sounded in her ears as she turned and ran headlong back down the pitch-dark corridors.

Without her torch, she was soon lost, and rather than run blindly through the Labyrinth, she stopped to take her bearings. A light glowed dimly from a side passage, revealing that she stood before the final painting of the chained demon. The unsteady light grew stronger till she recognized Varles running toward her with drawn sword and a freshly blazing torch.

"What happened, Jarryl?"

"A demon, Captain." Jarryl fought for breath. "The demon from the wall painting!"

Thick fog spilled suddenly from the painting beside them, filling the corridor. Shade's voice rose faintly in the distance.

"Free me, Captain! Ye need my help!"

The naked urgency in his voice contrasted strangely with his polite use of the formal *ye*. As Varles and Jarryl stood together, blades at the ready, something moved out of the fog and into the dim light. Fully a dozen feet tall, hunched over in the cramping confines of the passage, its bony head scraped the ceiling while massive arms drooped to the floor. It was long and lean, with a barbed tail that hung twitching past malformed flanks. There were no eyes, only dusty sockets where eyes had once been, yet it followed their movements nonetheless. Its gaping maw revealed row upon row of stained, serrated teeth.

The high-pitched tittering was strangely inappropriate for such bulk, Varles thought fleetingly as he dropped his torch into a nearby holder and then leaped to the attack, Jarryl at his side. Their blades sank deep into the demon, spraying foul-smelling blood across the floor and walls. It screamed, and an overlong arm sent Varles flying down the corridor to smash into a wall. Jarryl ducked the return swing and sprang under its reach to pierce the demonflesh that would hide a heart in any body less misshapen. It hissed, and Jarryl had to throw herself headlong to avoid wicked claws that dug furrows in the stone wall behind her. Varles staggered forward, and she screamed at him to free Shade. He gazed stupidly at her as she snatched his torch from its holder, touched it to another on the wall, and threw it back to him. His eyes suddenly cleared as he snatched it out of midair and then darted back down the corridor. Jarryl ducked the demon's petulant swing and retrieved her blade from where it lay sheathed in the demon's chest. She danced back just in time to be sent sprawling by a clawed hand that tore her cloak away and ripped a bloody track across her left shoulder. Blood splashed down her numbed arm. She spat out a curse and staggered to her feet again, pressing home an attack she knew to be hopeless, her skill weaving a web of steel between her and the demon. The wall torch was already burning low.

Varles tugged and twisted at the stubborn iron loop. Shade cursed dispassionately and pulled at his chains, which were so arranged that try as he might he could lift his hands no higher than his waist. As Varles paused to wipe sweat from his eyes, Shade suddenly tensed.

"Captain! Is there light in my cell?"

"Aye, Shade, how else could I see to wrestle with these damned chains?"

"Then free my eyes!"

"I haven't the time, Shade!"

Varles took the iron ring in both broad hands and put his shoulders to the task. With agonizing slowness, he felt the corroded metal stir under his grip. He jammed a fat against the wall to brace himself and threw his weight against the loop. For long moments, he stood straining, and then the stone gave, the ring flying from the wall in a cloud of dust and stone splinters. Varles lay sprawling as Shade reached up and pulled the blindfold from his eyes. He laughed triumphantly when a shadow fell across his face though there was nothing to cast it, and then he tore the heavy manacles from him as though they were nothing but paper. Varles staggered to his feet, but by the time he was up, Shade had already gone. He lurched back into the corridor, sword in hand, and snatching the torch from its wall holder, he hurried after Shade.

Jarryl swung her notched sword with aching arm, sweat running into her eyes, her blood making the floor slippery. She only just ducked the demon's lazy return swing and heard again its hateful titter. She knew it was playing with her but dared not retreat. With her gone, it might disappear back into the wall painting again, and there was no telling where it might choose to reemerge. She thought fleetingly of the painting on the guardhouse door and realized who had mutilated the dead guardsmen. The discarded jawbone swam before her eyes, and in a flash of inspiration, she understood the empty cells and why the city lived in fear. The King let the demon live by feeding on those prisoners it could reach. Only a thick iron door had saved Shade. In her musing, she let her attack slow, and again the heavy arm sent her flying. She lay exhausted, knowing she had to get up, but unable to force herself to her feet.

She stared helplessly up at the sniggering demon, and then her eyes widened as Shade stepped from the shadows beside her. The demon screamed shrilly and threw both gnarled hands to the ceiling. Flames burst between them, dull red with the stink of brimstone. The demon screamed again, and the flames crackled unsupported on the air. It seemed to Jarryl that the demon knew Shade, and in its own way feared him. Varles helped her to her feet, and she leaned on him a moment, before pulling away. She'd not miss the battle this promised to be.

Shade howled something in a tongue only the demon seemed to recognize, and it threw the flames at him. He darted aside, and Jarryl grinned with a savage joy as the sorcerous flames seared the demon's picture from the wall. It howled in agony as flames licked up around its bulk, but there was no longer any painting for it to disappear into. Fire roared in the narrow corridor, consuming the demon in a brightness too painful to look upon. It screamed in rage while it roasted, held fast in the passage by its bulk. As Varles and Jarryl watched, flames scorched along the walls, obliterating the paintings. The demon seemed to fall in upon itself, and soon the sorcerous flames had left nothing but a charred skeleton. The stench of burned meat hung heavy on the air as the flames flickered low. Shade loomed suddenly out of the shadows.

"We'd best leave; the sorceries of night have been called upon here, and I'd not stay to see the result of that calling. This fire is not the kind that can easily be banished."

He turned and ran down the corridor, leaving Varles and Jarryl to follow as the flames roared up again, eating into the very stone itself. With the heat already scorching their backs, they sped along the narrow, twisting corridors, just managing to keep Shade in sight, for he seemed to need no directions to lead him out of the Labyrinth. When he reached the portcullis, he barked a few words, gestured with a hand, and the iron grating rose obediently before him, hanging on the air as he sped under, and then falling slowly back again. Varles and Jarryl only just scrambled through the lowering gap. Jarryl shot a venomous glare after Shade but saved her breath for running. There'd be time for a reckoning later. Behind her, she could hear flames crackling and realized that although Varles's torch no longer burned, the corridor was still well lit. She risked a glance over one shoulder and cursed as she saw the corridor was already ablaze.

By the time they reached the final stairway, the flames were a raging inferno and no more than a dozen feet behind them. Sweat poured off them, and their breath came hard as they assayed the narrow steps. Shade stood in the guardhouse door at the top of the stairway, a grin twisting his mouth as he watched, making no move to help. Varles and Jarryl forced themselves up the last few steps with flames licking at their heels and burst into the guardhouse. Shade slammed the door shut behind them, sliding home the bolts. They lay panting a moment, regaining their breath, and Varles absently noted that the ancient painting of the demon on the inside of the door was naught but a patch of charred wood. Shade smiled.

"Be grateful ye're both good runners; another moment and I'd have had to slam the door on ye lest the flames reach me."

Jarryl glared at him. "Ye'd have done that to us, who freed ye?"

Shade shrugged. "If I'm to have partners, they must be my equal."

Varles got to his feet. "Partners, is it? Shade, ye swore an oath to serve with me in return for your freedom from that cell. Ye'll keep your oath, won't ye?"

He drew a silver dagger from his scorched sleeve. Shade regarded it thoughtfully a moment and nodded.

"As ye say, I swore an oath. Now let us leave; the fire will not long be balked by that door."

He turned, and pushing open the thick iron doors, left the guardhouse without a backward glance. Varles and Jarryl shared a look and then followed him out into the cool night air.

Aboard the *Revenge*, they stared back at the burning city. With sails full of wind, the ship was fast pulling away from shore, but still they could see men running to and fro fighting the blaze. Jarryl watched unmoved. She had little love for cities, and still less for Mhule, which fed its prisoners to a captive demon. Varles watched the leaping flames with dark and brooding eyes and did not turn as Shade joined them on the bridge.

"Aye, Captain, they'll long remember the night I worked sorcery in their city."

The words held a cold satisfaction softened by his sardonic grin. He stalked aft, and Jarryl watched him go, gingerly caressing her bandaged shoulder. "I'd no more trust that one than a starving wolf at my throat. Why do we need him, Captain?"

Varles smiled."If we are to gain the treasure I seek, we need the magic he possesses."

Jarryl growled softly, caressing her shoulder. "Your damn treasure had better be worth it."

"It will be, Jarryl. It will be."

The sails creaked under the urging wind, and they watched the burning city fall behind them as the *Revenge* sped out to sea on a rising tide.

This appeared in the British semi-prozine Fantasy Tales. It's a prequel to the previous story; and it's here at the end of the collection because this was the last short story I sold for almost thirty years. The markets dried up, the editors stopped buying. I concentrated on novels, and finally made a career for myself by selling my first novel to Ginjer Buchanan at Ace, in 1988. I was laid off from my job when I was thirty and was unemployed for three and a half years. During this time, I wrote morning, noon, and night, and had my work rejected endlessly. Finally, I got a job working at Bilbo's Bookshop, in Bath. I started work on the Monday, and on the Wednesday I got a letter from Ginjer, saying she wanted to buy my book Hawk and Fisher, and would I be interested in writing five more books featuring the same character? And that's how I got started. It wasn't until much, much later, that I was asked to write short stories again. Luckily, I still have a soft spot for them.

So here they are.

ABOUT THE AUTHOR

Simon R. Green is the *New York Times*–bestselling author of *Blue Moon Rising*, *Beyond the Blue Moon*, the Adventures of Hawk & Fisher, the Novels of the Nightside, the Secret Histories Novels, and the Ghost Finders Novels. He is a resident of Bradford-on-Avon in England.

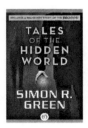

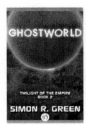

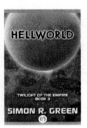

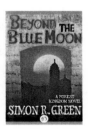

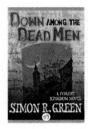

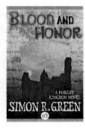

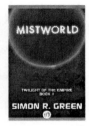

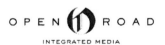

CPSIA information can be obtained at www.ICGtesting.com
Printed in the USA
LVOW07s0250100115

422261LV00001B/95/P

9 781480 491168